Five Years Later

Sarah Kraft

The characters and events portrayed in this book are fictitious. Any similarity to real persons, living or dead, is coincidental and not intended by the author.

Cover design by: Sarah Kraft
Printed in the United States of America

For Gudrun, an artist, dreamer, and survivor. Also my mom. I love you so.

In memory of Kim Gravelle (April 1941-2021), a traveler, fellow author, and legendary grandfather. You will always inspire me.

Lastly, but especially, for Tim... Hopefully, someday, you'll understand why.

Also By Sarah Kraft (Formerly S.B. Roozenboom):

PREDATOR GIRL

MARKINGS

XENOPHOBIA

Isn't it strange that the most gentle of hearts belong to all the souls on fire?

- *Michelle Schaper*

June 9th, 2017

THE RUN-IN

My mother used to tell me that during times of great chaos I should seek the little things that bring comfort, for one day I will look back and see that those little things were the big things in disguise.

It is this that comes to mind when my friend Shaya asks if I want to go for coffee and a morning jog on Friday. I hadn't seen my bestie since my twenty-third birthday, which was back in February, and thanks to the lingering aftermath of my parents' divorce I probably wasn't good company at the time (it's hard to be good company when your family dynamics have been shredded apart finer than a pulled-pork sandwich).

We agree to meet at our local Starbucks in Oregon City, the location of which I would later regret choosing, but there was no way to know this at the time. Shaya pulls up to the coffee house in a newer Prius. She's dyed her hair silver since the last time I saw her and sports an athletic vampire look consisting of black lipstick, blood-red leggings, and tennis shoes printed with flying foxes. A few minutes in her presence and I start to feel like my normal self again, like a person who has a life beyond work and family drama. After a barista hands me my coffee, I tell her I'm going to head outside and find us a table in the sun.

Side note before I continue: I try to be a considerate human being (usually). I'm the girl who holds the door open for frail old folk, the driver who waves when someone slows traffic to let her in. Hell, instead of killing the spider who made a web on my bathroom ceiling, I named her Betsy and steered house flies into her clutches. Being considerate is important.

So when I step out onto the sidewalk and spot a figure across the parking lot—one I could've spent the rest of my life without seeing again—it's out of character for me to loudly blurt, "Oh, fuck!"

My outburst interrupts two older women discussing the bible at a table nearby. They both turn in their seats, shooting me concerned looks, though whether that's because of my language or the fact I spasmed backwards like I'd just been electrocuted I'm not sure. A young mother covers her child's ears while hurrying him to their minivan but I barely notice.

My focus has gone entirely to the tall, wiry figure leaning against the side of a red Camaro that we used to call the Fugly Mobile. The car is still freaking ugly with its duct-taped taillight and discolored, nude model sticker clinging to the back window. Unlike the car, however, Tall and Wiry is as good looking as ever, all lean, long muscles and hair that shines in the sunlight like blackened steel. He turns his head to see why some woman is spewing profanities in a family setting and finds me. He visibly stiffens, blue eyes widening. I read his lips as he says, "Oh, shit."

My heart is pounding so hard I'm lightheaded. This was not the day for a double-shot latte. I nearly turn around and dive back into Starbucks but the only thing worse than looking panicked is appearing cowardly as well. *Toughen up, Elle,* some strong, little voice pipes up inside me. *He doesn't deserve to know he's unsettled you.* I straighten my back and lift my chin, trying to appear cool and confident while adrenaline rips through my system.

The door behind me opens and Shaya strolls out. "Jeez, people need to decide what they're ordering before they cork up the—Elle?" She comes a halt at my side, eyebrows scrunching up with concern. Following my gaze, she gasps and almost spills her macchiato. "Oh my God. That's not—is that?"

"Yep." There is no mistaking that figure, that face, that characteristically cold stare. "It's Scott." His name sounds dirtier on my tongue than any swear word I could ever use.

Scott quickly drops his sunglasses over his eyes and takes a long swig from the Monster Energy drink he's holding. *Probably swallowing the dozen other cuss words he'd like to shout.* He pushes off the car as the door to the pizza parlor across from Starbucks flies open. A redhead in an AC/DC shirt saunters out, twirling his car keys around his fingers. It's another blast from my past—Jordan Cane, Scott's best friend and the owner of the Fugly Mobile. He's laughing and talking but the look on Scott's face stops him short. Scott says something and Jordan's head swings in our direction. A big grin spreads across his face.

Oh no. "Shaya, unlock your car. Quick."

"Elly!" Jordan throws his arms in the air. "Holy cow, how are you, babe? You look amazing!" He laughs, eyes rolling down my figure like a kid whose spotted an ice cream truck.

"And time to go." Shaya jams her thumb into the unlock button for her Prius.

Scott tosses a hand at Jordan, clearly wondering what the hell he thinks he's doing, but as usual Jordan doesn't notice. "Thank you. Nice to see you." I don't want to be rude to him —*he's* not the lying sack who betrayed me—so I wiggle my fingers while trying to control my pace as I head to Shaya's car. I don't want it to look like I'm running away, even though that's exactly what I'm doing.

Scott sneers at the sky. He whips the Fugly Mobile's passenger side open and gets in, slamming the door so hard the mirror shakes.

"I'm having a party at the Blitz tomorrow night," Jordan calls. "You guys should come!"

"Thanks, but no thanks." I force a smile while circling the Prius. At least I hope it's a smile and not a toothy grimace since my face has a habit of betraying my true emotions. "See ya!"

"Wow, that was just… wow." Shaya stares at her windshield once we're in the safety of her vehicle.

I slump in my seat with a loud exhale then shove my sunglasses on, which I had inconveniently left in the cup holder. "What the hell just happened?" This is one of those scenarios that you imagine happening, but you imagine being prepared for it with the right body language and perfect things to say. I had neither.

"Are you asking if you just shouted fuck in front of two holy women and a new mother, or if you just ran into your ex? The answer is yes to both. By the way, I could hear your potty mouth from inside the coffee house." Shaya backs the car out of its parking spot, cheeks flushed. "Oh, God, don't look out my window."

Of course, the first thing I do is look out her window. Jordan backed the Fugly Mobile out of its parking spot at the same time she backed out. I watch as both cars pass and we get one last view of each other while leaving the shopping center. Jordan grins and makes some sort of hand signal that looks like *call me* to Shaya, who narrows her eyes in response.

Scott's blue eyes come right for me.

We pull out of the parking lot and circle around to a four-way intersection. Across the street lies the rolling hills of the community college grounds where we had planned to go for our morning jog. Shaya examines my face while sitting at a stop light. "You okay? You look like you're going to be ill."

"I'm fine." I hate that it's a lie. It's been five years since he and I were together—I *should* be fine. He's supposed to be a closed case in my life, someone who no longer affects me. I shouldn't feel like my insides are rotting just because we crossed paths.

"Isn't he supposed to be in California?" Shaya asks.

"Living with his dad? Yeah, last I'd heard. His mom still lives here in Oregon City though. He's probably visiting." It had better be just a visit and not a permanent thing, but I know his dad's lifestyle clashes with his own (big cities and political jabber have caused many fights between them). He only went to live there because it was far away from me, but I knew my existence alone wouldn't keep him away forever. He loved rain and mountain mist and the smell of deep, coniferous forests too much to not return to Oregon... I can only hope that after today he'll think twice about what part he lives in.

"Let's hope it's just a visit." Shaya speaks my mind. She gives me a once over as we park in the shared lot for the athletics center and college theater. "At least you look awesome today. No wonder Scott had to hide in the car after Jordan's nice comment."

I look down at my clothes. When I'd envisioned running into my ex again, my outfit involved leather leggings and a push-up bra—not an old tank top and sweatpants coated with visible remnants of dog hair. "Thanks, Shaya."

"Heck yeah, look at you! You've come a long way in the last few years—all twenty pounds smaller with those dark, luxurious extensions! You look stellar!"

Her effort to pump up my destroyed ego is appreciated, but it doesn't help. I pick at my clip-in extensions, knowing that hidden within them is my real hair, thin and damaged from years of bleaching. It was one of those life circumstances where I had to wave a white flag when I really didn't want to and return to my natural hair color, which was a dark turd brown. I hate waving white flags. I hate giving up on things I really want but seem destined to never have.

Why is it that just when we get our feet back under us, life waves its great hand of fate and floors us again? Is this some sort of test, a procedure to make us stronger?

April 6th, 2012

MR. DARCY

"Hi, Dad." I bounce into the front office of his automotive shop, smiling at where he sits behind the service counter. The office smells like new rubber today, mixed with someone's pine-scented car freshener.

"Hey there, Little Girl—No, I need it no later than tomorrow! Yes, part number B573—no, wait—B57B," my father, Jim Fox, yells into his Bluetooth headset, which is a near permanent fixture in his ear. Dad was the first person in line for a Bluetooth when they came out in 1999 and has been connected to somebody with car parts, cars for sale, or cars with unpaid expenses ever since. The only time the device is off is when he's sleeping or at church.

"Not little anymore," I remind him for the billionth time then trot upstairs to Dad's private office, a small, L-shaped room where his personal desk and the accounting desk are crammed together. As I walk in, a waterfall of blonde curls looks up from behind a tower of papers.

"Hey, I didn't know you were working today," Jan, the accountant, says brightly.

"Service day for the teachers. No school for me." I hang my purse on the coat rack then flop into a chair. Dad's desk is so heavily piled with sales receipts, thank you cards, and junk mail that I cannot see its cherry wood surface. A picture of me and my brother from a long-ago camping trip lingers on Dad's screen saver.

"You must be getting pretty excited," Jan says with a smile. "Only a couple more months and you'll be graduated. High school will be behind you."

I give an enthusiastic nod. "I wish it was behind me now."

She laughs. "Enjoy your time. The older you get, the faster it flies."

I scrunch my nose. "Can it fly now so that tomorrow is the day I accept my diploma?" I'm over taking tests and doing homework and being constantly pressured by teachers to be this high-performing, successful individual. Graduating and not failing algebra is success enough for now. "Dad said you have some filing for me to do?"

Jan grins a little too broadly and points to the twelve-inch stack of papers on the filing cabinet behind her.

Well. She's been busy this week. "That's going to require some go-power. Can I have a Frappuccino before I tackle that?" I grin hopefully. Jan always hoards coffee drinks in the mini fridge below her desk, mostly because they mysteriously vanish when left in the main lunchroom fridge but the auto mechanics insist they know nothing about it. I am one of few who has been blessed with the sacred right of mini fridge passage.

"You can, but you'll have to go downstairs and brave the lunchroom. My little fridge is busted right now thanks to your dad's desire to try and improve everything." Jan flattens her lips together, unimpressed.

"Oh." We both know how Dad has this incurable need to 'improve' everything. Fridge isn't cold enough? Let's modify it. Car has a scratch? Let's paint the whole thing. Your shoes don't fit? Let's buy five new pairs, because more is always better. At least, in his mind. "I'll be back in five."

The floor downstairs transitions from pristine, white tile in the customer waiting area to filthy rubber floor mats littered with fast food wrappers in the mechanics' lunchroom. Boxes of car parts are stacked against the wall like a losing game of Tetris and a stained poster of a pinup girl on a Shelby Cobra hangs above the sink. Being a mechanic is not a clean job by any means, but even though I understand the nature of the trade I'm still trying to figure out how it's *this* dirty. The fridge's handle is sticky with dark, greasy fingerprints so I use my pinkies to open it. The odor of rotting meat wafts out and about knocks me unconscious. I swipe the first Frappuccino I see and slam the door shut, suppressing a shudder. *So gross.* If Dad doesn't fix the mini fridge by tomorrow, I will be forced to bring an ice chest.

As I turn to go back upstairs I run smack into a figure passing through the doorway. A young man stumbles back, startled, and looks up from the work order in his hands. I'm hit with his icy-blue gaze. "Whoa. Sorry." He slides around me, walking out the side door to the workers' bays.

Whoa, hello. I catch a whiff of cologne left in his wake, a rich, almost burnt sandalwood scent that makes me think of spices and campfires on the beach. I start to walk back into the front office then spin around and go peek out the shop door's window.

Blue Eyes is working in the first bay, motioning a fancy Mustang in to be examined. He's the youngest mechanic in the shop and for sure a new employee because I'd remember a face like his. The boy is all tall, smooth muscles with a defined jaw-line and a pinstripe work shirt with Dad's company logo on the breast pocket. I squint to read his name patch but am too far away. Pulling open his toolbox, he sorts a couple of wrenches out then pops the car's hood. His dark hair curls out from under a flat-billed cap and a gem glitters in his ear.

"You meet Mr. Darcy yet?" Dad's voice is suddenly behind me.

I nearly jump out of my skin. "W—what? Oh, not yet. Wait, did you say *Mr. Darcy*?"

"Sure did." Dad gives a sharp nod. "Scott Darcy."

I snort. "Since when is there an automotive shop in a Jane Austen novel?" I'd never met a real person with that last name before, and a car technician with grease on his hands doesn't fit. "He looks awfully young to be a tech. How old is he, twenty-one?"

Dad expels a smug laugh. "Your age."

"He's not eighteen! You're joking!"

"Dead serious. He graduated early from the Clackamas High School and was looking for a summer job that might spur some career opportunities. His mom goes to church with me and is fresh out of a divorce. I get the impression they need the financial help, so I said I'd give him a chance." Dad grins as he watches Scott check the car's oil. He has this weird ego about hiring young, smart people and gets all excited when they don't quit twenty-four hours after they've been hired. "I just gave him his first starter toolbox. He's doing great for someone this young and inexperienced. I'm impressed."

That's saying something. Dad rarely ever uses the word 'impressed'. He also doesn't give his tools away to just anyone because they're from Snap-On and worth a small fortune. This Scott Darcy must have shown serious promise. Either that, or my father is having a mid-life crisis and realizes he doesn't need ten-thousand tools (unlikely). *Good-looking with a good name and smart.* A shiver runs through my core. We're both staring at Scott when the boy lifts his head and does a double-take at us. I stiffen but Dad waves. Scott raises an eyebrow, giving an uncomfortable wave back.

"Yup, I smell lots of potential in that one," Dad declares, then his hand flies up to his Bluetooth. "Hello, Mr. Carter. I'm well and how are you?"

After Dad leaves the lunchroom, I toss one last glance into the shop and my lungs hitch. Scott watches me while pulling on a pair of rubber gloves. His blue eyes rise and fall on what he can see of me through the window, making my face flush. I want to stop staring because I'm embarrassing myself but it's like I've been put into a trance. A flicker of a smile crosses his face before he ducks under the car's hood, out of view.

I'm surprised at how instantly attracted to him I am. I'm not a love-at-first-sight kind of person—unless there's a puppy involved. Love at first sight got me into trouble when I was fifteen, bringing Danny Larson from our high school's Lacrosse team into my life. After three weeks of nightly phone calls and hallway kisses, he left me for some big-boobed wallflower when he realized I wasn't going to put out and she would. After several weeks of crying, self-loathing, and way too many bowls of ice cream, I picked myself up and moved on but boys didn't look the same after that.

I peel my eyes off the window. *Cool your jets, Elle.* We haven't even officially met yet and already I'm preparing for things that might never happen. Just seeing someone shouldn't have me wound up like this. I walk back through the waiting room where some customer's kids are playing in Dad's newly added Kiddy Corner. I catch a glimpse of Sony Pictures' *Transylvania* playing on the television. The scene where Jonathon accidentally crashes into Mavis on the staircase rolls across the screen. I watch Mavis as she sits up and rubs her head then locks eyes with Jonathon for the first time. A flash of light swirls around their eyes, the infamous *zing*.

That damned scene replays in my head the rest of the day.

June 17th, 2017

DARK AROUND THE EDGES

AWW, brought home Baby Blue on this day five years ago! Happy fifth birthday, Bluey! Jeez, how time flies!

"You're telling me," I mumble, looking at the Facebook post of my long-time friend, Rena, and her Blue Heeler mix. Rena and I became friends in second grade after I told her how much I liked the puppy folder she kept her homework in. She told me she was going to adopt a dog someday, and even as that day came over a decade later, I was with her. Bluey came from a doggy-foster program in Portland. She seemed like such a sweet pup until she decided to pee all over my lap while staring triumphantly into my eyes, as if her seven pounds of fluff just dominated my hundred-and-thirty pounds of human. She was a handful to raise, but Rena's post makes her look like a model citizen now as she sits on her porch sporting a snazzy, plaid collar.

I lay my phone on the counter then stare out the windows of Portland Diamond Company where I've worked as a diamond specialist for the past three years. Vinyl gemstone stickers cover our front window alongside the words, *Feeling Stressed? Just Remember: The Most Beautiful Things Form Under Pressure.*

I sigh. Pressure might turn some people into diamonds, but it seems to have turned me into a piece of graphite, sharp and dark around the edges. While my love of glittering, timeless things is what drew me into this industry, working with those who want glittering, timeless things is a challenge not for the faint of heart. Portland Diamond has been owned by the same family for over a hundred years, so we have a reputation. Customers don't just happen upon our store like they do in malls or shopping centers. They seek us out when they have a jewelry mission, armed with high expectations of both their gems and their salespeople. There is a level of perfection that must be upheld, a level that requires a lot of time and energy—and occasionally blood and tears.

My coworker, Isa, peers over the top of her gemology magazine. "You okay over there? You're sure sighing a lot today."

"Headache," I mutter, rubbing my temple.

One of Isa's dark and perfectly shaped eyebrows lifts. "Like a headache from life or you drank too much again?"

I glare at her. When you work with eight people in a store the size of a cracker box, you're pretty much family and everyone knows everything. Isa knows my love of wine well, but she doesn't know that I'm burning out on my job—or maybe I'm just burning out on life in general. "I just need some water." I get up from the front desk and walk back to the stock room.

The stock room isn't just where we store the loot. To my immediate right is a small office occupied by two desks, several filing cabinets, and Rob and Mary—the company accountant and merchandiser. The left side of the room is our makeshift lunch area, a cramped corner where we've wedged the fridge in between the sink and main diamond safe. The safe itself acts as counter space for our microwave and toaster oven. What actual countertop we do have is reserved for the almighty BrewMaster, the king of all coffee and latte machines. It was a Christmas gift from our owner, Charles, after he realized that overworking four menopausal women and two PMSing ones nonstop during the holiday season might go over better with a steady flow of caffeine.

My coworker, Carrie, has come in to take the afternoon shift and is waiting for her coffee to brew as I walk in. She peers over the pearlescent rims of her glasses, watching me head to the water dispenser. "Would you like some sweet morning nectar of life?" She holds up the steaming coffee pot. "Or I guess I should say sweet afternoon nectar at this point, since it's almost twelve-thirty."

"No, thanks. My mom and I have a coffee date in an hour so I'm sticking to water." I pluck a paper cup from the dispenser and fill it up.

"You and I both know one cup of coffee a day isn't enough." She pulls a rhinestone-studded mug out of the cupboard. "Your client Mia Johnson called again, by the way. Did

Isa tell you?"

"Yeah, I'll deal with her tomorrow." I'd rather not deal with her at all. Mia had called three times already this week, asking if her half-carat sapphire ring was back from the appraiser yet. People might get crazy over their money but I'm sure they're crazier over their jewelry, which in most cases has a bigger sentimental value than it does a dollar amount.

Carrie rolls her eyes. "If she didn't want to be patient she shouldn't have had us send it out to be appraised."

"Nobody has patience anymore." While I think Mia's problem is a matter of trust and not patience, as is so commonly found in the jewelry world, it's true that I've dealt with a lot of impatient people in the past few years—myself included. I blame adulthood. Our daily lives are overly packed with responsibilities and worries and emotions.

"Tell me about it. Oh, also Anne just left for lunch but she wanted me to tell you to check your hold box. She says no way is she repairing the Linda Parsons ring. It's a big clusterfuck with a center diamond that looks like frozen shit." Carrie grimaces.

While gemstones come in a lot of colors, you'll never witness anything more colorful than the language of the people selling them. Or maybe it's just our people. Those that come to know us personally are always a little surprised when they discover that behind our little black dresses and beautiful sales pitches there is a swearing sailor in each of us. "We judge people on their morals," says Tessa, our assistant manager. "Not their mouths."

"I figured she'd decline that one. Probably came from corporate sales land." We often repair jewelry from large chain stores. Big stores draw people in with their lovely slogans and cheap prices, but the pieces themselves aren't always quality and many are ticking time bombs for disaster. The term *clusterfuck* in our line of work is usually code for *mayday, mayday, retreat.*

"You can tell Mrs. Parsons the best thing to do for that ring is throw it off a boat ramp and claim the insurance money. Then she can buy a real bridal set." Carrie is only partially joking.

"Got it." I sip my water and return to the sales floor, knowing it's just another day in the land of fine jewelry.

To prevent both of us from going into overtime, Carrie and I share the split shift. I leave the store thirty minutes later and head over to my mother's house, which is conveniently located right next door to my own thanks to my father's long-ago attempt at buying up our street block. He had succeeded in purchasing four houses side by side with the intention of mowing them down and building his automotive shop in their place. None of this went over well with the county as our block was strictly residential (pretty sure Dad is still listed as Public Enemy Number One to the county planner). My father eventually had to accept that there are some forces greater than him, so he sold two of the houses and we moved to the country. Eventually he moved his shop to a legitimate facility and the remaining two houses became rentals, one of which I now occupy. The other was taken recently by my mother in the divorce.

I walk through the side door of Mom's little red house. "Mom?"

"Why is it that your children always come looking for you when you're in the bathroom?" a muffled voice echoes from down the hallway.

"Sorry," I laugh, flopping down on the couch. Mom's house has a cozy, cottage feel with its stone fireplace and wood-paneled walls. Pumpkin-scented candles flicker in the dining room, making the wood of her table appear a warm gray today. The table was the first piece of furniture she picked out by herself after the divorce—an empowering purchase for a woman who'd spent twenty-five years letting her husband make most of the decisions. I look around the room at the rest. The couch is a huge, microfiber sectional that my father would've hated. It has a steady supply of fleece throws folded over its cushions and a selection of velvet pillows. A rack of seashells hangs over one side while three wooden whale cut-outs hang above the other. They were not there yesterday.

"Mom, you finally hung the whales!" They've been sitting in her closet gathering dust, purchased from an art show in Cannon Beach some time ago when our lives were still normal.

"I did! I got a wild hair and decided it was time." Mom walks into the room, admiring her work while weaving her blonde waves into a braid. "I might've hung them too close together since they're bumping into each other, but that's okay. I'll fix them later. At least they're up now."

"I think they're great!" They look like they're swimming through the air, making my mother's home even more magical. Each one is painted to look like the real deal, done by a human hand versus a three-dimensional printer. We both had a strong appreciation for handmade art, for the raw beauty of human expression.

"Sorry, I'm not ready. We'll leave in five." Mom disappears to find her tennis shoes.

"No worries." I wander into the kitchen. *This is good.* The more art she hangs, the more I know she's getting comfortable in her new home, her new life. A small stack of mail is haphazardly strewn around the bar and I snoop through it in search of coupons. While my mailbox seems to favor bills and junk mail, hers often receives sales ads for places like Kohl's and Macy's and I could use some new heels for work. My hunt through the pile is cut short by an envelope stamped with huge, red letters: FINAL NOTICE.

Mom has an overdue bill? That's not like her. I slowly pick it up. Its envelope is bright yellow, font bold and angry. There's another one hiding beneath a National Geo magazine. *How is this possible*? Mom hasn't gone shopping in months. She shouldn't owe on anything. Dad paid off the few debts she had as part of the divorce settlement. *Or did he*? I glance over my shoulder. Mom's zipping her Nike jacket and yakking about some nature photographer on Instagram. I quickly bury the envelopes under the Geo magazine. *If she'd wanted me to know, she would've told me.*

Mom slings her purse over her shoulder. "So, I really want to make a trip over to—what is that look for?"

Oops. I hadn't quite rearranged my face from the surprise yet. "Nothing. This is my I-need-coffee face." I head to the front door before she can read into it any deeper.

***

Oregon City was once a small, quaint town that marked the end of the Oregon Trail. A land of woodlands and fields with a sprinkling of suburbia, my parents thought it would be the perfect place to build their business and raise a family in the mid-nineties. It really had been, until ten years ago when suddenly everyone and their mother decided to move to Portland. Now we have been infected with a terrible strain of urban sprawl, resulting in constant bumper-to-bumper traffic, crowded grocery stores, and a zillion building projects that promise room for all.

The only good news is we now have more Starbucks locations.

I swirl the ice around in my drink, sitting beneath a forest-green umbrella outside my favorite coffee chain. I'm not usually an advocate for large, corporate companies but Starbucks has been running through my veins since childhood. From that first strawberry Frappuccino to the iced triple-shot vanilla latte in my hands, Starbucks and I have formed a deep and unbreakable bond.

I'm waiting for Mom to come outside with her mocha. I'm still warring with myself over whether I should offer her financial assistance—not that I have much to offer, but I would find a way. *It must be the credit cards.* My free hand curls into a fist on the table. *Credit cards that Dad was supposed to pay off.* It was in the final decree but getting him to do right by anyone other than himself in the damned divorce had been like pulling teeth. He kept the family farmhouse, two new rental houses plus the one I rent, and the automotive business—paying off Mom's two measly credit cards should've been pocket change. *And he* still *didn't do it.* I can't believe this is my father, that a greedy, angry narcissist was hiding beneath those sparkly, loving eyes all my life. *I can't believe how wrong I was about him.* I glance at my reflection in Starbucks' windows, eyes going to the long, white scar above my elbow. My throat tightens up as I touch the other arm, which carries an identical mark. *So very, very wrong.*

I'm still fuming when Mom finally appears. "Did you see the tattoo on the blonde barista in there? Really nice Celtic braid on her arm," she says.

I stop touching my scars and straighten up. "No, I didn't."

"Lew," Mom says after she sits down. Her voice is quiet but hangs heavy in the air.

I hate it when she calls me Lew in that tone, not because it reminds me of my full name, Llewellyn, but because it usually means she's about to bring up something serious and potentially emotional.

She looks hard at my face, searching.

I smile and try to laugh it off. "What?"

"You're flickering."

"No, I'm not."

"You are. Your eyes are ignited like sparklers on New Year's Eve. What's put you in such a rage today?"

I let out a sound that is half sigh, half groan. This is what happens when you're as close as we are—nothing stays hidden. I stare at my coffee for a minute. "Why didn't Dad pay your credit cards off?"

Like clouds passing over the sun, my words darken Mom's bright expression. Her mouth tightens into a thin line and she takes a long sip of her mocha to loosen it up. "Because he hasn't."

"That's not fair."

"Your father doesn't play fair when he's angry. He didn't want to be divorced."

Well, maybe he shouldn't have turned into a raging nutjob then. "Okay, well, can you pay them off using your settlement money?" She must've at least got that after the judgement, as Oregon is an equalizing state in terms of divorce and my father kept the big assets. "I know you're hoarding it for retirement and school, but can't you use some of it and then take him back to court for contempt or..." I trail off because Mom is giving me this sorrowful, unblinking look. I realize I'm missing something. There's something else she hasn't told me.

I am no longer the only one flickering as she says, "I would... if he had actually *paid* the settlement money."

My mouth drops so hard it should hit the pavement. "I

thought he already did! Did you not collect that at the end of the divorce?" We rarely talk about the final days of the divorce because it always ends in tears, depression, and the need to eat copious amounts of ice cream but this is serious. I had been sure that part, at least, had been sorted out for her, the money stowed away in an account somewhere.

"Part of the final judgement was that he had ninety days to come up with the cash to pay me off. Well, that ninety days ended a month ago." Mom gives a tiny shrug, eyes welling with tears. She tries to stop them from spilling over by looking up at the umbrella. Her hands shake against the table she's so angry. "Your dad hates when control is taken away from him. I left, so he feels I deserve nothing. He'll find some way to put as much time between now and the day he pays me as possible."

"No settlement money?" I can't believe the words coming out of my mouth. Who does Jim Fox think he is, denying my mother her equal share? It doesn't matter that she left first—how can he defy the woman who took care of him, his house, his company, and his children for over twenty years? It's not like she wanted to be divorced, either, but there are some differences that cannot be resolved. There are some actions that cannot be taken back (I squeeze the scars on my arms).

"I've already informed my attorney. He's on vacation this week but will get back to me as soon as he returns." Mom takes her bagel out of its paper bag. She starts to open her cream cheese then folds the lid down and puts everything away. She's lost her appetite.

And just like that, the topic of Dad's behavior has tainted

another afternoon. *I should've just kept my mouth shut.* I hang my head over the back of the chair and close my eyes, tired of watching her suffer at his hand. Her pain isn't just over unpaid debts and the very real threat of poverty, either. It stems from the deep, dark roots of self-blame and mourning for a life and family that has been ripped apart and will never be the same. It's like falling down a rabbit hole to another dimension with no way back. We're just stuck here now.

Mom frowns at the metal lattice work in the table. "Lew, I don't want you to bear this anymore," she whispers. "This battle is between me and your dad. It isn't yours. I'll be fine. Really, everything will be okay."

Her words sound recited, as if they came from a daily affirmations book rather than her own mind. "Why do you always say that it's not my battle? When two rulers from opposite countries go to war do you really think the citizens of those countries are told 'hey, it's not your battle'? No! Everyone is affected!" I want to remind her the entire family has been shaken by her and Dad's separation, not just me, but I hold my tongue. "I just think it's ridiculous that after two years he's still yanking you around financially when he's got enough money to fund—" I cut off because a red Camaro has caught the corner of my eye. I jerk around in my seat only to find that its taillight is fully intact and there is no nude model sticker on the back window. *It's not Jordan's.*

Mom makes a funny face then follows my gaze. "Okay, that is the second red sports car you've jumped at this week. What is up?"

I didn't tell her what happened when I was out with Shaya the other day. "It's just, I might've run into... Scott." *Speaking of men who broke their women.*

Mom chokes on her drink. "Oh, shit."

"Yeah."

"What did he say?"

"'Oh, shit.'"

"Well, I guess that's fitting."

I nod in agreement. "Especially since it gave me diarrhea afterwards."

Mom expels a dark chuckle. "Still can't stand the sight of him, huh?"

"Nope."

"So what else did he say?"

"Well, we didn't technically speak to each other. I just saw the words come out of his mouth across the parking lot. I talked to Jordan but not gladly."

"Oh, God." Mom's nose scrunches up in disgust. "How is the Playboy after all these years?"

"Still a good-looking Playboy." I watch an old, bald guy in joggers step out of the Not-Fugly-Mobile and head into a game store. "He was trying to get me to come out to the Blitz club."

"Seriously? Like you would ever go back there." Mom pulls her bagel and cream cheese out again, the change in conversation calming enough to reattempt it. "Nothing like picking up your underage daughter from a club after the police call and tell you to come get her. Boy, wasn't that a parental experience."

"I didn't know we weren't supposed to be in there." The problem wasn't exactly that we were in an adult club but that I showed up with the wrong crowd. Jordan and some of his creepier friends had been dealing drugs behind the scenes and the undercover cop finally witnessed it. They busted our entire group that night, a group that I was more than happy to leave behind. Partying had never been my thing and Scott only ever went to prevent Jordan from driving home drunk.

I'm lost in distant memories of neon lights, handcuffs, and a time when my parents weren't so complicated when a Starbucks barista walks outside. Mom tugs my arm. "Hey, she's the one with the ink I was talking about earlier."

I zone back into reality, peering over at the girl's Celtic tattoo. There's something about her petite stature and silky blonde hair that is familiar. As she tips to the side, I catch a glimpse of her sharp facial features and the freckles below her eyes. "Kacey?"

I hadn't said it that loudly but the girl turns around. Her eyes go wide. "Elle?"

"Oh my gosh!" I get up from my chair to hug her. She squeals, setting her drink down and throwing her arms around me. She smells like green tea and hibiscus, a scent from summer days of old when we hung out at random parks, swam in Oregon's lakes, and picnicked on pebbly river beaches. "I thought you lived out in Hood River! What are you doing in my neck of the woods?"

Kacey grins that pearly white smile of hers and lifts her left hand. I'm blinded by the large, glittering diamond perched on her ring finger. "I'm getting hitched, Elly."

"Oh, Kacey." I take her hand in awe. The ring is classic, a rose gold band with a single round brilliant stone. It's at least one carat and the way it sparkles in the light tells me it's a specialty cut. Whoever he is, he's serious about her. "Wow, that's a rock. When's the wedding and who is he and why did I not get an invite?"

"It just happened two weeks ago," Kacey giggles. "So no details on wedding dates or invites yet. I'm still in shock!"

That makes two of us. The last time I saw her we were eighteen years old, sitting in a café downtown talking about college submissions. Now we've hit that weird stage in life where everyone we know still feels like kids but they aren't. They're doing adult things now, like getting married or having babies or buying houses. "You're back in Oregon City, then? My mom and I were staring at your ink." I motion behind me to where Mom is sitting.

"Oh, thanks." Kacey smiles and waves at her. "No, we're in Molalla now."

"So you got yourself a good ol' boy then?" South of Oregon City lies the country—maybe a little *too* country—town of Molalla, notorious for its rodeos, dusty Chevy trucks, and boys in cowboy hats.

"No, not really. He did buy me a dirt bike though, and I

got my first fishing license this year." Kacey's pale cheeks turn pink as her lipstick. Her smile is almost more blinding than the ring.

"Wow, congrats." I have the urge to roll my eyes, which is sad because I really am happy for her. It's just a little hard to absorb her blissful radiation when a dozen black clouds still loom over my life.

"How are you?" Kacey switches subjects. "What do you do now? Any boyfriends? Are you still writing books?"

My eye twitches a little. I want to tell her that I've been doing incredible things since high school, that I really did become a famous author like I said I was going to and that I have a date with Chris Pine next weekend to discuss his role in the movie version of my latest novel, which just got named an International Bestseller... but that isn't the truth. The truth is that my novels are still unpublished, I have dropped out of college twice, and I am renting a four-hundred square foot house from my father who I can barely speak to so that I can be near my mother. "Not really. I work a lot right now. Life's been too busy for books or boys."

"Ah, that's too bad. That story you wrote about the guy who tracks paranormal creatures and stuff was *so* good! You should not give up on those skills!"

"Thanks." My face is starting to hurt from all the smiling. "Well, I'll let you get back to your break. It was really good to see you."

"Oh, wait! Let me get your digits before you go." She snatches up her phone and I give her my number. "I'll send you a text. Reply to me so I know I've got it right, okay?"

"Will do. And congrats on the wedding again!" I start to edge away.

She blinks at me longingly, like she doesn't want me to leave. Once upon a time, we were inseparable and it's nice to see a little of that connection still exists. "What are you doing for the Fourth of July?"

My heart rolls over. "I don't celebrate the Fourth." It might've been a perfectly good day to celebrate our country's freedom, but for my family it was a day to remember when everything went to hell in a handbasket.

"Really? Girl, you were the firecracker queen when we were growing up! What happened?" My only response is a shrug. Kacey purses her lips, a sign that the wheels are rotating and she's trying to figure me out. "I know this is super last minute, but you should come out to the coast with me."

Her offer catches me off guard. "Really?"

"Really! My fiancé Dustin's brother has this gorgeous house on Yaquina Bay and they do a big party every year. We stay out there all week and they have a private beach and the boys cook lots of food—oh! And Rena will be there!"

Rena. Rena whose Facebook post of Baby Blue I had just been looking at this morning. Looking at and reminiscing of a time when I had friends, when she, Kacey, Shaya, and I were the four amigos. I start daydreaming about all of us being reunited on the beach, roasting hotdogs over a campfire, and laughing at stories from high school. For a split moment I consider the trip, then remember that I'm an adult with a job now. I'm also socially challenged.

"I would love to, Kacey, but the Fourth is so close. I doubt I can get out of work."

"I get it, but if something changes, let me know? I'd love to take you! It would be just like old times!"

Just like old times. "Sure thing." I hug her one more time and we say our goodbyes. I return to Mom and my iced latte, which has become too watery to drink. "Sorry, Mom. I haven't seen her in forever."

"Isn't that the girl you used to run around the countryside with?" Mom rubs her temple as if trying to stimulate her memory. "You guys would go hiking and swimming in the summer and get massive sunburns on your shoulders. Every time I turned around I had to go buy aloe."

"That's the one." I burnt more than just my shoulders while running around with Kacey and Rena, and I'm fairly certain there is still a bikini with my name on it tied to a tree outside Bagby Hot Springs, but Mom doesn't need to know that. She lays a hand on my shoulder. I sigh, sensing she's about to say something else I don't want to hear. "What?"

"You should go on that trip."

"Mom."

"You should! You've endured a lot these past couple of years. A break from life would be really good for you." She tilts her head, giving me her loving-mom-eyes stare. "Go have an adventure. You're young! Have them while you can because, shit, it's a lot harder when you're older!"

"You know we don't celebrate that day. Besides, I have to work and I have dogs."

I've caused another shadow in my mother's eyes. "Then maybe it's time you make new memories of the holiday." Her tone is stern, almost demanding. "I don't think you have ever taken a vacation at your job. I'm sure Charles would let you go."

"Even if he did, how am I supposed to afford a vacation right now? What am I going to do with the dogs?" Her sudden financial predicament makes me want to hoard what little savings I have in case I need to help her. Who am I kidding? I *will* be helping her. Life is expensive and unfair and I will do anything to lessen her suffering.

"Pack your own food and go lay on a beach for a few days. How much money could you need? And I'll take care of the dogs." Mom leans forward on the table, triumph gleaming in her eyes.

I groan, sinking in my chair. "I'll *think* about it."

May 5th 2012

THE MAN MAGNET

"Cannonball!" Kacey screams, racing off the end of the dock.

Rena and I squeal from the lake as she leaps over our heads. For only weighing a hundred pounds, her impact still sprays half the dock and soaks our faces. I spit out the taste of river water and swim to our three-person floaty tube, which Kacey tossed in seconds before jumping.

Kacey surfaces and shoves her hair back. "Wow. The water is warm today!"

"You sure it's the water?" Rena jokes, smirking as she swims in front of her.

"Damn it, Rena, you better not have peed!" Kacey back-paddles, trying to get away.

Rena starts laughing so hard she can hardly swim.

I slither through the floaty tube's center hole and hop up into my spot. The float has three seats and four cupholders, making me wish I had a cold drink to stuff in the holder closest to me. I left my water bottle in Kacey's car. "Oh come on, Kace, you were just talking about golden highlights, weren't you?" I motion to her white-blonde hair that practically glows beneath the sun.

"You two are sick." She hops up across from me, ringing out her long locks. A line of red is already forming across her shoulders and face despite the amount of sunscreen she slathered on in the park's parking lot.

"Thank God. You wouldn't like us if we were normal." Rena throws her black braid back then smooths her bikini top, which is so heavily padded people might believe she has boobs.

We all sigh and drop our sunglasses over our eyes. I lean back, feeling peaceful—a rare occurrence for me. The sun shines over the reservoir and surrounding woodlands of North Fork Park, not a cloud in the sky. The air holds the warm scent of pine trees and fresh PVC plastic. For once I'm not dwelling on my worries, such as the upcoming algebra final or the fact I haven't applied for college yet.

"Guys, our floaty tube needs a name," Kacey says, bringing me back to reality.

Rena and I hum in thought. We had all chipped in on the float this morning during a pitstop at a camp store outside the rugged mountain town of Estacada. Its red and white stripes make it look like a giant peppermint. "Candy," I say.

Rena pets its stripes. "*John* Candy."

Kacey giggles. "We should call it Katy Perry because it looks like it belongs in the music video to *California Girls*."

"Guys, we could call it The Threesome." Rena spreads her hands out in front of her like she sees the name in lights.

"Rena, do you ever stop thinking about sex?" I chuckle.

Rena peers over the rims of her Michael Kors sunglasses, her focus on the dock. "Nope."

I turn and see exactly what I expect: four young men in swim shorts are standing where we just were. They set down a cooler and collection of fishing rods, getting comfortable. Rena's eyes have honed on a guy that looks older than the others with a luscious dark tan and long ponytail. He pulls a can out of his cooler and tosses it to a shave-headed kid with tribal tattoos. Tribal catches it one-handed, standing barefoot by a tall guy whose flat-billed hat is on backwards and a carrot-top whose loud voice catches everyone's attention. "Yeah, dude, check it out!"

They are gawking at the floating peppermint.

"The official name of this float is The Man Magnet," I state.

"Perfect. I call the one with the ponytail." Rena licks her lips and lifts her chest.

"Ever notice that Rena always calls the biggest, brawniest dude in the group? That doesn't always mean he's well-endowed, you know." Kacey smiles and does a fake stretch, giving herself a pin-up girl pose.

I slouch back in my spot, scratching my belly. "You guys are ridiculous."

Rena raises a finger. "Hey, one day you will put out and join our ri-dick-ulousness."

"Yeah right, Elly isn't going to put out until the guy drops to one knee with a ring in his hand," Kacey teases.

"Screw you guys. I like being a nun." It's true. My lack of sexual interaction has kept me focused on my writing and career goals. It has also saved me from the inevitable drama and heartache that dating brings. All three of us know the devastation breakups cause, turning even the liveliest girls into paralyzed couch potatoes. I don't have the time or desire to be a paralyzed couch potato, plus I don't relish the idea of sharing my body with someone else's. I'd never admit it aloud, but the idea of some guy's skin inside of mine freaks me out.

"Yeah, I liked being a nun, too. Really, I did." Rena holds up a hand, the other over her chest as if she swears by it. "But once you try meat in your taco, you find that a taco by itself just isn't good enough anymore."

Kacey cracks up. "Call me the vegan Taco then," I reply. "Now if the right meat comes along some day, I'll think about it. Maybe." Strong emphasis on the maybe.

The floating peppermint—er, Man Magnet—has slowly rotated so that I am now facing the gang on the dock. The boys are whistling and whooping while stringing their fishing poles and drinking from neon-colored cans. Rena wiggles her fingers at them. I start to close my eyes and ignore them all when the guy in the flat-billed hat turns around.

I shoot up in my seat so fast I rock the whole float. Kacey and Rena jerk to look at me. "What happened? Did you get bit by something?" Kacey squeaks and both girls yank their feet out of the water.

Now it's my turn to look over the rims of my sunglasses because I can't believe what I'm seeing. His hair flips out from beneath his hat, a gem glittering in one ear. His gaze lingers on our float, those smooth cheekbones rounded up by a smile that instantly turns my stomach into a butterfly factory. *Of all the places he could be right now.*

"Holy crap, do you know one of them? Please say yes." Rena is trying to pinpoint my gaze.

Scott Darcy tilts his head, taking us in. I pull my sunglasses up and hope there is enough distance between us to prevent him from figuring out who I am, that's if he even remembers my face. "Nope. False alarm," I lie. "Can we steer this thing the other way now?"

"Come on! You are the last person to freak out over nothing." Rena scans the group. "Which one is he? I'm betting it's the dude with all the tribal tattoos."

"No, no, he's too bald. I know Elle's type—it's the tall, broad-shouldered one with the flat-billed hat." There's no doubt in Kacey's voice.

Sometimes it's painful how well they know me. "Will

you guys shut up? We're not really that far from shore."

Carrot Top yells from the dock, "Whoo baby! Hot out today!"

"Nice float," shouts Tattoos.

Rena straightens up in her seat, lips puckered in a duck-faced smile. That face has gotten us into so many awkward and troublesome situations that I know exactly what it means: the game is on. "Thanks, we call it The Man Magnet," she calls back.

"Well, gee, it's doing an awfully poor job! I don't see any men on that baby!" Carrot Top grins from ear to ear. "Maybe you should let us check it out for you, make sure it's working right!"

"Sure! Your ponytailed friend there looks like a good float fixer! Why don't you send him out?" Rena teases, leaning forward. Her arms are clenched to either side of her ribcage, squishing her boobs together like balloons.

Ponytail guy steps forward. "Sorry, I've fixed enough floats in my time" –he waves his left hand in the air, a gold band shining on his ring finger—"but my buddy Scott here can fix just about anything, so I'm sure he can solve the problem for ya!" Ponytail slaps Scott on the back.

My muscles all tighten up at once at the mentioning of his name. "Oh, God, don't bring him out here." I don't want him so close, not when I'm this unprepared. I should've used waterproof mascara. I should've worn a less revealing bathing suit. I should've shaved my legs before we left. I should've, I should've, I should've.

"So it *is* the kid in the hat," Kacey chimes, proud that she was right.

Rena's sexy pout morphs into a frown at Ponytail's rejection. She gives Scott a once over as he laughs and shoves his married friend aside. Her eyes drift sideways as she turns to look at me. "Okay, this is your shot to call dibs on your meat."

"Excuse me?"

"Call dibs now or I want to call dibs. But if you call dibs? You gotta tell me where you met him and if there are more where he comes from because I could cook an egg with the heat radiating off that boy!"

If there was ever a time that I needed Rena to stop talking, it was right now. I feel weird about calling dibs on this. I've never really called dibs on anything because I prefer to share —share clothes, share front seat privileges, share the last piece of pizza.... Carrot Top and Tattoos stand on either side of Scott, motioning for us to come to the dock. Scott nods at us and gives a slow flick of the hand. It's like an invisible rope is tied between that hand and my pathetic heart, which pulls with his every movement.

Some things aren't meant for sharing.

"Fine. Dibs." At least it will keep Rena off him, though as I say it I have this sinking feeling and it's not because I'm leaning toward the edge of the float. When it comes to men, I'm not nearly as bold as she is and they aren't naturally drawn to me like they are to Kacey. Fidgeting nervously with the ties on my bikini bottoms, I realize the wind is pushing us back toward shore and we are about to get involved with the group.

Rena gets out first and slides gracefully onto the dock. I expect the group to swarm her like a million-dollar prize but instead they all step back, like she might be a grenade with a pulled pin. Carrot Top is the only one who doesn't shy away, quickly stepping forward to offer her a hand. "You, lovely lady, look like you could use a drink," he grins, pulling her to her feet. "I'm Jordan Cane."

Kacey climbs onto the dock next then spins to hold the float so it doesn't drift away with me. I almost tell her to let it go, let me drift. Rena is sure to embarrass us and while I deal with that on a regular basis, this time is different. *She'll embarrass you more if you disappear*. Exhaling a sound of frustration, I reach my hands out to brace against the damp wood and hoist myself out of the water. The smell of wet moss and lichen mixes with that of deodorant and tobacco as I stand up. My primitive survival instincts prickle to life as I remind myself that I might know of Scott but he is still a stranger to me, as are his friends. Kacey must feel the same way because she hovers abnormally close to my side.

Rena joins this Jordan Cane in the center of his gang. They're starting to warm up a bit, asking questions and making jokes about The Man Magnet. Jordan tosses her a Coke out of their cooler then asks, "What can I get you ladies? I've got Sprite, Coke, and good old pale ale."

"A Sprite, please. If you've got one to spare." Kacey smiles nervously.

"We have plenty to spare," Ponytail assures her, casting his fishing line into the lake.

I lean against the dock railing, watching Scott through my sunglasses. I've brushed my damp hair down over my front but still feel exposed. His attention is caught between me and Kacey and I bristle with jealousy as he yanks the Sprite out of Jordan's hands and extends it to her. Kacey beams, fingers brushing against his as she accepts the drink. He offers her a smile—not a flicker of one like he did with me at the shop, but a real one—and I don't miss the spark that ignites between them.

Great. The butterflies in my stomach melt into an acidic pool that gives me heartburn. Rena's forehead scrunches and I can tell she's wondering why I'm letting Kacey flirt with a dude that I just called dibs on. I decide that calling dibs on a human being is stupid and that a shy nun like me really has no business dating right now anyway. Kacey is prettier and much more experienced in this department and doesn't have a strict novel-writing schedule.

I'm in the middle of self-sabotage when the guy with the tribal tattoos nods at me. "Nice suit, Harley."

I glance down at my Harley-Quinn-themed bikini. "Thanks. Nice tats." I wave at the native-style totem stretching down his left side. "Is it a wolf?"

"It is," he replies, impressed that I guessed right. "Got any of your own?"

"Not yet, but I will soon." A black and white drawing of a hummingbird who carries the sun in her wings and the moon in her belly is taped to my mirror at home. I promised my mother I would stare at it for six months on paper before permanently inking it into my skin. We agreed that if I still wanted it by graduation, I could have it. "I'm hunting for the right artist right now."

"What are you getting?"

"A hummingbird. It's my own design."

"Ah, you should talk to Scott's brother." Tattoos fists Scott in the arm, making him spill the can of beer he's sipping. "He can do custom like you've never seen."

Scott wipes the spill off his chin, annoyed, then does a double-take at me. The hair on my neck stands up. He narrows his eyes, gears visibly rotating behind them, and the words I've been waiting for finally come out. "Hey, aren't you Jim Fox's daughter?"

He has a smooth, slightly husky voice. The neighboring hairs on my shoulders proceed to stand up at the sound of it. *So much for getting out of this unnoticed.* I push my glasses onto my head. No reason to hide behind them now. "Maybe."

Scott's eyes race around my figure, trying to decide if there's any chance I'm not. A hard pucker has appeared between his brows, like he dislikes that I've made him question his own judgement. "No, do not send her to Glen." That husky voice turns harsh and nonnegotiable. "Jim would rip me a new one if he knew my brother tattooed his kid."

Kid. He pretty much spits the word at me, like I'm some young, dumb child talking ignorantly of adult matters. Put aside that the term is insult enough coming from the mouth of someone my own age, the dismissive expression on his face like his boss' offspring is an annoyance unworthy of his focus brings my temper crackling to life. My mother calls this sudden burst of anger 'lighting the match' and it usually occurs about the same time the filter on my mouth breaks.

"Who are you calling *kid*? I'm no more a kid than you are! Nice beer, by the way, speaking of things that might cause Jim to rip you a new one. Hopefully you're smarter than the last *kid* he hired who showed up to work underage and hungover. That guy didn't last long."

The group falls silent. Ponytail's eyes go wide, probably because he's the oldest and the buyer of the beer. Tattoos is glancing between us, words stuck to his open lips, and Kacey and Rena are exchanging uncomfortable grins, probably questioning their decision to bring me into this. So much for thinking Rena would be the one to embarrass us.

I lean calmly against the railing, staring pokerfaced at my father's youngest employee. Scott says nothing but *you bitch* is written in clear, bold font across his face. He clamps his jaws together as if it's all he can do to hold back the fury-laden things he clearly wants to say to me, but fear rims his eyes. He doesn't want his friend in trouble. He doesn't want Jim's reputation of him soiled.

Deep down, I don't want those things either, but once my temper is set ablaze there is nothing left to do but wait for it to burn out. I'm not going to wait for that moment here. With the mood of the group thoroughly spoiled, I decide it's time to exit. My unfiltered mouth announces, "And with that, I need to pee." Sauntering off the dock, I head to the park bathrooms, disappointed in the situation and myself for reacting.

June 26th, 2017

TO VACATION, OR NOT TO VACATION?

I'm late to work thanks to an accident on the 205 Highway. Carrie and Tessa are stuck in the same traffic jam further back, so I'm the first salesperson to Portland Diamond.

I set up most of the sales floor by myself. Two customers walk in directly after I unlock the door—a pair of red-haired sisters in matching shirts who make snarky remarks about what poor service it is to open late. Their names are Elenore and Evelyn but Tweedledee and Tweedledum would've suited them better. Tweedledee has come in to pick up her bridal set that we soldered together and doesn't understand why the diamonds don't line up properly. I explain that not all wedding bands are created equal and that she should've ordered the match if she had wanted them perfect. She scolds me for not telling her that in the first place, though I was not the one who sold her the rings. Tweedledum has an appointment to size her ring but can't get it off her finger (she hasn't taken it off in ten years). After several attempts involving lotion, Windex, and the YouTube rubber band trick—which doesn't work worth a damn—I tell her we need to cut it off.

"Cut my wedding ring off? Are you serious?" She mutters something about needing ice to reduce the swelling and then the piece will come off like butter. They both leave the store in a huff and I pray they stay good on their promise to not come back.

Tessa's tall, blonde figure looms over me as the Tweedles walk out the door. She glares after them, mapping them in her memory as they climb into a shiny Land Rover parked in front of the store. "Don't you think twice about Bucktooth and Butt-Flap out there," Tessa growls. "It's not our fault one's too fat to get her ring off and the other is too stupid to have ordered a matching band. They're getting aggravation tax if they come back. Now go get some coffee." She all but pushes me off the sales floor.

My hands shake while pouring creamer into a mug. I shouldn't be mad. I've dealt with far worse customers, but the fuse on my temper is roughly the length of a tampon string today. I lift the mug to my lips and am about to sip when my phone dings and a new text message flashes on the screen.

Hi Elle! It's Bertie, inviting you to your Dad's annual Fourth of July barbecue. We're serving lobster and I just brought back this great chardonnay from the wine show in Napa! Try to RSVP because we have a lot of people interested. Hope to see you!

I growl at the ceiling. I never know how to take Dad's girlfriend's texts, the few of them that I get. We've only met twice and that's enough for me. *Lobster and Napa Valley chardonnay.* He's serving lobster, bought with money that should be going to my mother and her overdue bills. He's serving lobster when my mother can barely afford basic essentials. When I was growing up, he would hand Mom a hundred dollars a week and we had to make it stretch for four people, forget lobster. We hardly ever traveled and of the few parties I remember throwing—they were usually birthday parties—he missed most of them thanks to work. *Why is this woman so worth spoiling*? It's gut-wrenching, the idea that this new woman has something we never did, that she is worth something we never were.

I text back:

Already have plans, thanks.

I want to brush off the text and the knotting sensation in my chest, but I can't. Thinking of my father causes frequent bouts of *Iron heart syndrome*, a sensation that feels like I'm carrying a dumbbell around in my rib cage and it's crushing my lungs. I want to text him and give him a piece of my mind, tell him what a shitty person he is, but it won't do any good. It never does. All it does is give him and Bertie ammo to make me look like the emotionally disturbed relation I've become. "Poor Jim," I'd heard one of his cousins whisper at last year's Christmas gathering. Poor Jim, whose wife left him. Poor Jim, whose daughter so outwardly hates him. Poor, poor Jim.

If only they knew the whole story.

I'm trying to take some deep breaths when my eyes fall on the company corkboard. Among the various notes from vendors and emails from my boss, Charles, the yearly calendar is posted. The calendar is usually a donation from one of our bigger vendors, a thank you for making them so much money. This year's donation is from Gabrielle, a popular vendor who recreates vintage engagement rings. June's birthstone is pearl so this month's image features a hand holding a seashell filled to the brim with multicolored freshwaters.

I flip the page. July appears, flashing a woman's neck draped in rubies, her lips slightly parted and just as red. The first week of July is almost always reserved by someone going out of town for the Fourth, but this year those dates are blank on our calendar. No one has asked for time off until the fifteenth.

I think about Kacey. *You* can *go on that trip*.

Not that I really want to go, or do I? Maybe Mom's right and laying in the sand for a few days would be good for me. The last vacation I took was for my aunt's wedding three years ago and we spent the entire trip setting tables and serving cake. Maybe it would be good for Rena, Kacey, and me to reconnect. Friends are not something I kept in abundance and the list of enjoyable people in my life is short.

I plunk Kacey's number into my phone. *Just ask what the dates are. There's no harm in asking. I could go down for a day or two, just to catch up with everyone, then come home.* I've just hit the *send* button on a text when the stock room door opens. Carrie pops her head in and throws me this joyless grin.

"What now?" I grumble.

"Bob Kripston's wife is here. You know, Bob, who had the ugly family pendant made? She doesn't like the design and has some questions." Carrie rolls her eyes. "Gee, *big* surprise there."

Bob Kripston was one of my annoying clients who had become even more annoying when he'd decided that he had kickass jewelry design skills. For his wife's birthday in May, he'd had me put together a custom 'family pendant' and while I understood that he'd wanted the birthstones to be tiered a certain way to represent the family tree, the pendant had come out looking like a giant, gem-covered penis. "Tell her I'll be right out."

Carrie muffles a giggle then closes the door as my phone buzzes with Kacey's reply.

July 1st through the 6th! Are you able to come? :)

I stare at the screen. It would be good to get away from work. It would also be good to step back from my messy family and reassess how I'm going to help my mom. Picking up a pen, I scribble my initials on the calendar, marking out July 1st through the 6th. I leave a text for Kacey before going out to deal with Mrs. Kripston.

If my boss says yes, I'm in!

May 7th, 2012

APOLOGY

Since it's the final term of my senior year, I only have three classes. Third period history seems to drag on forever and by the time it ends I actually want to go to work.

I pull into the shop parking lot, which is a mess because Dad is an overachiever when it comes to how many cars his company can fix at a time. My skin prickles as I see Scott standing in my usual parking space. He's bent over the hood of a black Toyota Tacoma, standing beside a heavily tattooed gentleman who watches me debate on whether I'm going to squeeze into the patch of pavement beside them or not.

I huff loudly, hitting reverse. He probably took my spot on purpose. I backtrack and park behind the shop by the tire pile. My car isn't anything fancy but I think she's too good to be stuck next to a mound of greasy, used rubber. Dad's sitting at the front desk as I walk in, haranguing somebody on his Bluetooth about overcharging his account. His head service writer, Marcus, appears to be writing up parts orders but is really scrolling through Facebook.

Jan is also in an intense phone conversation involving money when I walk upstairs. We barely wave at each other. I sit down at Dad's desk and start organizing the piles of paper that have grown too large to comfortably work over. Shoes stomp up the stairs while I'm sorting out junk mail, trudge past Jan's desk, and stop directly behind me. I glance over my shoulder, assuming it's Dad.

It's Scott.

I startle out of my chair, dropping several envelopes on the floor.

"Jeez, sorry." Scott steps back, hands in the air like he didn't expect that reaction.

I didn't either. "Can I help you?" I don't mean to snap but I'm on edge from being caught off guard.

"Yeah, I think you can." He starts to snap back then calms his voice when Jan looks over at us. "Can we talk?"

I sense there is an unspoken *alone* at the end of that question. I slowly lay the fallen envelopes on the desk. *What could he possibly want to talk to me about*? After yesterday and the event on the dock, I'm the last person he should want to talk to. "Yeah, I guess."

He heads back to the hallway. My pulse pounds in my ears as I follow. The lunchroom is empty when we walk in, so he closes the door behind us. I sit at the counter, particularly close to the tray of knives because I've watched too many scary movies where the killer shuts and locks the door after the young, dumb girl has been drawn in.

Scott folds his arms, leaning against the door so that no one can enter. A frost settles over those blue eyes as he asks, "Did you tell your dad you saw me at North Fork yesterday?"

"No. Why are you asking?"

"Because he's acting weird around me."

"He acts weird around everyone. It's called being *bipolar*."

"Look, I know you don't know me and I don't know you, but I need this job, okay?" Scott's words are angry but also desperate. "I'm sorry if I did something to piss you off but I don't want your dad thinking he's hired some young, drunken loser. So if you could just not say anything about yesterday and put it behind us, I would appreciate it."

Oh. I think back to my words on the dock. *Hopefully you're smarter than the last kid he hired who showed up to work underage and hungover. That guy didn't last long.* I scan him up and down because I *would* tell my dad if I thought he was wasting his time. Scott's gaze is crystal clear, his eyes neither sunken nor red and puffy, and his stance is perfectly stable. His hands are blackened by fresh grease and two work orders are tucked into the pocket of his work shirt. Nothing about his behavior suggests he's hungover or wasting anyone's time. "He doesn't think that," I assure him, feeling bad that I insinuated otherwise. "I owe you an apology. However, treating me like some annoying child in front of your friends and mine *was* the move of a loser. You might not know me, either, but that's not how you should've treated your boss's daughter on the first go round."

Like a cobra lowering its hood, Scott's guard falls a little. A confused look crosses his face—does he not recognize how cold his behavior was?—and he blinks at the wall. After a moment, he says, "I guess I didn't talk to you very nicely."

"You guess," I chuckle, unamused. "What did I do to make you dislike me that suddenly? Are you against tattoos or something?"

"Definitely not. And I'm sorry for calling you kid when I should've..." He trails off. A momentary silence hangs between us, then he lets out a sound that is somewhere between a laugh and a snort.

"What?" Did I miss the funny part here?

"I don't know your name." A flicker of an almost-smile crosses his face, but he quickly hides it. "The techs all call you *Boss Daughter* and your friend Rena kept referring to you as *The Firecracker* but I've yet to formally meet you."

"Oh." I had secretly worried that Rena had called me something far more humiliating after I'd left the dock, like the vegan taco or the nun with irritable virgin syndrome (that's her new favorite). Scott holds out a slow hand, gesturing for me to speak. "Oh. You want me to just tell you my name?"

"Were you expecting me to guess?"

"If you want to formally meet me, you can introduce yourself first." Since my father is terrible about proper introductions, especially regarding new employees, I either make it my business to introduce myself or ignore them all together. Since I haven't been able to ignore Scott ever, a real introduction after yesterday seems like a fair punishment.

Scott blinks, waiting to see if I'm serious. When I continue to sit there quietly, he shifts uncomfortably on his feet, pale cheeks taking on a redder hue. Exhaling an overly controlled breath, he steps away from the door. He wipes the grease on his pants and holds out a hand. "Hi. My name is Scott Darcy."

"Much better." I stand up and flip my hair back, clearing my throat. "Hi, Scott. I'm Elle Fox. It's so nice to meet you." I shake his hand despite the grease.

Scott's tongue is pressed into the side of his cheek. He's either extremely amused or annoyed—I don't know which. I don't care, either. After the shake, he doesn't let my hand go. "So are we good now or am I supposed to kiss it, too?"

"You tell me. I can only tell you that my good opinion once lost *is* usually lost forever, Mr. Darcy." I smirk, assuming he—like my father—won't catch the Jane Austen reference and will give me another confused stare.

"Well, I can't have that now, can I?" He bends at the waist like an eighteenth-century gentleman and pulls my hand to his face, brushing a quick kiss over my knuckles.

My jaw hangs as he releases my hand. "*Whoa*, a gentleman! Rare occurrence in this industry." The auto mechanics I'm accustomed to are grubby, don't care if their butt cracks are hanging out of their pants much less flashing the customers, and often compete in belching competitions out in the work bays.

Scott makes a clicking sound with his tongue. "I have many shades, Miss Fox." He flicks his brows at me before heading to the door. "Oh. Before I forget." He fishes in his shirt pocket, pulling a black square of cardstock from the folded work orders.

"What's this?" I ask as he holds it out.

"My brother's business card. If you're serious about getting a tattoo and you want one that doesn't suck, you should go see him. Just do me a favor and don't tell Jim who told you to go there."

The card is painted with roses atop a bird skull and reads, EAGLE EYE TATTOO, GLEN DARCY. It's located near the Clackamas shopping mall, barely ten minutes from here. "Oh. Thanks." If Glen Darcy is responsible for the art on the card, as would be expected, his style is right up my alley. "You seem pretty sure that my dad hates tattoos."

"Oh, trust me." Scott shoves the sleeve of his work tee up. A tattoo that looks like armor peeks out. A raven hovers in the center of the design, wings covering most of his shoulder. The bird clutches a knife in its talons, blade pointing down his arm. "I'm *very* sure your dad hates tattoos."

July 1st 2017

THE HOUSE, THE HOTTIE, AND THE HOLY SHIT MOMENT

My vacation time was approved at work.

I'm up early trying to clean the house before Kacey arrives to pick me up. The nice thing about living in a tiny house is that the cleanup is quick. I finish loading the dishwasher then vacuum the floors and make my bed all within thirty minutes. A small shadow moves around on my bathmat while I brush my teeth. Dobby, my littlest dog, is pacing circles into the fabric. Named after one of my favorite Harry Potter characters, he was my quarter-life crisis dog, brought home the same day Mom started packing up her belongings at the farmhouse. By the time I put my toothbrush away, his whole body is shaking and his eyes are so wide they're bulging out of his head.

"Dobby," I groan, wishing he wouldn't do that. This behavior is the precursor to one of his doggy anxiety attacks, which are usually triggered by changes in his environment. He must sense that I'm leaving, so now his hair is going to fall out and there will probably be diarrhea and chewed shoes all over the house by the time Mom gets here. "Stop it. Just stop, okay? It's only a few days." He cries and stamps his leg which isn't much bigger than a chicken bone. "Oh my God." I pick him up and tuck him in his front-carry pouch, which is basically just a baby sling for dogs. The pouch has been a saving grace because it keeps him out from under foot and he can go more places with me, but people always stare. Everyone in our neighborhood knows the Dog Pouch Lady, especially my neighbors, Mr. and Mrs. Marigold, who often watch me from their porch while drinking their afternoon bottle of wine. I can tell by their expressions they think I need to hurry up and pop out a baby. The thing is, I don't want a baby. Babies makes me nauseous, especially when I see the drool running or smell the loaded diaper. My Mom Chip has crossed wires and only activates in the presence of animals.

I haul Dobby around while packing a bag of snack food. Meanwhile, trying to open the zipper on my suitcase is the other ruling force in the house, Piglet. I scoot the small dog away and she wanders off to check out my rain boots, which I've just set by the front door. Despite her Disney-inspired name, Piglet is brave. Too brave at times. She was given to me at four weeks old because her mother had birthed an abnormally large litter for a Chihuahua and couldn't provide for all the pups. I had still been speaking and working with Dad at the time and raised her out of a blanket-filled Amazon box beneath his desk. Under my care, she grew from a sickly, one-pound runt into a wild, five-pound terror who now steals socks and sleeps on my face at night.

I'm digging my flipflops out of the closet when my phone

buzzes. A picture of a rather stoic-looking young man pops up on the screen. His hair is pulled back in a low ponytail and he's wearing a Legend of Zelda shirt.

I smile. *Matt.* I open my brother's text message.

Heard you're not coming to Dad's wing ding for the Fourth. Bertie's pissed.

My smiles flips. I make an annoyed sound then text back.

You want to know what I'm pissed about? Dad spending Mom's settlement money on wine and lobster. Did you know he's fighting the divorce decree he signed?

It's several minutes before he texts back. I wonder if he's finding that as hard to swallow as I did.

Not surprised. Dad has this extra bitter attitude about *everything* right now. Him and Bertie got in a fight over what kind of toilet paper to keep in the house, for God's sake. The second I apply for community college, I'm out of this place.

I tell him that I hope he stays true to that. Matt should've moved out of the family farmhouse when Mom and I did instead of watching it descend into Bertie and Jim Land, but he was afraid that Dad would take his college fund away if he left. Once upon a time, I would've told him don't be silly—Dad is our dad he will always be open to helping us—but these days I really don't know. His mental state is too unstable.

Matt suddenly adds:

Dad said he tried to call you last week but you didn't answer. Are you ever going to talk to him again?

My stomach goes all wobbly.

I don't know. Probably not. I gotta go. I've got a friend coming over. Talk to you after the Fourth? I love you little brother.

Back in the day, my brother would've left it at that but not today.

Love you, too, Sis. You know it was an accident, right? What happened between you and Dad? I know that doesn't excuse it, but still.

I don't respond. Just what I need: my brother throwing rocks at my heart right before I leave for vacation. I've just laid my phone face down on the kitchen counter when I hear a car pull into my driveway. Dobby kicks me in the chest and shoves out of his pouch. "Okay, okay!" I catch him before he can fall to the ground then rip the pouch off.

Both dogs bark up a storm as I try to bar them from the front door. There's no question as to why the neighborhood kids avoid my house every Halloween. Through the front window, Kacey can be seen strolling up the broken pavement of my sidewalk. She's smiling at my tiny house, at the pansies and snapdragons blooming by the front porch. The flowerbed is probably the only redeeming quality about this place.

I wrestle both dogs into the bedroom then open the door. "Hey." I smile.

"I love your little house," she gushes. "Oh my gosh, it's so cute! Is it yours?"

"My dad's. I just rent it." I should start giving my rent money to Mom, tell Dad I am paying for his debts and he'll have to find some other way to afford his lobster parties, but I don't have the energy for another war yet. "It's a tiny, crappy little house but it's home for now."

"It's not crappy! Why would you say that?" She mills around my kitchen, touching the pink hand towels and the ugly silver backsplash. Her foot lands on one of Piglet's squeaky toys. "And obviously you have puppies!" She gestures toward the ruckus behind my bedroom door.

"Two spoiled, rotten terrors more like." I'm happy she likes my house, but I want her out before she notices the peeling countertop, the stains on the floorboards, and the fact we literally had to cut a hole in the bathroom wall for the water heater to fit. "Suitcase in the trunk?"

"Oh, yes!" She skips out the door then pauses. "Can I meet your babies first?"

She spends an abnormally long time fawning over my dogs before we finally leave. It hurts my heart to close the door on their tiny, inquiring faces, knowing I won't be back to hold them tonight. *Mom will have to hold them for me.* Kacey pops the trunk of her Subaru and we stuff my suitcase in alongside three of hers.

"Wow, Kace, did you pack your whole closet for this trip?" I joke.

"Hey, a girl needs options," she giggles. "One of them is Dustin's. My honey-bunny can't come down until the fourth, so I'm taking his suitcase for him." She winks at me. "I can't wait for you to meet his brother."

I'm not sure what that's supposed to mean.

After years of being apart, I'd worried that it would be difficult to reconnect with Kacey, but we seem to pick up where we left off. She tells me about Hood River, an arid town on the Columbia River whose rolling hills are known to grow some of the best fruit and wine in Oregon. She spent three years working in a bistro that changed into a winery, then met her fiancé at a summer rodeo through a friend. Their connection quickly became serious, so she left Hood River and they bought a house in Molalla. A week ago they went to a fancy dinner where he'd asked her to marry him.

My stories aren't nearly as exciting or joyful, but I tell her about my job at Portland Diamond and the growing challenge of working with the public. I tell her about how Piglet snores when she sleeps and Dobby helps pull weeds in the garden (he also pulls out freshly planted bulbs, but we're working on that). I touch only briefly on my parents' divorce and our divided family. I try to prevent her from asking questions by saying, "Anyway, Dustin sounds really nice."

"He is. I am *so* lucky." A flirty smirk shapes her lips. "So you are seriously still single, huh?"

I don't like how she said *still*, like she automatically assumes I haven't dated anybody since Scott. "Seriously."

"I'm sorry."

"Don't be. Some of us are better at being single."

A weird expression crosses Kacey's face. "You always were good at being single—that is *not* an insult, by the way. I wish I had your independence. I've never been single for longer than ten minutes."

Her comment takes me by surprise. She and Rena had always poked fun at my chronic singledom, for being the 'nun' while they were out hunting and testing out men in the hopes of finding their perfect matches. For some reason, it's important to me that she appreciates my independence. "That's better than Rena, who's never been single for longer than five."

Kacey giggles. "Au contraire. She is single as we speak."

I huff a sound of disbelief. "No way."

"That's what I said!"

"There must be a guy somewhere in the background."

"Nope. She's coming alone on this trip. I asked her if we needed to make room for her boyfriend, Jake, and she proceeded to tell me 'there is no boyfriend'. So yeah."

"Wow." Just when I think I've heard it all. "So what do you and Dustin do for fun? What does he do for work?" I quiz her like I do my future brides, trying to gauge how serious and long-term this marriage might be.

"He works at Cane Steel Fabrication as a welder. When he's not working, we go fishing or ride dirt bikes. Sometimes we'll go check out local events in town. We have a lot of fun together." Kacey glows.

A bell goes off in my head. "Cane Steel Fabrication?" I find something discomforting about the name, but Kacey doesn't clarify. Some must-hear song from our high school days has started playing on the radio and she excitedly turns it up.

We cross the Yaquina Bay Bridge, a long highway across the water whose metal arches are the color of The Statue of Liberty. A large storm cloud is rolling in but the sun shines through it, casting pale rays on the ocean. The scent of salt and seaweed drift through my window, a wild, clean smell that triggers some slumbering part of me that hasn't been awake in a long time. The dumbbell that's been sitting on my lungs lifts for the first time in months and I can breathe again. For the next five days, there are no schedules or responsibilities, no customers or problematic family to be concerned over. Just friends and a good time. Suddenly I want to lay in the sand, see Rena, and explore the Newport area with my friends. *Whoa, am I feeling happy*?

The Subaru cruises through town and turns off on a side street that follows the bay. I crane my neck over Kacey's steering wheel to see the water shimmering beyond tall patches of dune grass and old, weather-worn houses. She laughs as my eyes follow a large heron flying over the road. "Still a bird nerd after all these years, huh?"

"I am right now." Birding is a growing pastime in Oregon, and I have been fortunate enough to fall in love with the hobby. I pat the front of my backpack and feel the hard edge of my travel binoculars still tucked behind the fabric. It's been months since they've been taken out.

We turn onto a one-way gravel road heavily lined with ferns and ponderosa pines. My beloved, salty air is given a woodsy stain that is reminiscent of my childhood. The forest opens to reveal a squared patch of driveway against the side of an enormous, cedar-shingled house.

My eyes widen. "Whoa."

Kacey giggles, then unbuckles and gets out.

The house is built on a slope, facing a well-groomed yard just below the driveway. Two towers, one on either end of the home, are layered in stone-colored brick and the dormers in the house's middle are so huge they each have their own balcony. I hear voices coming from the covered outdoor patio as I get out of the car. Four figures lounge by a fireplace in plush-looking furniture.

"I'm underdressed." I should've shown up in glittering sandals and a dress, not flipflops and jeans.

"You are not! Trust me, they aren't as fancy as they look." Kacey hands me my suitcase then drops two of hers to the ground. "Now follow me and come meet the gang." She leads the way down the gravel steps.

Adrenaline rushes through me like it always does when I meet new people. It's easy to socialize at work because deep down I really don't care what the customers think of me but out here, with potential friends, I'm a little nervous. Upon closer inspection, I see there are five figures on the deck: three guys and two girls, all in a conversation about boats and fishing and the time someone's nipple got pinched by a crab. As we approach, one of the girls turns around and starts squealing. Her brunette hair and padded boobs give her away instantly.

"Elly!" Rena races up the steps and throws her arms around me.

The impact of Rena's body mixed with the weight of my suitcase knocks us over. We topple down the last three stairs, nearly wiping Kacey out, and I land face-first on the patio. Rena falls half beside and half on top of me. I must've blacked out for a minute because when I come to, I'm staring into the brown eyes of a rather gorgeous stranger.

"Elle?" He says my name. "Elle, can you hear me? Do I need to call an ambulance?"

"No," I manage to spit out. "I'm okay." I can't feel my legs and my head is pounding, but I'm fine. I have to be fine because if I'm not this will be too embarrassing.

His eyes fall on my mouth. His own mouth is rimmed by a five' o'clock shadow that curls around a chiseled chin with a dimple in the center. One of his ebony curls is hanging near my face, his hair a sexy mess that smells of barbecue smoke and tropical paradise. "Kace, she split her lip. Can you grab the First Aid kit from the guest bathroom?" His voice has a slight accent, maybe European? Canadian?

I reach up to touch my lower lip and my fingers come away with blood. "Oh, shoot."

"Elle, I'm so sorry!" Rena comes into view, hands on her cheeks. "Oh my God, I'm so, *so* sorry!"

"I'm good. Really." I push myself into a sitting position. My vision goes sideways for a minute before evening out. I try to lighten the situation by saying, "I guess I know how to make an entrance."

Brown Eyes chuckles, pulling over a wicker chair from the outdoor table. "Hey, better to be remembered than forgotten, right? Here, let me help you." He offers me his hands, which are linked to golden-brown, muscular arms.

"I've got it, no worries." I wave him off and crawl into the chair in front of a full audience of strangers. There's a skinny dude who looks about thirty standing by the fireplace with a woman whose pink swimsuit and golden waves make me think of Legally Blonde. Lounging on an outdoor couch is a thickset guy in Hawaiian-print shorts and a shirt that reads: WARNING: MAY CONTAIN WHISKEY.

"Can I get you anything? Water? Pepsi? Shot of Tequila?" Brown Eyes quirks a sorry smile.

My heart goes kind of fuzzy. "Thanks, I'm okay. I mean, if you see my dignity anywhere on the ground grab it for me, but other than that I'm good." I'm cupping my lip as it continues to leak blood. I've dripped all over my jeans and have stains on my sweater. What a way to start a vacation.

Brown Eyes chuckles, handing me a stack of napkins from one of the outdoor tables. "I'm Noah."

It's a good thing I've stuffed napkins around my mouth because I'm grinning like an idiot. "Llewellyn. I go by Elle, which I guess you already knew."

"I've got the kit!" Kacey rushes out of the house. She opens the box on the table and pushes clean paper towel into my hands.

"Do you think she'll need stitches? Oh my God, I'm an awful friend," Rena cries.

"It's not that bad—I'm just a bleeder. And a friend that is *that* excited to see someone is not an awful friend. My suitcase is the jerk." I glare at it, covered in sandy dirt laying by the stairs. I should've brought my weekender, the smaller one with better wheels. Noah walks over and picks it up, then shows us inside to the bathroom so I can clean up properly.

The sliding glass door opens into a kitchen that is straight out of Pinterest with its marble countertops, polished oak floors, and vaulted ceilings. Kacey steers me down a hall-way that has that clean hotel smell and into a guest bathroom that could easily fit the contents of my entire living room. The split in my lip isn't that deep but the skin around it is already swelling.

I'm sitting on a wooden toilet seat rimmed in gold plat-ting when Rena barges in with a wine glass. "Here. Noah sent you a glass of his best champagne."

"Oh, thanks. That was nice of him." I take a sip, the drink

crisp and cool in my mouth with the lovely aftertaste of pears. "Mmm, this is good. Who is this Noah anyway?"

Kacey smiles mischievously. "He's the one I wanted you to meet. That's Dustin's older brother."

"That dark, hot mess of curls owns *this* house?" It's hard enough for millennials to buy a small, crappy house in Portland much less a mini mansion near the sea. "How does he afford it? What does he do for work?"

"Inherited," Kacey answers. "Well, sort of. His grandmother lives downstairs, but the boys' grandfather passed away six months ago and left it in their names. It would've gone to their dad if he hadn't drunk himself into an early grave. Here, Elle, I pried some clothes out of your suitcase." She hands me a sweater and a pair of leggings.

"Noah is a *great* guy." Rena widens her eyes at me in a *hint, hint* sort of way.

"Yes, he was very nice to me as I bled all over his expensive patio." My skin gets all hot as I think of the smile he gave me, which felt like a hello-I-want-to-know-you smile.

I'm about to take off my clothes when I hear a car horn beep. Kacey jerks her head up. "That sounded like Dustin's Honda."

"I thought he was driving his truck down on the Fourth," Rena says.

"That's what he said, but I'm just going to go check." Kacey goes to the door. "I'll be right back."

"What's your opinion on this Dustin?" I ask Rena as

Kacey's footsteps fade away.

"He's nice. I think he's fine for her." Rena throws my bloody paper towels into a garbage bag, making a scrunchy face. "He has this subtle, I don't know, underlying snob attitude. They had some real issues a year ago. I didn't think they were going to make it—don't tell Kace I told you that. Then the boys' grandpa died and they both inherited some money,"—she rubs her fingers together to emphasize just how much—"so now Dustin has a house and they're engaged. The house is gorgeous, not something you see our generation buying every day."

"Well, hopefully that works out for them." I strip my clothes off and pull on the new, clean set. Funny how money enters a relationship and then suddenly all the serious issues get swept under the rug. I cringe as Dad and Bertie come to mind. "So, what about you? How's life? Who's your current flavor of the month?" I still can't picture Rena without someone on her rope.

She gives a dark laugh, washing her hands. "No flavor this month. I know. It's shocking." Her voice teeters a little toward the end. She keeps her eyes on the sink.

I wonder if this is about that Jake guy. I'm not sure what to say because I've never seen Rena get emotional about a dude before. Back when I knew her, they usually came and went like the tide. "Well, at least we have wine."

Rena laughs. "I'm so glad you came. I was really worried you wouldn't because you know that Dustin works for Dale Cane's steel shop."

That terrible, warning feeling I'd had in the car comes back. "Wait, Dale Cane? As in—"

"Rena!" Kacey's voice ricochets off the hallway walls, cutting me off. We both jump as she bursts into the bathroom. "We—uh—can you come outside for a minute?"

Rena furrows her eyebrows, confused, but exits the bathroom. I start to follow but Kacey throws her arm up. "No! Just hang out for a minute, will you? Just hang out and relax. I will be right back!"

"In the bathroom? Really?" Not that it was a bad spot to hang out but still. "Kace, what's going on?"

"Everything's totally fine, I just need you to hang out for a minute while I go organize a few things. Okay?" Kacey grins a little too widely. "Here, have a seat at the bar. Noah designed it himself, did I tell you that? The carvings in the wood were all his design."

I allow myself to be directed into the kitchen, but I don't stay put. As soon as Kacey and Rena disappear outside, I wander over to the sliding glass door. *Is there some problem with me being here*? I can't quite see the parking lot but I do see Noah and his friends looking at it as they lounge on outdoor couches staged around a granite table with fire glass burning in the center. Their expressions are unreadable.

Wait a minute. Dale Cane. Dale Cane, as in father to Jordan Cane? No. No, that can't be, because if it's true then that means Dustin works alongside Jordan, and given their age group and Jordan's vivacious nature they are probably friends. And this is a weekend for friends to be together, which means

—

Holy shit, no.

I fling the sliding glass door open. My heart leaps into my throat and blocks my airway when I see it: a junky red Camaro is parked by Kacey's Subaru. Her blonde ponytail waves in front of his tall, red-headed figure. She's blocking him from the stairs. *No, no, no*. My right leg hurts from the tumble I just took, but I still take the steps two by two. I don't care that Jordan and Dustin are friends. That doesn't matter. What I care about is that Jordan rarely goes anywhere without his *best* friend, and there is no reason he would've left him behind for a trip like this.

Rena stands beside Kacey and her shoulders visibly rise when she sees me coming. Kacey turns toward me. Jordan bursts out laughing. "Elly! No way, you're here, too?" He holds his hands out like he's going to hug me.

I toss my arm up like it's a big stop sign. His clothes reek of marijuana and peppermint gum and I swear if he touches me he'll be the next person with a bloodied lip, payment for screwing up my long overdue vacation that I was just getting excited about. I hawk-eye the passenger seat of The Fugly Mobile, but there's no one inside. "Where is he?"

Almost as if on cue, the crunching sound of tires over gravel penetrates the parking lot. A black Toyota Tacoma growls out of the trees and into the driveway. Its windows are too dark to see inside, but the sticker on the back window with a raven clutching a knife tells me all I need to know. As the dumbbell returns to weigh down my lungs and crush my heart, the Tacoma parks and the engine dies. I give Kacey and Rena my best what-in-the-fucking-fuck-is-going-on-here face but neither give a response. They stand like a pair of awkward statues with their hands over their mouths.

The door opens and the driver steps out. He's wearing what used to be my favorite outfit on him: a pair of 501 Levi's and a fitted, black tee shirt. Tattoos run in colorful patterns down both of his arms and there's a black stud in his left ear.

Scott stands in his open door for a long moment, then finally pushes his sunglasses up. Those blue eyes come right for me.

I want to tear them out of his head. I want to tear everyone's eyes out of their heads because this should not be happening.

"What the hell is *he* doing here?" I demand.

"I didn't know." Kacey's voice is shivery and mouselike. "Elle, if I had known—"

"I was invited." Scott speaks up, interrupting Kacey. He slowly walks toward us, never blinking, never breaking eye contact. "What the hell are *you* doing here?"

"*I* was invited," I retort.

Scott throws Jordan the same hostile look I just gave both girls, like this is some sort of sick setup and he does not find it funny. Jordan holds both hands up in a don't-blame-this-on-me way.

I'm breathing so hard I'm either going to burst into tears or smack the shit out of someone. It's amazing that after all this time he can still draw out the beast in me like no one else can. I step back from the group and gather myself. *I am not going to have a meltdown. I am in control. I have all the tools to deal with this. I am* not *going to lose it.*

"Look, we're all adults here," Rena chimes in, stating the bloody obvious. "Clearly there has been some miscommunication, but this house is big enough for twenty people so I'm sure we can find some way to fit you two into—"

"No," Scott and I say at the same time.

"Why don't you just leave?" I suggest.

He shoots back, "Why don't you?"

"Because I was here first and I plan on having a real vacation for once!"

"Congratulations! I've been friends with Noah for years and I just drove here all the way from Ridgefield." He dares to step closer, just inches away from me. "So if you think I'm getting back in that truck, you are mistaken."

He's so close that the smell of cigarette smoke and Old Spice clouds my head. Memories that I thought I'd gotten rid of go dancing through my mind, stirring up sensations of bliss, pleasure, and long forgotten comforts. It hurts. Hurts like heartburn on a hundred-degree day mixed with a full-body sunburn and a hangover. It's probably my imagination, but for a split second I swear those memories reflect in his eyes.

Seeing the holes that have appeared in my armor, I back down and head for the stairs. Kacey's footsteps trail behind while Rena stays and tries to reason out the situation. The group on the patio all watch with silent questions as I pass by. Striding into the kitchen, I pluck my wine glass off the bar. I'm busy chugging its contents when Kacey walks in.

"Elle, I'm so sorry," she whispers. "He hardly ever comes to these things. When he does, it's usually with Jordan and I was told Jordan was working this week."

The last of the champagne burns my throat on the way down. I set the glass on the marble counter then search Kacey's face. *How could she not tell me they all know each other*? Her expression radiates pure honesty; she really didn't think they would be here.

"Please don't let him ruin this trip. I'll have Noah put you in the furthest part of the house away from him—just promise me you won't leave," she begs, hands clasped together. "Rena and I have so many fun things planned and I have no idea when we might get this chance again! Please don't call a cab, Elle."

I lean against the bar, debating. The fireplace on the patio is crackling outside, Noah's group of friends smiling and laughing as they enjoy its warmth. Legally Blonde throws her arm over the shoulders of the tall, scrawny guy who vaguely resembles a Ken doll. I wonder how long they've all been friends. It's important to have good friends, true ones. We need people we can count on who can count on us… I don't have very many friends. This is my chance to reestablish bonds with two of my oldest companions.

I'm not going to let Scott ruin it.

"I won't leave," I declare.

Kacey let out a huge sigh. “Good! Because we’re going to make this the greatest time ever! Really, we are!”

I exhale at the vaulted ceiling. Maybe it’s the champagne, but I’m suddenly a little calmer. “Sorry I lost it up there.”

“Don’t apologize for having emotions. I would’ve done the same thing,” Kacey assures. “Now let’s go talk to Noah. We need to get you settled in for our amazing weekend!”

***

While the house is big enough to comfortably accommodate twenty people, there is one small problem: almost all the bedrooms are on the third floor, including the room that Jordan and Scott apparently like to stay in, which is right next to Rena and Kacey’s. There is a master bedroom on the main floor, but Noah already has Ken Doll and Legally Blonde (their real names are Allen and Betsey) set up there, and I refuse to let him move them. It wouldn’t be right and it would embarrass me even more.

“Honestly, I am great on a couch. I’d be happy to set up camp in the living room.” I say, trying to convince Noah as he leads me down the basement stairs.

“It’s just so close to the kitchen, I’m worried we’ll wake you up too early. Chris and Allen like to get up and go fishing before dawn.” He knocks on the door at the bottom of the steps. “This is my grandmother’s studio apartment. She has lots of room down here.”

"Your *grandmother*? Oh, no, no! Don't make your grandmother make room for me, oh my gosh. I've already imposed enough as it is!" Like falling down the patio and getting in an argument with my ex didn't make me look like a great new guest to have, now I'm going to impose on his elderly family member. "Really, I can sleep on the couch! It's fine if the guys are up early I have no problem with that!"

"It's okay. Nana loves company," Noah insists.

Now I've done it. I'm shifting uncomfortably when the basement door opens and a little brown-skinned woman appears. "Ninito," she exclaims, reaching up to pat his cheeks. He's at least two feet taller than her. "Come in, I just made fry bread!"

"No, thank you, Nana." Noah bends down and kisses her forehead then motions to me. "This is Elle Fox. I'm running low on rooms upstairs. Can I trouble you to let her use your spare down here?" He says something else, but it's in a language I am unfamiliar with.

I give an awkward wave. *This poor old woman should not have to be saddled with me.* Nana shuffles into the hall, peering into my face. Her eyes are like vats of melted chocolate, dark hair thicker than my own and braided down to her tailbone. She smells like rosemary and cooking oil. The edge of her wrinkled lip pulls up. "She's good. She may stay." She flicks a hand. "Come, child."

I don't thank Noah as I leave him at the door and enter the old woman's apartment. He still smiles and nods, like I'm some reluctant kid who needs encouraging.

Nana leads the way down a hallway decorated in carved driftwood and beaded murals. The hall exits into a daylight basement with an open floorplan. Like upstairs, the kitchen is all oak cabinets and steel appliances but while the countertops above play host to iPads and phone chargers, Nana's has live plants growing out of coffee cups and up the windowsills.

"You know Noah long?" Nana asks.

"No. He seems very nice though," I reply.

"He is a good boy. Smart, unlike his father." She pushes a door open in the living room, gesturing me in.

Her guest bedroom is small, the queen-size mattress taking up half of it. A handmade quilt and some type of animal fur are draped neatly over the sheets. The dresser is jammed in the closet and is missing its top drawer while the bedside table is home to half a dozen candles. No lamp. *Home sweet home*. I drop my suitcase.

"I have only one rule." Nana holds up a ring-laden finger. "Respect Speaks With Seas." She touches the painting beside her, which features a pissed-looking Indian chief holding a spear in his hand. "And no noise after ten."

That's two rules, I think but don't say. "Thank you, Nana. You really don't have to do this I feel bad invading your apartment."

"Nonsense." She waves a hand. "You make yourself at home."

"Do you go by something other than Nana that I should know about?"

"Everyone calls me Nana." She smiles. She has one of those endearing, old lady smiles that makes me think of Christmas cookies and bedtime stories.

"I'll do my best to not be a nuisance," I promise.

She bursts out laughing and leaves, and I can't decide if it's a don't-be-silly-there-are-no-nuisances sort of laugh or the laugh of you're-young-you're-automatically-a-nuisance. Finally alone, I close the door and flop onto the bed. It's an old spring mattress so my body jiggles while the wires adjust. The popcorn ceiling stares back at me as I try to grasp everything that just happened. I'm already regretting the loss of my composure in the parking lot.

So much for thinking you were over it. The reality is, that day at Starbucks was all the evidence I needed to know I wasn't a hundred percent over Scott. I don't know if it's the stress or the glass of wine or just the sheer lack of rest in my life, but I start to doze off. Of all the things swarming through my head, I start dreaming about tattoos.

May 9th, 2012

THE TATTOO

I tell Dad I'm busy studying for finals and can't come to work, but it's a lie.

I pull into the parking lot of a sketchy-looking strip mall not far from Clackamas Town Center. The light is out in the L of the Plaid Place sign, which sits on the mall's left side, so it reads *Paid Place*. Two women in short skirts and stilettos walk out and I question if the store has more than one purpose. At the end of the strip next to a Teriyaki joint is a tattoo shop. The shop's window is covered in a giant decal of a golden eagle with a crown on its head, a sword in its claws. Above the bird is a line of letters in big, bold font that reads, EAGLE EYE TATTOO.

A bell jingles as I open the door. I've only been inside a couple tattoo studios and they had all looked the same: flash art on the walls, pleather couches, coffee table holding a book of the artists' work. Eagle Eye is different: a faux brick fireplace decorated with matching candelabras and two vases filled with painted glass eyeballs takes up the left wall. Two Victorian style chairs sit before it, the velvet of their cushions matching the drapes in the window. The most striking part of the room is painted on the wall: a woman, arms and legs carefully positioned to hide her more intimate features, peers out at the studio's guests through a feathered mask. She wears nothing but a series of tribal-inspired tattoos. An eagle, wings spread behind her, perches on her shoulder.

"Can I help you?"

A young man, inked from the neck down, is sitting at the front desk, sketching. He doesn't look at me but his haircut and the rich sweep of landscape inked across his arm have met my eyes before. He owns the black Toyota Tacoma that Scott was working on at Dad's shop.

"Hi. Um, yes, I want to see about pricing a tattoo?"

"What are you wanting?" He brushes some eraser debris off his page. The outlines of a giant rose—it must be going on somebody's hip or chest—with a skull peeking out of its center take up the paper before him. Still no eye contact.

I pull out my own, much punier sketchbook from my bag. Stepping forward, I flip to the hummingbird drawing. "I'm looking to have this put on my shoulder. I was told to come see Glen?"

He holds out a hand for my book, the other hand still sketching. I reluctantly pass it over. His eyes roam the lines in my design, around the sun hidden in my bird's left forewing and the moon in her right. "Do you want it black, grey, and white like this?"

"Yes, please. So you must be Glen?" I know the answer before he gives it. He has the same vivid blue eyes as Scott ... not to mention the same closed-off attitude.

"The one and only." Glen's pierced eyebrow quirks, mouth almost tilting into a smile. He traces a finger down the trailing wisps of the bird's tail. "I'm guessing this is supposed to be like, a celestial hummingbird?"

I nod. *I'm guessing nonchalant assholism runs in your family*? Scott had made it seem as if his brother would be the right person for this project and while I hadn't expected Glen to jump for joy at the chance to tattoo somebody else's artwork, I had expected better customer service. He's running a business after all. I'm about to tell him I'll take my business elsewhere when the bell on the door jingles.

Scott walks in with a Subway bag in one hand and his phone in the other. He looks up at the counter then does a double-take at me, standing stiffly near Glen's drawing table. "Hey," he says, surprised, then glances at Glen who is still examining—and probably picking apart—my hummingbird. "So much for studying for finals?"

Blood rushes to my cheeks. "Studying's overrated."

"Indeed." He drops the Subway sandwich on Glen's desk then leans over his brother's shoulder, peering at my sketchbook. "Did you draw this?" I nod. "Huh."

"Hey, just because it isn't your taste doesn't mean it's not someone else's."

"No, it's a cool concept. You should let Glen fix up some of your line work though." Scott's pinky traces the sun rays in the bird's feathers. "You don't want these melting together over time."

"Melting? What do you mean?"

"Your skin is going to stretch and change as you get older," Glen explains. "You don't want your lines to be too close together." He points to the word WANDERLUST tattooed on his forearm. The W and the A are starting to shrink into themselves, and the E has attached to the R.

"Oh." I see where some of my inner wing work may become a problem in the future. I drew a few of the feathers close together as well as some of the finer details, like the stars hidden in her tail.

"Let Glen redraw it," Scott insists.

I purse my lips, thinking of the hours that had gone into the drawing, how many erasers I had used up and how much concentration and technical effort it took. "But then it won't be mine anymore."

Scott snorts. "It'll be yours, just more functional. Trust me."

I look hard at my work. I really wanted my own personal art on my body but perfectionism is another of my strong traits. My eyes drift back to the woman on the wall. Her color saturation is so lush, every highlight perfectly placed, every shadow elegantly executed. Each feather on the eagle is evenly detailed and matched. That mural took ten times as many hours as my hummingbird, and the artist was probably a lot more devoted to his craft.

"Did you paint the woman on the wall?" I ask Glen.

Pride glimmers behind his pupils. "Every inch of her."

"Then I guess I'm going to trust you to fix it."

"Alright. I'm going to eat lunch, then I'll get to work on it. Give me an hour?"

I do, and I park myself in one of the Victorian style chairs by the fireplace while the brothers share a foot-long. I suppose most people would've gone and found something to do, but I'm staying to monitor the drawing's progress because I want to make sure the important details of the piece are not removed... and I'm secretly observing Scott in his natural environment. For two people who remind me of the human embodiment of hermit crabs, they seem perfectly comfortable with each other, sharing food and drinks and mumbled conversation. Every now and again they crack a smile. Traffic rumbles lightly outside and prevents me from hearing most of their conversation. Having Scott around seems to have lightened Glen's mood because suddenly he addresses me. "So, Ella."

My heart jumps.

Scott corrects him. "Elle."

A mischievous smile curves Glen's mouth. "You would know." Scott punches him in the shoulder. "Ouch! Hey, that's my drawing arm." He rubs his arm, the freshly inked scales of a Chinese dragon flickering beneath the sleeve of his tee. "I hear you're the force to be reckoned with down at Jim's Automotive, *Elle*."

Uh oh. I'm wound as tight as a batter's hand, but my voice is almost lazy as I reply, "I'm a force to be reckoned with in general."

Both boys' eyes lift to examine how much force and I realize they don't have the same eyes at all. Glen's are far more penetrating, like I'm being x-rayed. "I can see that," he says thoughtfully. "Is that why you threatened my brother's job?"

"Glen." Scott's voice is a warning.

Great, he told him about our conflict on the dock. "If your brother is to ever lose his job, which is highly doubtful given how much pride my father currently has in him, it won't be because of me," I make clear. "And just for the record, your brother is an equal—if not more difficult force—to be reckoned with."

Glen takes a bite of his sandwich. "Oh, trust me, I already knew that." Another mischievous smile. "Which is why I find it interesting that you've made such an impression on my seemingly-unimpressionable sibling." He slaps Scott on the back.

Scott pelts him in the face with a chunk of onion. "Don't listen right now, please," he pleads with me as heat is visibly crawling up his neck.

Glen suppresses a grin as Scott gets up, shaking his head

as he disappears down the hallway. The sound of water rushing echoes throughout the studio.

Keeping my poker face intact, I shake my own head like they're just silly boys and start scrolling through Pinterest on my phone. Meanwhile, my heart is running laps around the question, *what kind of impression*?

I'm just starting to calm my nerves when Scott heads for the door, car keys in hand. He pushes on the handle like he's going to go out then stops and turns toward me. "Are you getting tattooed today?"

"If Glen has time." I've been dreaming about it for months and had planned to have it done before high school graduation in two weeks. It would be a mark of success, a reminder that I have completed a major milestone and will be soaring into the next chapter of my life and I desperately want to show it off at the ceremony.

"He'll make time." Scott seems sure of that. "See you at work."

The bell jingles as he walks out the door. It takes all my strength to not turn around and peer out the window. *He's not anything special. Just another boy, an acquaintance,* I remind myself. *An acquaintance who clearly talks about what a beast you are behind your back.* My brain keeps trying to pick apart Glen's words in the hopes of finding positive potential, but if I had been an outsider looking in at this situation I would've seen it for exactly what it was: a big brother trying to protect his little brother. Despite Glen's fantastic artistic skill, I should've gone somewhere else for this.

Fifteen minutes pass and Glen has gone back to ignoring me. The whole situation grows more embarrassing in this new stretch of silence so I say, “Glen.”

“Yes?” Still not looking up.

“You know, you don’t have to do my tattoo if you don’t want to. I’d understand.”

Now he looks at me. His brows are quirked in confusion. “Do you not want me to do your tattoo?” He sounds offended.

“I’d love for you to do my tattoo. Your work is amazing. But if it’s too weird because of the apparent bad blood between your brother and me, I wouldn’t be upset if—”

“Bad blood?” He sounds generally shocked, then barks a laugh. “Girl, you wouldn’t be sitting here if you and my brother had bad blood! Why would you think such a thing?”

“Uh, did he not complain about the loud-mouth cow he pissed off up at North Fork Park who just so happened to be his boss’ daughter?”

“No.” Glen is trying not to laugh as he draws. “But he did say his boss’ daughter showed up in a bikini and caught his dumb, underage ass drinking beer in public and she might make him pay. Most people don’t threaten others for no reason, so of course my first question to him was, ‘well, were you being a dick?’ He had no response, so I assume he provoked you in some way.”

“Yes, thank you!” *He mentioned I was in a bikini*?

Glen nods. "Oh, I know my brother."

"He's not a very warm, fuzzy type."

"Not really. Try to go easy on him though. He's been through a lot recently, trying to help our mom through her divorce, watching our dad skip town with his new lover. He's shouldering a lot right now." Glen blows eraser shavings off his sketch, brushing them aside. "He wouldn't have sent you here if he disliked you. He also wouldn't have asked me to squeeze you in today on my catch-up day. Next time, you're going on the waiting list like everyone else."

"Whoa, hold up! Scott *asked* you to squeeze me in?"

"As I said: he can't dislike you that much." Glen holds up a piece of translucent paper. "Now quit worrying about my brother and come look at this."

My lips round into an O as I approach the table. What took me weeks to accomplish Glen has outdone in a matter of minutes: my hummingbird went from being two-dimensional to being *alive*. He's taken the design and amplified it, bringing it to life in ways that I never could. The best part is that I can still see my ideas and patterns, only now she feels more like a masterpiece from a famous gallery and not a two-dimensional creation from high school art class.

"You like?" Glen asks.

"I love." It's more than I could've asked for. I want her to be part of me, right now, flapping those sunray-filled wings across my shoulder. "When can we start? What are you going to charge for her?"

"Where do you want her?"

"Here." I touch the back of my right shoulder blade.

"I'll give you the family discount." Glen winks. "Hundred-fifty sound good?"

"Let's do it." I whip out my wallet and slam three fifty-dollar bills on his desk. He swipes my money off the table and sticks it in his shirt pocket, then passes me a form to fill out.

I follow him down a hallway painted with Oregon-inspired foliage and flying skulls. We step into a room that's almost all windows and velvet curtains. He has me sit backwards in one of his tattoo chairs while he prints off a peel-and-stick version of my bird. From where I'm sitting, the front desk is straight ahead and a flash of movement catches my eye beneath it. I sit straight up, praying it's not a rat or I'm out of here. Two beady eyes peek down the hall.

It's a small, pale dog. A grin spreads across my face. "You have a little chihuahua?" Glen just went up twenty points in my book.

"More like the little chihuahua has me," Glen says. "Usually she stays at home with her little pug brother, but she's incredibly pregnant right now and I don't want to leave her alone."

I wiggle my fingers, which captures the small creature's attention. She crawls out of her bed to waddle down the hall, belly dragging against the floor. "Wow, she's *super* pregnant."

She sniffs my ankle while I pet her head. I receive a small tail wag as thanks. Her collar reads, TATTOO SUPPORT DOG. "How many puppies are in there?"

"Vet thinks four, which isn't common for a dog of her size." Glen grabs my bird off the printer. "I've got the clinic on speed dial for when it happens. I don't want to risk anything happening to my little Cheerio." He blows kisses at her. She whines, watching him like the entire world revolves around his presence.

Cheerio gives my hand a final lick of approval then waddles back to her bed. "She's absolutely darling. I've always wanted a chihuahua but never had the chance."

"Well, you're in luck. Despite my wife's pleading, I'm not keeping her entire brood. You want one, you can have one."

"Really?"

"Really, really."

"I might take you up on that offer." If only I can convince my parents. They did ask what I wanted for a graduation gift. "Is your pug the father?"

"No. I have no idea what the father looks like. I picked her up off the streets of Mexico when I was there. She was skin and bones, hiding behind a taco cart I had just bought food at. The cook in the cart came out to shoe her away and she ran right to me. The guy got all defensive and said, 'Sir, is this your dog?' I don't know what came over me, but I bent down and picked her up. 'Yes,' I said. 'Yes, she is.' So we shared tacos and I took her home on the plane. Didn't realize I was actually taking home five dogs, but I still wouldn't have changed my mind."

My lips are parted in awe. I take back the thought about him being a nonchalant ass. "What a beautiful story."

"She's a lucky pup. My wife spoils her." Glen waves a finger at my jacket. "Unzip. Let's get this party started."

We place the hummingbird a couple of different times before it sits right. Glen wets the paper and a purple image appears on my skin. I shiver with delight. "Perfect."

"Now the real fun begins." Sitting on a bench with wheels, he rolls around the room plucking color from a wall of ink bottles and organizing tiny plastic cups onto a tray. My stomach coils when he pulls a packet of needles out of a drawer. They're much longer and pointier than I imagined.

"Nervous?" Glen asks, watching me blanch at the needles.

"Not at all," I lie.

"You ever been tattooed before?" He pulls on a pair of rubber gloves. I shake my head. "Didn't think so. I'll go easy on ya. It's not going to be a walk in the park though."

"I'm aware." When I was younger, I used to pinch myself and hold it until deep half-moons were indented in my skin, telling myself a tattoo was going to hurt worse. My mother got her first tat when she turned forty, an atlas moth across her lower back. She'd described it like someone scratching you really, really hard. My godmother, Debbie, said it was like being stung by a bee over and over again.

He squirts ink—which is so thick it looks more like paint —into the plastic cups. "Why a hummingbird with the sun and moon?"

"It represents change, the dusk of one chapter in my life and the dawn of a new one," I explain. "I'm graduating in a couple of weeks. My future is wide open, though a little unknown."

"Good choice, seeing as the hummingbird in a lot of cultures represents enlightenment. You going to college next year?"

"I might take a couple of years off to write. I wrote a novel for my senior project." Under the guidance of my English teacher, I was also learning what it takes to get one's book into the hands of a reputable publishing company.

Glen nods, impressed. "Let me guess: romantic fiction?"

"No." *Please, God, tell me I didn't do something to make him think I'm a sappy romance writer*. "Paranormal."

"Ah, my favorite. You'll have to tell me if it gets published." Glen picks up his tattoo gun and hits the peddle, testing the machine. It emits a shrill, metallic sound that sets my teeth on edge. "Deep breaths," he says, watching my shoulders tense up. "Relax. You'll make this more painful by being uptight. I'll start with small lines first, let you get used to it."

"Okay." I rub the seams of my yoga pants between my fingers, trying to distract myself.

Glen's fingers rub circles into my shoulder, preparing the skin. "Ready?"

I inhale loudly. *Here's to the future*. "Ready."

July 1st 2017

CONFESSIONS

"Elle!" I jerk awake on the hard spring mattress. The smell of corn oil and the picture of the Indian chief remind me that I'm not at home. "What?" I call, not fully awake.

"We're going to Mother Shuckers Seafood House on the beach! Hurry up!" Rena calls from the other side of the door.

"Mother what? What time is it?" I feel around for my phone and smack my hand on the nightstand. "Ouch!" I hunt for a lamp or a light switch, then remember Nana's guestroom is like something out of the eighteenth century and there's no obvious electricity.

"It's a bar by the beach! Now come up and get ready with us," giggles Kacey.

"Be there in a minute!" My phone is crammed between the nightstand and the bed. I rip open the drawer and find a box of matches. Picking through my suitcase by candlelight, I pull out my sequined jeans, a silk top with long sleeves, and my makeup bag.

The girls are in the upstairs bathroom getting ready when I arrive. Kacey has on a form-fitting black number with rhinestone straps and her hair is a waterfall of gold and platinum curls, which I envy just as much now as I did when we were teens. Rena, who I expect to be wearing a short skirt and a top that is two sizes too small to show off the size of her fake boobs, is in jeans and a surprisingly conservative t-shirt that covers most of her cleavage. She pulls out the same undereye cream my mom uses and I glimpse just how dark the circles below her eyes are before she covers them up.

We decide to take Kacey's car. My body tingles, on full Scott Alert, as we exit the house, but he's nowhere to be seen. The Fugly Mobile is sitting in the driveway but the Tacoma is missing. *How did he even get the cash to buy a Tacoma*? Even the older models go for what Dad calls "stupid money" and the last time I spoke to Scott he was in debt.

Mother Shuckers is a log cabin built by the beach. White lights glitter across the roof and old rock music reverberates off the front doors, which are ornately carved with starfish and other sea life. A waitress leads us out to a covered patio table with a Jack Daniels umbrella over it and sets down three menus. The air is just warm enough to sit outside and the plastic wind guards protect us from the cool evening breeze. My soul stirs as I hear the crash of the ocean waves, smell the sandy dunes and clam chowder.

Kacey and I order wine and Rena gets an IPA. We instantly launch into full-blown girl conversation: where did Rena get her shoes? Did we hear the downtown Macy's was closing? Have we been out to the new winery in Aurora? I let

Kacey and Rena do most of the talking because I'm staring at the sea, busy in my own brain. This is the first time I've stepped back since the divorce started, stopped to examine all that I've lost and accomplished.

"Elle?" Rena's voice brings me back to the table.

"Oh, sorry," I say.

"I was just asking about your books."

"Oh. They kind of, uh, got put on hold. I haven't felt much like writing."

"Where did you say you were working again?" Kacey asks me.

"Portland Diamond Company." I'm grateful for the change in subject.

"Isn't that that little family-owned jeweler in downtown Portland?" Rena rubs her chin. "The one that's been around forever? They're famous for their wedding designers or something."

"We're very well known for our wedding rings, yes." Maybe it's the wine talking again, but I add, "Honestly, ladies? I don't know what I'm doing in the bridal industry. I don't know what the hell I'm doing in general."

"Well, thank God, you're with the right crowd! Cheers to not knowing what the hell we're doing!" Rena lifts her beer and we all clank our glasses together with a laugh. "One thing I do know? It's so good to be back with you two."

"You've gotta tell us what happened with Jake." Kacey

says.

Rena's smile falters. It's too subtle a movement for Kacey to notice but I see it. She wrinkles her nose and shrugs. "He just wasn't right for me."

"Bummer. He seemed cool. I'm sorry it didn't work out." Kacey sips her wine then stands up from the table. "I gotta pee. If the waitress comes back, I want the fish and chips and another glass of Noir!"

I give her two thumbs up as she skips off to the bathroom. Rena chews her lip, fussing with the candle on our table. "Rena?"

"Huh?" She perks up.

"What happened?"

A long moment passes between us. She holds my gaze until her eyes start to water. Releasing a deep breath, she whispers, "You always saw straight through me, Elly. How do you always know?"

"I'm magical."

"Psh, clearly." She tries to pass off the subject with silence but I wait. "Don't say anything to Kacey, okay? She's all love struck with the ideas of weddings and babies and houses. I don't want her to think badly of me."

I'm not convinced that Kacey could think badly of anyone, but I say, "My lips are sealed."

Rena rotates her glass around on the satin tablecloth. Her crumbling expression and the tension surrounding it almost makes me wonder if she's going to confess a murder. "It's been hard for me, Elly. My dad got sick not long after we graduated. I gave up college to work full time and help my parents pay the bills so we could keep our house. We spent two years barely scraping by. Plus, giving up college in the middle of the term resulted in bad grades, and it screwed up my financial aid. I took out a lot of loans, got into a lot of debt.

"Then I met Jake at Red Horse Pub where I worked. We got pretty close for a while. I didn't really want anything permanent but he really liked me and he was cute so I thought why not give it a chance? I may have given it an *unprotected* chance one night after a few too many drinks..." She trails off.

I piece the rest together myself. "Oh, shit. Rena, I'm so sorry."

Rena sniffles, shaking her head at the sky. "Don't ever say it feels better without the condom off. Just saying." She lets out a choked laugh.

I laugh, too, but only to lighten the mood.

"You're the first person I've told besides Jake." She dabs the tears out of her eyes with a napkin before they ruin her makeup. "God, it was so terrible. I'm terrified my parents are going to find out. You know how Christian they are. They'd disown me if they knew, even after everything I did for them. They would disown me and call me a child-killer."

Her tears are threatening to become sobs. I put a firm arm around her shoulders, as if I could protect her from her parents, this Jake guy, and all the world's judgements. "They would not, Rena, they love you."

"Everybody's love has limits." Rena tries to pull herself together, glancing around to see if anyone had noticed her outburst. "I just couldn't bring a child into my debt, my messed-up family. I know it makes me a bad person and a coward, but I couldn't."

"It does not. You need to quit beating yourself up with this." I hand her my napkin because she's already destroyed hers. She blows her nose. "Sometimes you have to do what is right for you and not what is right in others' views."

"It's just been eating at me. I feel so horrible for it." Rena looks around again for signs of Kacey.

I open my mouth to tell her that she can choose to have regrets and suffer, or she can have choices that she chooses to live with and go on with her life, but Kacey pops up in my peripheral vision. I quickly take Rena's napkin and help clean up her face as she's making a mess of it. "It's going to be okay, Re. I'm here for you."

Rena nods then bestows upon me one of the most genuine, loving smiles I've ever seen her give. "Thank you, Elly."

Kacey flops down into her seat. "Whoo! Jeez, don't go in the last stall. It's out of toilet paper and the toilet seat covers do not make a good substitute." Her eyes dart between us. "Uh oh. What did I miss?"

"Oh, you know." Rena slaps a hand on the table like she's going to say something brilliant, but nothing comes out.

I take over. "Just talking about how hard life is sometimes."

"Ain't that the truth?" Kacey tips her wine glass back and sucks the last few drops out of the bottom. "And with that thought, where's the stinkin' waitress? We need another round if we're going to talk like this!"

"I'll go find her." Rena stands up a little too quickly and wanders into the bar. Instead of going to the bartender, however, she veers off for the restroom. Kacey doesn't notice. I hope she isn't embarrassed by telling me the truth. I am the last person she should be embarrassed in front of, especially after falling down the stairs and having a faceoff with Scott.

Speaking of which. "Kacey?"

"Yes, ma'am?"

"You don't think Scott's staying for the whole week, do you?" I need her to say no, because if I have to walk around Noah's house on Scott Alert all week, my butt might remain permanently puckered.

Kacey grimaces. "I don't know."

Great. "I feel bad that I'm imposing on Noah's grandmother. Do you think Noah would be bothered if I just moved into the living room? Why didn't he want to put me there in the first place?"

"Probably because he likes you, and Nana *loves* company. She was raised with six siblings and is used to a full house. I really think living here by herself half the year is too lonely for her."

Noah likes me. The warm fuzzies come to life below my skin. I wonder if she's assuming this or if he said something to her. "If you really think Nana's okay with me staying in her spare room, then I guess I'm fine."

"Yes, I really think Nana's happy to have you. She's a little different, if you didn't figure that out already, but she's wonderful." Kacey taps her acrylic nails against the table, narrowing her gaze. "Can I ask you something? Since we're talking about deep stuff and I sense more wine will arrive soon."

Please don't be about Rena. "Okay."

"I was in Hood River when, well, when you and Scott broke up. What happened, Elle? You two were crazy in love. I feel like it ended so abruptly."

I hesitate. From the moment I'd heard the black Tacoma rumble into Noah's driveway, my intuition said someone would ask about us before this trip was over. The night we broke up is blurry and comes back in fragments. "It *was* abrupt," I confess. "And it taught me that if I want someone who can be faithful and loyal forever, I need a dog. Not a man."

May 17th, 2012

MEMORIZED

I frequently fight with Dad's upstairs computer at the shop. It always has a problem with the internet, and I don't know if it's because he's cheap and won't buy a better Xfinity package or if he opened a bad email again and gave it a bug.

I'm so involved with trying to get Firefox to load that I don't hear the footsteps walking up behind me. I shake the mouse in frustration. "Piece of useless crap son of—"

"Hey."

The mouse goes flying as I jump, then tumbles to a stop against Scott's boots. He picks it up and sets it back on the desk.

"Good God, were you Batman in a previous life? Make some noise when you walk up the stairs," I snap, my hand still over my pounding heart.

He holds both oil-stained hands up. "I'm just looking for your dad. I thought he'd be up here at his desk but apparently it's just you and a soon-to-be-busted computer." He throws a sideways glance at Jan's desk, which is empty because she's gone on vacation.

"I haven't seen him and the computer is already broken. Call his cell phone." I straighten my shirt and am consumed by the worst itch on my newly inked shoulder. I immediately slap it a few times because Glen told me to not scratch. Slapping makes it worse.

Scott squints. "Isn't that your tattooed shoulder?"

"Ugh, yeah. Is it supposed to itch like this?"

"Not like that." He eyes the red patches spreading over my collar bone. "Have you put anything on it?"

"Everything. Nothing is working." I don't tell him that the itch wakes me out of a dead sleep sometimes and leaves my whole arm twitching. I don't want to look like a wuss after my first tattoo.

He chews his lip. "Can I see it?" I pull back the sleeve of my tee shirt. He hisses through his teeth. "Wow, it's really mad. Mine never got irritated like that. You should have Glen look at it. I'm heading over to pick up his truck for new tires if you want to ride along."

Some of the staff watch as we walk out the door together. I wonder if they'll say anything to Dad or if he'll care. Scott leads me to the front of the parking lot where he unlocks a Honda Civic with a big spoiler on the back. It sits so low to the ground I half fall into the passenger seat. "Gee, talk about a low rider."

"Don't buck it till you try it." Scott starts the engine and it snarls to life. The Honda's interior is black and grey faux leather and smells like tacos and tobacco. Besides a crumpled paper bag on the back floor and a wadded-up sweatshirt on the seat, it's cleaner than most of the other auto mechanics' vehicles. He pulls out of his parking spot and I'm all too aware of his hand on my headrest as he twists around to see out the back window. That spicy sandalwood cologne wafts through the air.

The Honda buzzes down the road like a hornet, loudly revving up every time it changes gears. The momentum yanks me flat against the seat. The radio is blasting Queen and it's no time at all before my ears start ringing. Our seats are close together, traditional sportscar style, and all that separates his arm from touching mine is an emergency break.

"Besides the inflammation, how do you like your tattoo?" He asks. My response is a grin, which makes him laugh. It's a velvety smooth sound that sends shivers through my core. "Worth the redraw, huh?"

"Your brother is an amazing artist." So amazing as a matter of fact that I'm considering going back for round two.

"He's pretty kickass when it comes to tattoos. He can't fix a car to save his life, but he can decorate skin like nobody's business."

"Sounds like a fair trade."

"For now. Until I run out of skin or he buys a new car

with a warranty."

"Looks like you've got plenty of skin left." Besides his shoulder piece with the raven, his arms are blank. I wonder if there are other tattoos hidden below his work shirt or jeans. Heat flushes my cheeks as I realize where my thoughts strayed.

His eyes flick to my own clothes, appearing to wonder the same thing. "What inspired you to get a hummingbird? Wouldn't a fox have been more suitable?"

"Hardy har, you're so funny. I've always liked hummingbirds. It was the first truly magical animal I saw as a child, one that made me believe in impossible things." My mother used to tell me that hummingbirds are the guardians between this world and others, carriers of faeries and spirits. It's why they're always found in forests or gardens, places where these doors are rumored to exist. "Speaking of impossible things, how on earth did you catch my Austen reference the other day? You don't dawn on me as a historical romance fan." I'm still secretly swooning over the way he bent to kiss my hand in the lunchroom.

He rolls his eyes, neither offended nor amused. "I'm dark-haired, blue-eyed, and my name is Darcy. Do you think you're the first person to throw an Austen reference at me?"

I imagine a troop of high school girls all watching him from across a classroom or in the gym, making up all sorts of daydreams about a modern-day Darcy. "Touché."

The Honda grumbles to a stop at a four-way intersection. With traffic still speeding through the light, he turns to look at me. *More than look.* A stare this intense would generally be viewed as sexual admiration but Scott's searching for something. I'm not being admired; I'm being memorized. "What?"

He shrugs, eyes returning to the road. "I can't decide if you hate my guts or if fair to partly bitchy is just your general forecast."

I laugh, surprised. "Hey now, it pays to be well-rounded when you're one of the only girls in an all-male work environment."

"Ah, so that's what they call it now: well-rounded."

"Look, I don't *hate* you I just—" My tongue presses into the side of my cheek, trying to prevent me from smiling. He notices, the smirk on his own face rising. "You're annoyingly charming from time to time and I find it.... annoying."

"Annoyingly charming," he chuckles, rolling the words around on his tongue. "Wow, I don't even know what to say to that. That's a new one for me."

"Say nothing. And don't let it go to your head."

"Oh, it's too late for that." He eases off the brake pedal as the stoplight turns green. He starts to say something else as we cross the intersection but never gets the chance to finish—our conversation is cut short by the white trail blazer that blows the stoplight. I'm thrown against my seatbelt as the Honda goes spinning across the intersection. Glass chunks explode over our laps. The airbags go off and my head is slammed so hard into my headrest I black out.

July 2nd, 2017

DARK AS THE OCEAN FLOOR

I wake up Sunday morning on the carpet, not in bed, wrapped up in blankets like a human burrito. I sit up with a groan and rub my kinked neck, cursing how much I drank at Mother Shuckers. The front of my head feels like someone swung a hammer into it and I need to pee like a racehorse.

I stagger to my feet, wearing a nightgown that I don't remember putting on. Cracking the door to my room open, I inhale the glorious aroma of maple and butter. Nana moves around the kitchen, stirring bowls and scooping things out of jars.

"Good morning," Nana chimes as I try to walk normally through the bar area to get to her bathroom. Her smile makes her already high cheek bones lift a little further. "You sleep okay?"

"Yes, thank you. Can I just use your bathroom for a minute?"

"You don't need to ask. You are welcome to everything in

this house." Nana waves a hand around then points to the bar. "For you."

A tall glass with a lemon wedge hugging the rim sits there. "Oh, thanks. What is it?" The glass' contents are thick and red as tomato paste with flecks of some sort of green foliage mixed in.

She leans over the counter and whispers, "Nana's legendary hangover cure."

My mouth rounds into a big O. "Wow, that's so nice. Thank you. I'll be right back." I close the bathroom door and slap a hand over my face, wondering what I did last night to make this poor old woman feel she needed to mix me a hangover cure. How out of control had I been when we came home? My last memories of our evening involved me crying into the tablecloth about Scott and asking the waitress why she was bringing me chowder when clearly I needed a piece of chocolate cake and another bottle of wine.

I glance in the mirror but that's a mistake; I'm puffy-eyed and pale. My bottom lip has crusted over where it split but should be concealable with a good coating of lip gloss. I return to the kitchen, desperately wanting to go hide in my room, but instead I take a seat at the bar. It was too kind of Nana to mix me a drink... even though it smells like heartburn.

"Kacey and Rena went to Farmer's Market. They came down to get you but you were sound asleep," Nana says, pouring batter into a frying pan. "How many pancakes you want?"

"Nana, you don't have to make me breakfast. You're too kind." I sip the drink and hold my throat so I don't spew it back out. I was right about the tomato—and the heartburn. Traces of banana and vinegar linger on my tastebuds as well.

"Nonsense! I haven't had anyone to make breakfast for since the holidays." She hands me a plate of freshly scrambled eggs.

"If you're sure. Thank you." I pick at my eggs, remembering a Facebook article that recommended them to anyone who has consumed too many adult beverages. My stomach calms after a few bites and suddenly I'm ravenous.

"How long you know Kacey and Rena?" Nana asks, flipping a pancake over.

"Since grade school. We were the three amigos for a long time—well, four if you count our friend Shaya, but she couldn't come. After graduation we all kind of spread out and went separate ways." I think back to what Rena told me last night, and then I think about Kacey with that big diamond ring on her finger. High school, which looked so close to us a few days ago, appears further behind me all the time. "Life is weird."

"Life is full of mystery, strange at times and wondrous at others," Nana says brightly. "Either way, every day is a good day for a lesson."

"Yeah." I'm not sure where she's going with this, given our morning so far. Was today's lesson that I should not talk about emotional situations and drink at the same time? Maybe so.

Nana hands me another plate, this one cradling a golden pancake and an unlabeled bottle of syrup. "You have big plans today?"

"Definitely not." The sun is blazing through the sliding glass door behind her and I'm aching to lay on the beach. I hope it's as warm as it looks. "I'm just happy to be away from my real life right now."

"It is good to step back from our lives. Helps us to look at ourselves, our choices, our happiness." Nana scrapes burnt batter and grease off her pan with something that looks like an oversized guitar pick. "There are fresh towels in the bathroom for you to take a shower. You want another pancake?"

"No, I'm full. Thank you so much." She takes my empty plate before I can offer to wash it. I listen to her hum an eerie yet lovely little tune as she begins loading her dishwasher. The sound pulls at my heartstrings for reasons I can't quite pinpoint.

I accept her offer and use the shower. I take a short and intensely hot one, which does help my headache, then dry my hair and reinstall my extensions. I probably put on too much makeup for a girl whose plans consist of nothing more than laying on a beach, but there's just something about the risk of seeing one's ex that makes a person want to look extra smashing. That same idea applies to my choice of clothing: a pair of skinny jeans and a lacey V-neck that clings to every curve of my pushup bra.

I walk upstairs into the main kitchen and find Noah perched at his counter, a cup of coffee in one hand and a newspaper in the other. He looks up as I walk in and takes his glasses off. I don't miss the full body scan he gives me. "Hey there, Gorgeous. How'd you sleep?"

"Like a log." I wait to see if he says anything about how emotional and drunk I was when I came in last night. I hope he wasn't present for that. Even more so, I hope Scott was out of the house on his own night on the town when we returned.

"Rena and Kace ran up to the Farmers Market. Sounds like you guys had a wild night." He winks at me. So much for hoping that he didn't know anything. "They should be back soon. You hungry? Allen and Betsey just cooked a ton of sausage on the grill."

"No, thanks. Your grandmother just stuffed me full of pancakes and thought-evoking conversation."

He chuckles. "Ah. Yeah, she's good like that." A dark and perfect curl falls over his brow as he bends to sip his cup. "You're doing okay downstairs then?"

"I'm good. I'm sorry I've caused so much drama already. It's not my forte, I swear."

"Nonsense. You haven't caused any drama. If I'd known you and Scott had history, I would've made him come another weekend."

You would've made your friend wait to come over for me, a stranger? "Don't say that. If anyone should've come another weekend it should've been me, but I had no idea you knew Scott. Small world we live in."

"Smaller than we think. And nah, he comes down a couple times a season. He could've come another time." Noah walks over to the coffee machine and holds up the pot. "Coffee?

Or would you prefer a latte or a cold brew?"

Pretty and *he speaks my language*. My brain elbows my heart in a hint-hint sort of way. "Coffee is fine." I was tilted in the direction of the door, intent on exploring the property while I waited for the girls to return, but now I turn and pull out a stool. Shaya used to say the fastest way to trap a white girl is to offer her a latte and I dare say there might be some truth in that. He pours me a mug and hands over a bowl filled with tiny creamers. "Noah?"

"Yes, ma'am?"

"How did you do it?"

He laughs. "Do what?"

"Make such a beautiful vacation home, or is this your permanent home?"

"It's my vacation home, though Nana lives here permanently. Luckily, my company is doing well enough that I'm able to keep this home as well as my permanent residence in Portland."

"Oh." So he's not a millionaire but financially well-off. Still, I don't know anyone in their twenties that can keep one home in Oregon much less two. Our real-estate is quickly becoming the new prized pig of the states. "Sorry about the losses of your dad and granddad. That's too bad."

Noah shrugs one shoulder. "It is what it is. My grandfather was a cool dude, but my dad and I weren't that close. He spent most of his time at his casinos, rolling in cash and expensive prostitutes. We parted ways when I turned eighteen. I got a full ride scholarship at Oregon State where I studied business and marketing. He died the night before my graduation."

"Ouch." Poor relationship or not, that must've been a damper. I wonder how I'd feel if my dad died suddenly like that. The last time we spoke was at the annual Christmas gathering hosted by Grandma and Grandpa Fox and it had been extremely uncomfortable. "Parents are complicated. My dad and I aren't friends, either."

Noah opens his mouth to reply but we're interrupted by the squeak of the sliding glass door. I look up, fully anticipating the return of Rena and Kacey, but it isn't them.

Scott steps inside then freezes, seeing us at the counter. He's wearing sweatpants and a shirt with the sleeves cut off, hair tussled like he just rolled out of bed. His eyes dart between Noah and I. "Oh. Sorry, am I interrupting something?" His tone is sour.

If I had hackles, they'd have shot straight up. Noah must sense this because he gives my shoulder a gentle touch and replies, "No. We were just having some coffee. You want a cup?"

"You mean there's actually some left after *she's* been in here? That's a miracle," Scott scoffs, strolling into the kitchen.

I'm torn between going outside and remaining in my chair. If I get up, he'll think he has the power to clear me out of any room simply by being in it. If I don't get up, I risk upset guts from blending coffee with anxiety. *Screw it, I'll risk it.* I take a deep breath. Leaning over the counter, I let my pushup bra do its job as I reach for Noah's newspaper. Offering a flirty smile, I steal it away. He smiles back and sips his coffee, unbothered.

Scott observes us. His tattooed shoulders bulge and the veins in his hand pop out as he grips the handle of the coffee pot. I peruse the headlines of the Newport Times, pretending to be totally unfazed by his presence. Scott slowly pours his cup, throwing in two creamers but no sugar. I pretend to be engrossed in some article about native wetlands and wait for him to leave the kitchen. To my continued discomfort, he leans against the counter and stays there. A couple minutes pass. Now Noah shifts uncomfortably.

I can't take it. I slap the paper down. "Noah, how far is the beach from here?"

Noah starts to speak but Scott cuts him off. "*Your* beach is about a hundred miles that way." He points toward the northern coast where my family used to vacation. "If you leave now, I bet you'll reach it by lunchtime."

"Elle, you are welcome to walk down to our private beach on the bay. It's just down the hill," Noah interjects. He mouths the word *stop* to our fellow house guest. "You can follow the bark dust trail."

"You sure you want to lay on a beach with *that* rash?" Scott waves a finger at my chest.

I've broken out in nervous hives. He knows that's what they are, too. Between that and the fact I've had no good comebacks to anything he's thrown at me, I start to come apart inside. I'm either seconds away from a sobbing fit or a bout of uncontrollable rage. *You're stronger than this. It's okay. You've got this.*

"Noah." My voice comes out surprisingly calm.

"Yes, love?"

"Can you give us a minute?"

He gives a single nod, then heads for the glass doors. On the way by, he slaps Scott on the shoulder. Hard. The door makes a gentle *clink* as it shuts behind him, leaving the kitchen in burning silence. Scott tries to act relaxed as he sips his coffee, but his movements are too slow and controlled to suggest he's truly at ease. I take this time to really look at him, to see what he's become these last five years. He's still lanky and broad-shouldered but the muscles in his arms are a little more pronounced than I remember. His shoulder armor with the raven and sword has extended down his whole arm into new, realistic panels and the chain link work beneath them is phenomenal. *Glen outdid himself*. His other arm is a conglomeration of tribal designs mixed with tradition flash art. I notice the trees across his lower forearm are just outlines. The lines are dull and faded, a sign they've been there a while. *Why hasn't he finished them*? His hair is shorter on the sides and longer on the top, more modern and less skater-boyish.

My intense staring finally breaks his composure. "What?" he snaps.

There's so much I could say, so many reactions for me to choose from. I really want to walk over and dump the whole pot of coffee on his head, watch it sizzle and burn his flesh. I want to throw my cup and have it shatter against his face. I want to touch his tattoos and his skin and see how much warmth is still under that icy exterior.

"Look—" My stupid voice cracks. *Damn it.* I clear my throat. "I know that we've apparently pissed off somebody in the universe or picked up somebody's bad karma and it's landed us in the same beach house at the same time, but haven't I suffered enough because of you?"

He rolls his eyes.

I get up from the bar. "I have been through the wringer these last few years, okay? I don't want to fight anymore. I don't want to fight with you, I don't want to fight with my dad, I don't want to fight with myself! It's exhausting and it's painful. So can we just try to accept that this is the current situation and try for a decent vacation with our friends? Because I don't know about you, but I really needed this trip." I whip my cup of coffee off the counter and dump it in the sink, standing inches from him. He doesn't shy away, which pisses me off more. I'm rinsing the soap out when suddenly I feel it: a pressure on my shoulder.

His fingers have bravely reached out and touched my hummingbird, tracing the lines that Glen inked into my skin so long ago. Strange sensations blaze through me. I turn my head while wearing a what-the-hell-are-you-doing expression but he doesn't notice. It's as if the bird has put him in a trance. A sadness as deep and dark as the ocean floor is sitting in his blue eyes. I know that kind of sadness well—it's the same kind that lives in me.

It's loss.

Suddenly Scott snaps his fingers back, aware of his actions. Without a word, he turns and leaves the kitchen, disappearing out the sliding glass door. I finish washing my mug, still in shock over what just happened, then walk out to the patio. Noah is walking down the stairs but he's alone. Behind him is a newly empty parking spot.

The black Tacoma is missing from the driveway.

***

Kacey and Rena arrive minutes after the Scott confrontation, carrying a latte and lemon scone for me. The confrontation left me so exhausted, I'm grateful for a second chance at caffeine. I don't tell them about what happened and let them assume that my dim behavior is due to a hungover.

We spend the first half of the day doing exactly what I've been dying to do: hang by the bay. Noah's beach is small but it's our own private paradise, a strip of golden sand protected by young shore pines and long, shimmery strands of beach grass. Six lounge chairs overlook the water, shaded by big striped umbrellas mounted in the ground. The girls both snag a seat, but I throw a towel in the sand and sprawl out.

I doze off at one point and start dreaming. I'm walking on a patch of land between sea and woods. The world smells fresh, like salt and Sitka spruce. The sand is cool and sticky beneath my toes, then suddenly dry and fading. Tiles appear on the beach, their navy patterns crisscrossing like those of the farmhouse. I look up.

I'm in my parents' kitchen.

"Get off! Get away from me!" My mother's panicked voice cries out.

I race into the entryway between the front room and the basement stairs. Mom is on the ground, Dad towering over her. I don't understand what I'm seeing—is he trying to pull her up or keep her down? It doesn't matter. I lunge into action as if I'm about to defend her from an intruder, except this is no invader. This is a man I share a house with, blood with, a man I have known all my life and suddenly don't recognize at all. My fingers dig into his arms then turn to jelly. I can't harm him. I can't fathom that this situation is really happening and the truth sucks all the strength from my body. People always talk about being paralyzed with fear but nobody can understand what that means until they experience it.

Aware of my jelly fingers loosely sticking to his skin, Dad throws his arm out to shove me back and catches me in the jaw. I go plummeting to the floor—except there isn't one. Mom screams my name as I fall down the basement stairs, hitting the metal lips with my arms first. A mind-blowing sensation races through me, a pain like nothing I've ever experienced. I lay in a heap at the bottom, unable to move either arm. *What just happened*? *Did that really just happen*? I'm too numb to process it, to even get up off the floor.

"You stay away from her! Damn it, Jim, I will *kill* you!" My mother's shrieks mingle with the sound of Dad's footsteps, racing down the steps.

I try to tell him off as he gathers me up but apparently I'm crying too hard to speak. Crying and my arms won't move.

"Lew." Dad's voice shudders as he carries me up the stairs. Tears are streaming his face. "Lew, I didn't mean to. I'm so, so sorry."

I jerk awake, kicking sand everywhere.

"Oh, Sleeping Beauty has awoken!" Kacey giggles. "Just in time, too, bird nerd. Look up!"

Discombobulated, I look around the sky and catch sight of a large, blurry shape soaring overhead. My eyes focus on a bald eagle flying over us. The bird's shimmering call echoes over the beach before it soars above the dunes, disappearing behind the house.

"Oh, pretty! Look at that!" Rena watches the eagle then does a double-take in my direction. She hisses through her teeth. "Girl, you might want to come put some aloe on that back. You're going to look like a walking lobster."

Besides the stinging in my eyes thanks to the horrible dream, I'm aware of a far more painful sting across my back and in the cracks of both butt cheeks. My skin feels like someone slapped me repeatedly with a wooden paddle. How long had I been asleep?

"You remember that summer Shaya passed out by the pool?" Rena whips out her aloe bottle as I crawl over to her chair. She pops the cap and starts smothering my back in the chilly, jell solution. "She cooked like an egg."

"Yeah, then tried to cover it up with fake tanner for her cousin's wedding. She looked like a scrawny Oompa Loompa." Kacey bites loudly into a potato chip from the stash in her beach bag. "We spent the rest of the week asking her which way to Willy Wonka's chocolate factory. Oh, the good old days."

"Weren't they just yesterday?" I chime in, desperate to remember the better parts of my past that have nothing to do with my family. "I mean, seriously. How is it possible that we're all twenty-three and Kacey is getting married and I've had enough time to drop out of college twice?"

"Way to make me feel old, Elle." Rena flicks my sunburn. "At least you attempted college. I've worked in restaurants for the past five years listening to people complain about their ex-spouses and their kids and how I put too many pickles on their burgers." Her fingers pause to touch the backs of my arms. "Whoa, what happened here?"

I instantly fold my arms over my lap, attempting to hide the long, pale scars near my elbows. I'm so used to hiding them under long-sleeved shirts and jackets that I don't have a response. "Uh, you know." I shrug. *Lew, I didn't mean to. I'm so, so sorry.* "Too much wine mixed with clumsy feet."

The girls titter with laughter but the sound is unsure. I give another casual shrug and act like big, pale scars are just a natural part of life and not another trigger for bad memories. A few dark dots pepper the bay so I seize my chance to change the subject. "Kace, will you hand me that?" I point at my backpack. She pulls it from the sand and passes it over. Unzipping the front pocket, I pull out my faithful pair of travel binoculars.

"What'cha see out there?" Kacey asks.

"Buffleheads." I smile, glad I haven't lost all my ornithology knowledge. The flock of tiny ducks look to have white and black faces, but a wiser watcher knows that in the sun those dark feathers shimmer with alexandrite hues.

"*Bufflehead*? That sounds like a medical problem. Avoid that guy, ladies, he's got a bufflehead!" Rena chuckles. Kacy bursts out laughing.

"No, my gutter-minded friend, it's a type of duck, one not commonly seen on saltwater lakes." They tend to prefer fresh water. I hold my binoculars high, catching the green-purple scintillation on a duck who is shaking his head. They were always one of my favorites, seemingly simple from far away but exotic beauties up close. Then again, the same can often be said of people when you look close enough.

"Well, I don't know my ducks. I know my men, though," Rena proudly assures. "If Mr. Haynie's science class final had been about world's hottest men of 2012, I would've aced it."

"I bet Elle aced that one," Kacey remarks.

I hesitate to respond. "I was excused from that final."

"Wait, weren't you in an accident or something?" Rena tries to remember.

I don't know that I want to remind them much less remember, but I'm not going to lie. "I was in that car accident."

"Oh," both girls say it like it hurts. The car accident had been previously labeled as Unspeakable Scott Subject Two-Hundred-And-Four.

I drop my binoculars into my lap. As unspeakable of a subject as it is, I notice that since I stood up to Scott this morning, it feels a little easier to talk about him. "Actually, I missed a couple of finals because of that."

Kacey asks, "Didn't an old lady blow a stoplight or something and hit you guys?"

"Yeah." An eighty-year-old woman in a trailblazer who should not have been driving had snuck out to the grocery store while her caretaker was busy. In her hurry to get back, she ran a red light. Scott and I walked away with minimal injuries and minor whiplash, but his Honda had been totaled.

"That's right." Rena remembers. "And you were the nice person who drove Mr. High and Mighty to work when he didn't have transportation."

"Yup." That was how our awkward acquaintanceship bloomed into a cataclysmic love spell that consumed us both. *Or, at least, it had consumed me*. I should've let him get a rental or take an Uber while he looked for a car, but no. Being a lovestruck teenager, I'd jumped at the chance to drive him back and forth while the insurance companies worked things out.

"Guys, I think I'm going to ask Noah if we can have the wedding here," Kacey says, thankfully changing the subject.

"That would be beautiful," Rena exclaims, reaching into Kacey's beach bag. She pulls out a colorful handful of M&Ms and throws them in her mouth. "How many people are you expecting? The yard could probably handle fifty if you're wanting an outdoor ceremony."

"Shouldn't be more than that. I mean, we have a ton of people that want to come but I plan on keeping it small. Closest friends and family only." Kacey sighs dreamily at the sky. "I'm thinking August, an evening event. Strapless dress. Swarovski-covered sandals. Let's shop." She whips out her cell phone and starts browsing, Rena leaning over her shoulder.

Maybe it's because weddings and brides make me think too much of work, but suddenly I'm fidgety. "Are there any walking trails on the property?" I glance toward the woodlands behind the house.

"Not really. There's a few at the park down the road though," Kacey says.

"Would you mind if I walked down there for a bit?" I don't want to sound like I'm trying to get away from our girls' day, but I'm ready for an hour alone.

"It's a long walk. Take my car," Kacey offers. "Just don't crash it, okay?"

"No accidents to date—knock on wood." I smile, hoisting my beach bag over my aloe-covered shoulder. "See you guys in a bit!"

The Subaru has a button instead of a key to start the engine. Driving Kacey's car makes me nervous as it is newer and fancier than my own. There's a screen in the dash that I don't know how to use and the steering wheel has several buttons I keep accidentally pushing. Kacey must've spent a fortune on this vehicle. She really has done well for herself since high school—nice car, big diamond ring, financially well-off fiancé. She's the jewelry industry's favorite kind of girl: a Traditional.

As I'm driving down the road, I come across a young couple trying to cross the street to go to the park Kacey was talking about. I slow down and let them go. The gentleman flashes me a grin, Nike shoes so white and unsoiled they're probably new. His wife waves, jewelry glittering in the sun as she folds an arm over the baby strapped to her chest. The driveway they've come out of spirals up to an enormous house on the hill with a professionally landscaped yard and two fancy cars not much newer than this one. It all reeks of society's seemingly inescapable adult standard: marriage and money and children.

My parents believed in the standard. And it never made them happy. Maybe that's why I'm so strongly against following the norm—I'd rather write my own rule book for fulfillment versus use someone else's, though it's a lot easier said than done. Society makes it difficult to step out of line and leave the well-walked path behind. It seemed more accomplishable when I had someone at my side who also believed in blazing their own trail.

And it's moments like this, when I reflect on how much we had going for us, that I hate Scott the most.

June 1st, 2012

CASCADE LOCKS

Historic Oregon City is basically an enormous hill grid-laid with narrow streets and old houses.

I slow down on Monroe and pull into the driveway of an old yellow house with a roof that has more moss than shingles. The low fence out front has been eaten by blackberries and a garage with wood rot that could never fit a modern-day vehicle sits at the end of the broken pavement. Scott's totaled Honda lays crunched at the curb, only adding to the beauty of the property.

I walk up the decaying porch steps, hoping I won't fall through. The front door is cracked open, the smell of cheese and eggs wafting out. "Scott?" I call down the hallway.

"Two seconds!" His voice is muffled like his mouth is half full.

I growl, letting the screen door slam shut. I don't feel like waiting. Scott comes out a few minutes later, jogging down the stairs with a jerky stick hanging out of his mouth and an energy drink in hand. He slides into the passenger seat, the aroma of paprika and sodium nitrate wafting off him and into the fabric of my vehicle. "You couldn't have eaten that beforehand?"

"Someone showed up early, so nope." He takes a big bite and chews loudly.

Usually I pick him up after third period around twelve-thirty, but I've been in a mood all day so I skipped my last class. I rip out of Scott's driveway and speed back to the 99E highway, deciding that I'm not going to survive this day without coffee and there's a Starbucks five minutes from here.

"Jeez, who pissed in your coffee this morning?" Scott looks over his shoulder at the streetlight we just passed. "Tell me if I'm wrong, but isn't the shop the other way?"

"Why yes, it is."

"O—kay. So where are you going?"

"To get caffeine because, speaking of coffee, I haven't had any yet today." And if somebody dares to piss in it, heaven help them.

I circle to the bottom of the hill and pull the Suzuki into the shopping center. The drive-through line wraps around the Starbucks building like a stream of colorful ants. Scott watches me lean back in my seat and rub my face, releasing a heavy sigh. "You know, you didn't have to pick me up if you didn't want to. I could've taken the bus."

"It's not you," I mutter.

"What's the problem then?"

As if on cue, my eyes start watering. *Oh, God, don't cry.* I squeeze them shut. The last thing I want is for him to pinpoint me as one of those overly emotional girls, the kind that outwardly vomits their feelings all over people they don't know. Not that we're strangers anymore since I've been his chauffer since the accident, but we aren't exactly friends, either.

A clicking noise comes from the glovebox. Something nudges my arm so I open my eyes. He's holding out a rumpled Starbucks napkin because, alas, my stoicism has failed and there are tears on my cheeks. "Don't worry, it's not my jerky stick hand," he assures.

I huff a laugh. "Thanks. Good to know."

"Are you going to tell me what's wrong?" He closes the glovebox.

"Well, you see, every twenty-eight days or so a woman goes through this thing—"

"And I'll stop you right there." He holds up a hand.

Funny how men can handle blood and gore and death on television, but the second a woman mentions her monthly cycle their ears slam shut. "Scott?"

"Huh?"

"What is it like having divorced parents?" We have never breached this subject before. Glen had made it sound like it was a touchy one for him, but I don't know who else to ask and I need to talk to someone. After the fight I witnessed between my parents last night, it might soon be my reality as well.

He hesitates then gives a slow nod. "It sucks. And it makes everything and everyone complicated."

"Great." I sink in my seat. *What were you expecting, Elle, a comforting answer*?

"Your parents having issues?"

"They've always had issues, but I think it's getting worse. They had a huge fight last night. Something about a large loan that Dad signed and never told my mom about. If he defaults, we lose our house. We've already lost one TV, an IKEA lamp—which went through the TV—and my mom's voice. She yelled so hard she sounds like a raspy, old lady today." And Matt and I said nothing. She was under the impression we couldn't hear what happened down in the basement, but the air ducts in our house transfer more than just heat; Matt and I sat at the duct in my room for over an hour, petrified by the voices coming out of it. Neither of us could sleep afterwards. I've never felt this level of insecurity before.

Scott is quiet, absorbing this. "Has he taken out these kinds of loans before?"

"I have no idea."

"Are you worried he'll default?"

"Yes." I shouldn't be sharing these kinds of details with an employee of the shop, but it feels better to talk about it with someone who doesn't live in the same house. *A house that might not be ours anymore*. Maybe Dad already defaulted on the loan and that's why Mom was so angry. Maybe she's trying to figure out how to tell us we're going to be homeless.

I'm trying to hide a panic attack when we finally make it to the order board. I'm so distracted I forget what I want. I can't remember the name of the new drink I had planned to try so I order my usual iced grande macchiato with extra caramel drizzle. I ask Scott if he wants anything and he replies by popping the lid open on his energy drink. We're three cars from the pick-up window when he says, "Who threw the lamp into the TV?"

"Mom, but it wasn't on purpose. She was aiming for Dad's head." I'm starting to sweat so I switch the cold air on in the car. An unpleasant dampness is noticeable inside my shirt. "Can I have two more napkins out of there, please?" He digs two more out of the glovebox. I jam them down into my bra. His eyebrows shoot up. "What? My boobs sweat when I'm stressed, okay?"

He runs a hand over his mouth, lost for a response. Shifting his legs, he turns to his window like he can't focus on the conversation if he's watching me. "What was your dad's reaction?"

"Angry. He kept turning it around on my mom: she's not being a supportive wife, she's hindering the progress of the business and therefore the progress of our family, blah, blah, blah. Not once did he sound worried about losing the farmhouse. He sounded even less worried about losing her." It was the first time I'd heard him truly yell at her as if she were an enemy, not a spouse of twenty years. It scared me, almost more than the chance we would lose our home.

I pay for my drink and a pretty barista with auburn curls hands my card back through the window. Scott smiles at her and she nearly drops my coffee while passing it over.

"Can you maybe, I don't know, *not* smile that stupidly attractive smile at the barista when she's handling my precious cargo?" I huff as we leave the trail of coffee-deprived ants behind. Pulling one of my boob-sweat napkins out of my shirt, I wipe the spill off my hands. "That was three sips that girl just lost me."

He widens that stupidly attractive smile.

"Shut up." I jam a straw into my macchiato.

"Your dad's an unpredictable creature." He returns to the original subject. "It's well-hidden in front of his customers, but he's different with his employees. I saw him gently schmooze this lady into buying a new Nissan then seconds later go into the parts room and cuss Darren out for screwing up somebody's tires. It was like watching two different people emerge out of the same body."

"That sounds like him." Mom once called him The Man of a Thousand Masks. For every person, place, and event in his life, my dad seemed to pick out a different personality to wear. I've ignored this reality for a long time because I love my dad and am fairly certain that we see the real person he is inside—a loving, devoted family man trying to do what's best for his family—but after last night...

"Have you spoken to your dad since this happened?"

"No. I don't know what to say. Honestly, I'm dreading the fact that I'm going to have to see him in a few minutes and pretend I know nothing of last night." I hated hearing him yell, hated witnessing him turn into one of those other personalities that I thought we were all exempt from. To know that he struck fear into my mother so deeply that she felt the need to throw a lamp makes me sick to my stomach.

"Why didn't you just stay home from work today?" Scott asks.

"I had to pick you up."

"I already told you that you don't have to."

"I wanted to." The words come out too serious, like picking him up is the most important part of my day. *Shoot.* The ice in my cup crunches loudly as I stir it around with my straw, looking for any way to appear nonchalant.

Scott's expression is blank as he stares out the window. It's impossible to know how far he's read into my words. The fact that I've suddenly lost his attention makes me worry he's read plenty and doesn't know how to respond. Worse, he doesn't know how to say that he's not interested. God, why doesn't life have a rewind button?

Suddenly he says, "Pull over."

"What?"

"I said pull over. Your back tire is making a weird noise."

I hesitate, listening to my vehicle. I don't hear anything. "Are you serious?"

"As a heart attack. Here, pull off after the exit."

The pavement widens beneath the overpass just enough for a single vehicle to take a break from the highway. Scott waits for traffic to pass then gets out. For a moment, I think he's going to walk past the tail end of my car and keep going. My imagination dies down as he circles the Suzuki. He doesn't kneel or bend over to really look at anything. Of course, this close to the road, he shouldn't. I don't know why he wanted me to pull over here. We should just get the car to Dad's shop if we can. Stopping at my window, he motions me out. "I'm going to drive for a few."

"You're not insured. And you've already crashed one car this month, pal."

He rolls his eyes. "Shop employee—I'm fully insured. Now get out."

If my car is about to do something weird like blow a tire, I guess I'd rather not be the one behind the wheel. He slides into my seat and I take his, noticing how warm he's left the pleather. He fusses uncomfortably, knees jammed up under my dash. "Damn, you're short." He grabs the adjuster and pushes the seat back as far as it will go.

"Would you prefer me tall?" *Would you prefer me in any way*?

"Definitely not." He shifts the car out of park. "You're intimidating enough as it is."

It's weird seeing him in my driver's seat. Sunlight spills through the windshield, catching the gem in his ear which is partially hidden by a wave of dark hair. A small birthmark stands out on his collarbone, his lashes darker and longer than previously analyzed. I clear my throat to hide the sudden need for air. "So, what do you think is wrong with my car?" Dad will freak if it's something big and expensive. I've been good about coming in for oil changes and general inspections. Maybe it will be under warranty.

Scott shrugs. "It's fine."

"*Fine*?" It seemed very not fine a moment ago. The exit for the shop approaches quickly and is left behind once again. I frown at the rearview mirror. "Are you taking the long way for some reason? Don't you think that's a bad idea if I have a tire problem?"

He takes a long sip of his energy drink then calmly replies, "Who says we're going to work?"

I wait for his expression to give away some sign that he's joking. The mischief in his eyes has trickled down to his mouth and he's holding back a deviously charming smile. *He's hijacked you*. Hijacked my vehicle and... wants to play hooky with me? My stomach flip-flops. I listen to my car, to it's completely normal hums and clicks and the normal squeak of the breaks.

"I think we could use a break from work, don't you? Unless you've changed your mind and you really just want to go see your dad."

I don't. He's going to act like absolutely nothing went down last night and I won't be able to take it. I can't go to work like this. *You can't just run off with Scott, either.* His desire to steal me away from responsibility is more than just a little flattering, but I don't know him that well. Despite the number of days we've driven together since the accident, he's stayed sealed up like a clam. His real thoughts and intentions about most things remain a mystery. I open my mouth to tell him no, we can't do this.

"Okay." I'm a weakling. A pathetic, love-struck weakling. Why do I so desperately want to see how this plays out? *You might regret this, oh cat of curiosity.* "So where will we go instead?"

He skips over into the fast lane and hits the gas. "You'll see."

We continue down the 205 Highway into southeast Portland, passing several large shopping centers where clusters of people carry bags and nibble mass-marketed food items. The shopping centers quickly become graffiti-covered neighborhoods where a lot less people are mingling. A park that would've been pretty if it weren't for all the garbage strewn across the ground comes into view. Homeless camps are strung between the trees to form webs of tarp and plastic. I recognize the painted benches and recall that this was the same park on the news last year where two women joggers were found dead from knife wounds.

"Nervous much?" Scott's arm is resting on the center counsel and he waves a finger at mine.

I'm twisting the hem of my shirt into little knots. "Not at all. I'm just sitting in my hijacked car driving off into Graffitiville." I eye the multicolored spray-painting of the words *Fuck Global Warming* on the underside of a passing bridge.

"You don't trust me?" He sounds offended.

"Frankly, no."

"Why not?"

"What legitimate reason have you given me to trust you? Notice that we're in the part of Portland most commonly on the news, and not in a good way." I hit the lock on my door as we come to a stop light. A collection of strange people loiters on the sidewalk, uncomfortably close to my car. One of them is missing his front teeth and shoes. Another dances to inaudible music outside my door while a third screams unintelligible words into the air with a raised fist.

"Don't worry," Scott says. "We're just passing through."

Sketchy Portland does eventually come to an end and I take a breath as we veer off on an exit I have never taken before. The neighborhood goes up a few notches then disappears altogether, taken over by fields of tall grasses and several species of leafing trees. We pass a nicer-looking outlet mall and a more inviting park with a sandy beach. The hills grow and reshape into tree-covered plateaus that curl around the wide expanse of the Columbia River.

I crack my window. The air is clean and fresh and full of green smells. "Where are we?"

"The Columbia River Gorge. Have you never been?" Scott can't believe that.

We pass a plateau of red rock covered in moss, tree roots draping like long, witchy fingers into the ravines between. A stream zigzags through one of the larger surfaces, carving a deeper V than should be possible for such a small amount of water. It spills over the edge and is blown away before ever reaching the ponds below, where ducks and other dabbling birds are swimming. Rays of sun dance between blankets of pine and evergreens, the land dipping to form valleys and then stretching in points toward the clouds. There is an enormity, an ancientness here that cannot be felt within city limits. I have seen the natural beauty of Oregon, but I have never seen it like this.

I am instantly in love.

The highway follows the river and stretches into the horizon, weirdly exitless. At this rate, we're going to end up in another state by sundown. I should've made clear that this drive has a time limit and I need to beat Dad home, especially since I just left him a text saying I'm studying for finals and am staying after school.

Wildflowers grow in broad patches off the roadside, covering the ground like colored confetti. I spot two deer grazing in the shadow of a plateau, their figures bent over rusted train tracks to nibble young clover. Scott has relaxed, his shoulders have dropped and the hard lines in his face are disappearing. *He's comfortable out here*, I realize. This place is important to him.

He catches me observing. "Yes?"

"Nothing. Just thinking how wrong I was to peg you for a city boy."

His nose wrinkles. "I can endure city life, but I'd far rather live in the middle of nowhere than the edge of somewhere."

An exit from the highway finally appears. We take it and pull into a tiny town built alongside the river called Cascade Locks. There is only one way through town, a two-lane road called Wa Na Pa. We follow it down past a couple of restaurants, a big one that you can tell is aimed at tourists and a smaller, more rundown one with letters missing that the locals probably favor. A rustic-styled Best Western greets us from beside the river, as do many little businesses that look to be run out of peoples' homes. A tiny chowder house has drawn customers in by the dozens, the line wrapping around the building and into a roped-off parking lot where two native men are selling whole salmons out of the backs of their trucks.

Scott turns into a gravel drive behind an old western-style building. Old English script dances across the wall: THE BIG LOCKS BREWERY. He parks by the only other vehicle in the driveway, a silver Passat with a rainbow sticker on the bumper. "We're here," he announces.

For being called The *Big* Locks Brewery the interior is surprisingly small with more tables than it can comfortably manage. The wood panels on the walls and ceiling are home to a variety of animal furs, rusted mining tools, and framed photos from early America. Florida Georgia Line's *Good Girl, Bad Boy* plays over the speakers as Scott heads for the bar, acting like we're not underage and sitting in a no-minors section is completely normal.

"Hey, Scotty, my man!" A girl with a blue ponytail peers out from the kitchen.

"Nat the Tat, what's up?" Scott shouts, getting comfortable on a stool.

I'm awkward as a rat at a cat's convention while pulling out the stool next to him. Two elderly men at the other end of the bar take notice of us. If I don't stop acting so stiff I'm going to give us away. Flipping my hair over my shoulder, I straighten my back and cross my legs like I've sat at a hundred bars. I'm fine. I'm chill. This is totally normal. My elbows fold over the countertop, knees pressing against rough ridges. The bar's underside is an ornate carving of a wolf sniffing the hand of a woman with feathers in her hair. The forest resides at the wolf's back and a camp of teepees dwells behind hers.

The blue-haired girl, Nat The Tat, walks out to the bar, wiping her hands down her apron. She's built like a Sports Illustrated model, black tank hugging her chest, pockets dangling out from the edges of her jean shorts against narrow, fatless thighs. Black eyeliner and big, mink lashes line her eyes, which wave like butterfly wings every time she blinks. Tattoos decorate most of her body, running from her neck down to her toes. Her skin features everything from naked mermaids to roses to winged eyeballs and voodoo dolls. What little blank skin she does have is smooth as coconut cream.

"Where have you been, boy?" She leans over the counter and wraps both arms around Scott's neck.

"Everywhere I want to be." He pats her back but doesn't really hug her.

"Everywhere except here! We've hardly seen you." She makes a pouty face, protruding her studded lip. "Jake was just saying you guys haven't been out on the boat since last summer. You and Glen missed the spring fishing trip!"

I open my menu, trying to hide my sudden and intense onset of envy. *So this is the reason we drove all the way out to Timbuktu.* No man in his right mind would drive this far to sit in a cramped restaurant that smells of burnt oil and steelhead just to order a burger. *This was a damn setup.* And here I'm thinking that he was drawn by some sense of adventure and desire to get to know me versus the need to come stare at some tattooed centerfold.

"Nat, this is my friend, Elle."

Nat gives me a tight smile and I return it with one that is equally forced. "Hi." I offer her my hand, trying to be the bigger person. She gives it a weak shake, eyes flashing around my figure. If she's looking for signs of competition she need not look any further: her hips don't curve, her boobs are twice the size of mine, and there isn't a newly formed zit on her forehead. She has me beat.

"Well, I'll give you guys some time to decide," she says, sounding put off by having to say *you guys* instead of just *you*. "I'll bring some tater tots. On the house."

"Thank you, Nat." Scott opens his menu. "Are you hungry, Elle?"

"Not really." My newfound insecurities have stolen my appetite. *I'm such a fool.* I should've known better than to hand Scott my car keys and believe it'd lead to some sort of memorable adventure. I check my purse to make sure I have my phone as well as my wallet while trying to figure out how to get out of this. How bad would it be if I just left him here and drove home?

I'm starting to pull my debit card out when Scott's hand folds over mine, eclipsing it like a bear paw. "You've chauffeured me around ever since the car accident. Don't even think about paying for anything."

Blood charges into my face. His skin heats up my cold fingers. "I can take care of myself. Really."

"I'm sure you can, but you're not going to today."

Nat smacks a paper cup with a lid down in front of him. Tossing a straw on the countertop, she whispers, "If anybody asks, that's root beer. You know the drill." She stalks off, casting him a dangerous glance over her shoulder.

My eyes slide sideways to the seemingly harmless paper tube with the plastic lid that Scott pulls toward himself. The contents beneath the lid are too pale and amber colored to be Pepsi. "Do I want to know what's in the cup?"

"Probably not." He takes a long sip. "Want a taste?"

Honestly, I don't, but I don't want to look like a wuss, either. The drink fizzes in my mouth with a hoppy, bitter flavor that makes my eyes twitch. "That's disgusting. Oh my—is that *beer*?"

"Shhh," Scott scolds, peering around to see if anybody heard. Luckily, the two oldies have fallen into conversation about sports and are no longer paying attention. "It's just one and it's not a big deal."

"Not a big—are you serious?" I whisper hiss. "In what world is serving alcohol to a minor in a bar not a big deal? There is no way you are driving my car after this!"

"Okay, okay, just keep it down." He props his menu open on the counter, hiding the cup inside. "They have really good fish and chips here. Or, if you don't like fish, their Northwest Burger is excellent."

"I'm not that hungry."

"Please tell me you're not one of those girls who orders a salad and a glass of water when she goes out."

"Do these thighs look like I eat leaves?" I'm not a big girl by any means, but my thighs have always been the reason I have to go up a pant size even if my waist could handle a smaller pair.

His eyes deviate from the menu long enough to trace up my calves and across my jeans. His smile says, *I'm smart enough to not answer that.*

Nat comes back to take our order. She tucks our menus away but instead of returning to the kitchen like a polite hostess she starts talking Scott's ear off about Glen and the tattoo shop and how she's going to adopt one of Cheerio's puppies when they come of age. As she leans over the counter, breasts falling halfway out of her shirt, it dawns on me that almost all her ink carries the dark sweeping richness of Glen's hand.

I try to read Scott's body language as she continues to make moves that no uninterested girl would pull. As usual, he's a foreign language to me. I fully expect to see him show interest since clearly she's the reason I got dragged out here, but he does nothing to immediately imply this. She finally sashays off to help some new customers and I try to carefully pry into his thoughts with an oh so delicate conversation starter. "Does she always try to shove her tits in your face like that?"

He chokes on his beer. "Wow, are you always so subtle?"

"As a gun."

"She's like that with everyone. She gets good tips out of it."

"Oh, she's hoping for more than a tip. Every time she looks at me it's like she's hoping I'll drop dead so she can pull you over the counter with those black, glittering talons. You two clearly have history."

He grits his teeth. "It was a long time ago and nothing came of it. I'm not her type and she's not mine."

"Oh, really?" I snap, because there it is: clear evidence that they had a past. "You know, if you'd wanted to drive all the way out here to see her, you could've just asked my dad for a loaner car rather than steal mine."

Scott's face scrunches up in confusion. "I didn't come here to see her. I came here because it's one of the best places between Portland and Hood River to grab lunch. And we're out here in the Gorge because we both needed a break from life, remember?" He tilts his head thoughtfully, confusion melting off his face. "You're jealous," he realizes, surprised.

"What am I, twelve? No, I'm not jealous," I lie, voice so strong and convincing I can almost believe it myself. "I just don't like feeling used. To think that I ran off to escape my responsibilities with someone who really just came out here to hook up with his long-lost girlfriend is sort of degrading."

He rests his chin in his hand. "So I should hook up with you."

Heat rushes straight up my core and into my hairline. "No—yea—wait, what?"

He laughs. "Like I said, I'm not her type. I'm not a chick."

"*What*?"

"She prefers girls over guys. Most of the time," he clarifies. "You're more her type than I am. Speaking of which, you should probably pull your shirt up."

I peer down at my V-neck, which has fallen and is showing off the irritated, red-splattered skin of my cleavage. I adjust the hem but there is no hiding my discoloration... or the embarrassment that caused it.

The chowder I ordered is loaded with chunks of salmon and shrimp, the broth a perfect consistency with flavors of butter and brie. Despite my lack of appetite, it's so good I eat it all. I guess I can see why this place is a local hotspot. Scott eats his fish but takes his chips and leftover tater tots in a to-go box. He loudly sucks down the last of his beer then chucks it over the bar into an open garbage can. When we stand up to leave, Nat circles the counter like a vulture, swooping him into a hug. She pecks his cheek. "Stay out of trouble, bro."

I'm still not convinced that she's into girls.

"Take a left at the next turnoff," Scott directs once we're back in the car.

Apparently Cascade Locks is known for Thunder Island, a small land mass separated from the mainland by a canal carved out in the late 1800s. The canal was designed for ships who were trying to avoid the Columbia River's rapids, which were often influenced by the extreme winds that roll through the Gorge. Now Thunder Island is a public park. I curve into a paved lot guarded by a pristine, white building with a sign that reads, HISTORIC MUSEUM. A cement walking bridge sits before us, stretching over the canal to the island. Shrouded in a thick coat of mist beyond the island is The Bridge of the Gods. When the sun slips through the clouds, The Bridge glows like a silver lining across the Columbia, a connecting vein between Oregon and Washington.

Scott gets out of the car and starts walking. A nippy breeze rolls off the water as we step onto the canal bridge. I suppress a shudder, folding my arms to my chest. "Do people fish here?" I motion to the large nets laying on the flat, cement slabs below us.

"The natives do." He hops down the stairs, following a trail through the trees. Realizing his legs are longer than mine and he's out-walking me, he pauses. I race to catch up. "Are you cold?"

I shake my head. "No."

He looks at my arms, uneven with goosebumps. "Yeah, right." He shrugs off his hoodie and holds it out.

"I'm fine. You don't have to do that."

"I run warm." He shakes the jacket until I take it. The fabric is infused with tobacco and Old Spice and the inside is rough, worn from age and too many trips through the washer, but I don't mind. It's better than freezing.

Pine and dogwood dot the crest of the hill, overlooking the river. Layers of basalt stair-step their way across the Washington side, towering like ancient monuments amongst our modernized world of cars and bridges. I wander along the trail, marred by human sneakers and dog paws, thinking about the bare feet of the natives that used to walk the grounds of Cascade Locks long before settlers arrived. In a grassy clearing, I sit on an old wooden platform, wondering how many people have stood here and played music, or preached holy words, or said *I do*.

Scott sits down beside me and taps my knee to get my attention. He points to a large, red-headed bird pecking the tree over our heads. "What is that?" I ask.

"Pileated woodpecker. They're not really rare but we don't see them often."

"How is it you know this and I don't?" Scott seemed like your average car guy, one who could raddle off makes and models from a hundred paces away. I didn't expect him to be that way with birds.

"My grandparents were biologists for the State of Washington. When Glen and I were kids, our parents worked a lot so we often stayed at their farm. My grandfather performed detailed birding surveys for Clark County." He glances at the raven in his tattoo, peeking out from under his t-shirt.

"That's really cool." The woodpecker gets annoyed by all the attention and flicks off to another trunk.

Scott smirks. "Still wish you were at work?"

"No. You were right—we needed this." Regardless of whether he'd had alternative motives for this trip or not, I am thrilled to discover this island, Cascade Locks, and the Gorge. Who knows how much longer I would've missed out on this beauty if he hadn't kidnapped me?

He leans his elbows back on the platform's wood planks, releasing a sigh. "Do you ever feel like modern life is choking us?"

"How do you mean?"

"Like we're too absorbed in our cities, jobs, and money and we forget that the natural world exists all around us without any of that? Some people seem to forget that the natural world exists at all."

A pair of chickadees sing from the branches of a nearby aspen. I look at them and think how some have never really looked at a chickadee—just like I've never really looked at a pileated woodpecker—even though they can be found outside most Oregonians' front doors. "Yeah. My dad's a prime example of that. He could walk through a desert and say it's an ugly wasteland full of nothing while my mother could walk through the same desert and see the patterns in the sand and the bits of life hidden in plain view. She'd think it was incredible."

"Life is all about perception." Scott's expression becomes unsettlingly intense. "What would you see?"

"In a desert?"

"In any natural-born landscape without human interference. Would you see nothing?"

I shake my head. "That's when I see everything. Nature is this series of small, intricate pieces, seemingly separate but strangely all connected, one part always influencing another. We might forget but we're part of that, too, strands of the universe in infinite, marvel-worthy motion."

Scott sits up out of his slouch, gaze landing on me as hard and heavy as an open drawbridge. "Do you ever go hiking?"

"I used to." More like I used to run laps around the outdoor track at school, but it's the same idea, right?

"Would you go with me?"

I inhale sharply. "Um, right now?"

"No, right now we need to hit the highway before five' o'clock traffic. Next Saturday?"

A ripple of energy goes up my spine. "Like, just me and you?" He nods. A low giggle escapes my throat. "What's the catch? Is there some tattooed tour guide with bigger boobs that I need to chauffer you to next?" I'm trying to be funny but now I do sound like a jealous twelve-year-old.

He sighs, dropping his head back in disbelief. "You are impossible." He stands up and offers me his hand. "Actually, there is this tattooed chick with a big mouth named Elle that I want to get to know if she'd stop making it so hard."

"*I'm* hard to get to know?" I let him pull me to my feet. "How about you with your impenetrable barrier, Mr. Ten-Foot-Wall? Do you think you've made it easy for me to get to know you?"

"I might be a ten-foot wall, but you're an active volcano

—I never know what's going to come out of your mouth or what your temperament is going to be like. People should receive a hard-hat and a First Aid Kit for wounded egos when they meet you." His hand leaves mine and goes to his pants pocket. He starts a slow saunter back up the hill.

I'm still standing by the stage. *Am I really that bad*? How about all the conversations we've started that he just dropped out of or cut off? How about the questions he never answered or the sarcastic looks and responses I've received time and time again?

I slowly follow him up the trail, crossing the bridge back over to the parking lot. I must be unusually quiet or maybe something changed on my face because he asks, "Did I hurt your feelings?"

"No." I unlock my car. *Just making me realize that some of our failed interactions might be my fault.* He might be on to something, saying how life is about perception. "But I'm a little worried I've injured yours with my volcanic behavior."

"Nah. Ten-foot wall, remember?" He slides into the passenger seat. "You might hurt my feelings, however, if you get cold feet over hiking next weekend. You can hike, right?"

"Of course I can hike." I hiked three flights of stairs when the mall elevator died during a blowout sale at Nordstrom, then hiked back down them with four bags of clothes and shoes. Normal hiking can't be that grueling. "Where are we going hiking?"

His gaze flicks over my head, to the mountains beyond town. “You’ll see.”

July 2nd, 2017

PATIO GAMES WITH FOX AND DARCY

I bypassed the park and drove down to the beach.

By the time I start walking up the dunes, the sun has sunk into the sea. I've witnessed a handful of pelicans, sandpipers, and loons who remind me that I don't take enough time out of my days to appreciate nature and all its wonders like I used to. I sat for a while on a driftwood log with a pen and notebook, attempting to summon my magical writing powers after years of nonuse. A vacation seemed like a good time to try again, but I ended up with three pages of crossed out paragraphs. My ideas all sucked. Storytelling used to come so effortlessly, so naturally, but not anymore. I'm a computer with a broken circuit board, a typewriter missing its keys. This isn't just writer's block; this is writer's *wall*.

The sky is colored like a raspberry and lavender mojito as I steer Kacey's Subaru into the driveway of the beach house. Fire flickers on the patio where several figures move and the roar of hysterical laughter billows up the stairs. *Looks like the drinking started without me*. The group is grinning and wiping tears from their eyes as I approach. Smoke coils out of Noah's Traeger, the aroma of beef and hot dogs almost tempting my stomach. Rena and Kacey wave from a couch where they've saved me a seat. A figure sitting in a wicker basket chair peers over his shoulder.

Scott's eyes are hard, reflecting the flames of the fire.

"Ah ha, there's our woman of the hour! Grab a glass and a plate, Elle!" Jordan motions to the outdoor table, where huge buckets of ice cradle a half dozen wine bottles. Glasses and paper plates circle a platter, piled with enough cheese and meat to feed an army.

Scott stares at me. *Not leaving*, his expression warns.

I pick up a glass. *Me neither*. He's ruined enough of my time here already. I offer Noah a smile, pushing my beach-blown hair back. "What all do we have here?"

"Anything and everything!" Noah gets up out of his chair. His hair is wet like he just got out of the shower and he's wearing a native style tee with a coyote on it. "I've got a great chardonnay in this bucket, two pinot noirs and a Sauvignon Blanc from my uncle's winery in Cali. Tell me what you want, Gorgeous."

"I'll take the chardonnay." I lift my glass as he uncorks a bottle with the disconcerting name of *The Showdown*. He catches me off guard as he reaches for my hand, pulling it and the wine glass toward him. His fingers are gentle over mine, smooth and warm and perfectly tanned. "Thank you."

He smiles, brown eyes glittering in the firelight. "Of

course."

I grin. I don't even mean to—it just happens. Noah's smile is contagious, and he kind of has this Jon Snow thing going on with his dark curly hair and stubbly chin that draws me right in. Lifting his drink to mine, he says, "Cheers."

"Cheers." We clank glasses and sip.

"Did you have a great adventure?" Kacey scoots over, making room for me on the couch.

"Any good bird sightings?" Rena asks.

I plop down between them, trying to act like I'm right at home versus uptight from the unwanted company sitting three chairs over. "Yes, sandpipers on the beach and pelicans in the waves. Even spotted a loon. It was cool."

"Oh, super cool," Kacey beams, even though she doesn't have a clue what I'm talking about. I appreciate her enthusiasm.

"Did you go down to the beach to bird watch?" Ken Doll —er—Allen questions, one eyebrow slightly quirked. In a whisper, he says to Betsey, "Isn't that what your dad does on Tuesdays with the retirement center?"

"Yes, I did," I say in an excited tone like it's the greatest activity on the planet and not just a boring hobby for old people. "We have a lot of migratory species right now, stuff you don't always see like Surf Scoters and Western Grebes. I'm thinking about making a trip to Alaska next year to see some of our native birds' nesting grounds."

"Oh." Allen nods slowly, lost for a proper response. "So

you've been doing this for a while then?"

"A few years now."

"Who got you started on that hobby?"

My eyes involuntarily dart toward Scott and the slightest snort flares his nostrils. My bubbly demeanor falters. "Somebody I used to know."

"Have you ever been down to the Winter Wings festival in Klamath Falls?" Betsey asks. "It's amazing how many different kinds of birds pass through that area, and I'm not even a birder!"

"It's on my bucket list." Which seems to increase in size all the time but never decrease. I haven't checked off any notable adventures in years. And the problem with Klamath Falls is that it's a small town at the southern Oregon border, nearly five hours from Portland, and people would rather bang their heads on a concrete wall than put up with my squirming impatience to get out of the car. Three hours in a moving vehicle is my max.

"Stop it, you guys, all this talk about birds is making me want chicken," the thickset guy speaks up. I think his name is Chris. "Hey, Noah, when your brother finally gets here we should all go check out that new barbecue joint in Lincoln City! Best barbecued wings on the coast, I hear."

The boys settle into a conversation about food and local hot spots while I drop back with Rena and Kacey. Rena pokes me in the hip then tries to nonchalantly point her head at Scott.

His aura drifts between chair legs and across the pavement like toxic fog, but I ignore it. I have the sudden urge to make him as uncomfortable as possible because I'm horrible like that and ready for a challenge. Our couch is seated not only near the burning fire glass but beside the outdoor fireplace, the perfect seat to roast marshmallows... or fake a hot flash. "Wow, it's hot right here," I say, unzipping my jacket.

"We can move the couch," Rena suggests.

"Nah, it's okay. The couch is heavy. I'll just take this off." I shed my jacket, still wearing the bikini top from our morning of sunbathing. I don't even care that my scars are showing. Unlike Teenage Elle who'd thought a villain-themed, poor-fitting bikini top was cute, Adult Elle has style. I adjust the straps on my push-up balconette then pretend to dab a fallen drop of wine off my boob. I lick the nonexistent drop off my finger.

My trick catches more attention than it's meant to: Chris has gone from salivating over the Traeger to looking hungrily in my direction. Jordan is openly gaping, and Noah's eyes are a pair of wandering travelers that don't seem to know where to land.

Scott glares. Almost unnoticeably, he shakes his head.

Chest up, chin high, I smile at him and give my glass the lightest lift. In attempt to be even more awful, I say, "Hey, Noah?"

"Yes, Gorgeous?"

"Who owns the boat at the end of your little beach?"

"Well, who else?" He holds up both arms like it's obvious.

"Do you want to go for a ride?"

"Can I?" I giggle.

"Of course you can. Tomorrow. You name the time."

I'm about to produce another sugary sweet comment but Scott finally cuts in. "Don't be out too late, Noah. Aliana's arriving tomorrow. Unless you want *me* to entertain her and then you can stay out all day if you want." He flicks his eyebrows in a seductive fashion.

"Psh! She's all yours." Noah waves a dismissive hand. "She'd rather hang with you than me anyway."

"Well, we both know why that is," Scott laughs, tipping the rest of his beer back.

"Oh, no. *No*!" Noah covers his ears. "Don't say it! I don't even want an inkling of what you and my baby sister do together when she's here!"

My wine suddenly tastes like acid. Noah has a sister? And not just any sister. *Some plaything of Scott's.* You'd think that his being with another girl, especially after this long, wouldn't nudge my cold heart but it does. It's another stabbing reminder that I wasn't good enough. If I was smart I would get up and leave. Now.

I'm too pissed off to do the smart thing.

"Oh, I didn't know you had a sister! What's she like, Noah?" I ask.

Noah starts to speak but Scott answers, "She's a model in California, a six-figures-a-year goddess who has better curves than a coke bottle and definitely makes good use of them. Oh, sorry, Noah." He pats Noah's shoulder apologetically.

Noah unplugs his finger from his ear. "What did I just say? I don't want to know!"

That makes two of us. I'm losing willpower fast and the nervous shakes have started in my thighs. *Not good enough, not pretty enough, not worthy*. I suck down two more gulps of wine, ignoring the heartburn. "She sounds very accomplished! Good for her." My voice comes out deceptively positive. "Though Noah, you might want to tell her she has terrible taste in men."

Chris bursts out laughing. Allen and Betsey snigger.

"I've already tried, trust me," Noah chuckles, his turn to pat Scott on the back.

"You should probably tell her to take some of that six-figure salary and get some penicillin shots," I suggest, glancing at Scott's pants. "Herpes will not make for a long-lived modeling career."

The crowd around the fire pit is equal parts silence and muffled laughter. Nobody knows how to take my comment. Kacey has choked on her drink. Rena nudges my shoulder and whispers in my ear, "Burn 'im, Tiger."

Scott stands up from his chair. For a moment I think I've won, but he wanders over to the cooler parked between Jordan and Chris and grabs another beer. "Sounds like you're speaking from experience." He takes the end of his lighter and jerks it beneath the beer's lid. It releases with a loud *pop*. "But since I'm pretty sure herpes can't be cured with penicillin, maybe it's *inexperience*. What did you guys used to call her, the nun with irritable virgin syndrome?" He wags a finger between Rena and Kacey.

Both girls sit like statues while my grip on my glass tightens. "You told him the nun joke?" I whisper through clenched teeth. When and why had they done that? It couldn't have been anytime recently because I haven't been a virgin for *five years*.

Kacey sinks into the cushions. "Might've slipped out once?"

"What kind of friends are you people?" I hiss.

"Good ones," Rena murmurs then straightens out of her slouch. "On the other side of that coin, we used to call you Dented Dick Darcy," she hurls at Scott at full volume.

The patio roars with drunken laughter. He rolls his eyes while taking a swig of beer and I love witnessing the cracks appear in his ego. *Justice*.

"You're never going to live that one down," Jordan assures, wiping a tear from his eye.

Scott smacks the back of his friend's head. "Shut up, J-Fraud," he orders, using an old nickname that Jordan had earned after getting drunk one night and stealing women's underwear from Walmart.

"Anyways, Elle," Noah says, trying to steer the conversation around, "don't worry about my sister. Just tell me when you want to go out tomorrow and we'll go. I'm here all day." His brown eyes sparkle in the firelight.

There's a warm security in his tone, a reliability that makes me think I could ask for anything and he'd give it. It soothes the hateful buzz coursing through my veins. "I'm usually up around nine, so I'll let you know."

"Oh, please, she *hates* boats," Scott snarls.

"Uh, correction: I hated Glen's boat," I fire back, bothered that he's interrupting a conversation that no longer includes him. He must be thinking of the time we all went camping and Glen had taken us out in his old speed boat which would buck like a bronco when he'd hit the gas. It also had a habit of dying when we were in the middle of the lake, and after being towed to shore by strangers twice I refused to get back in it. "That does not make me anti-boat. And how would you know what I do and don't like these days?"

Scott looks at Noah. "She screams when fish jump out of the water."

"I do not!"

"Glen used to call her *Flying Fox* because she'd fly to other side of the boat if she saw anything move in the lake."

"Yeah, and he used to call you Sir Fish-A-Lot because you couldn't keep a fish on your hook for love or money."

Scott narrows his eyes. *Sure you're talking about fish*, his expression reads. "Not true."

"Should I call Glen and ask him?" I smirk. My head is starting to buzz a little from the alcohol.

The chitters of laughter die down. Every pair of eyes shuffles over to my ex, expressions pitiful. Scott is, finally, lost for words. His gaze darts to the ground and he lets out a carefully controlled breath. "If only you could." His tone is dark, distant.

"And why can't I? Pretty sure I'm capable of lifting a phone." Glen's number is still somewhere in my contacts list. I go to sip my wine and nearly spill it as Kacey elbows my arm. A deep frown carves her features as she shakes her head.

Scott looks up from the fire at me, sharp and unblinking. "Pretty sure the dead can't."

It's like someone dumped a bucket of water over my head. "What?"

Without another word, he lifts his beer to the crowd in a goodnight salute and wanders off the patio. I peer around, confused and waiting for someone to speak but they're all quiet and giving each other sorry, awkward looks. "What is he talking about?"

"Glen died last year, Elle," Jordan answers.

Pins and needles shower across my skin. The air comes whooshing out of my lungs like someone kicked me and it's hard to inhale. "*Died*? What happened?" Glen seemed like a relatively healthy individual. It must've been an accident, something unexpected.

"Don't know." Jordan shrugs, but his tone says otherwise. "He doesn't talk about it."

So that's what triggered this morning's weird episode. Scott bravely touching my tattoo, the deep, dark sadness in his eyes when he did it, none of that was about me. Scott's shadow starts to disappear down the trail to Noah's beach. I have this absurd urge to go after him, to tell him I'm sorry for his loss and I know what it feels like even though my loss is different, but I don't get up from the couch.

Conversation trickles back in around the fire but I no longer hear it. I spend the next while trying to suppress memories of woodlands and tents, boats and lakes, of Glen singing funny songs while cooking over a campfire and the warm perfection of his brother's body next to mine. These memories bring up others that I've been trying to avoid like those of vacations with my parents and our family friends, of sitting in a circle around a bonfire much like I'm doing right now. Loss is so hard, no matter what form it takes. What is it designed to do except turn us into hollow shells of the people we once were?

"Elle?"

Kacey's voice catapults me back into reality. "Huh?"

"Rena and I are going to go play blackjack with Allen and Betsey," she says, standing beside the couch. Rena is at the wine table, refilling her glass. "Do you want to come?"

I had been so distracted I hadn't realized they'd left. "Oh. Uh, where's Noah?" I tilt towards his chair but it's empty, too.

"He's on a long-distance call with his mom. She travels so I don't think he hears from her much." Kacey's lips turn down at the corners. "Are you okay? I didn't even think to tell you about Glen. I'm so sorry."

I feel a pang of annoyance at how many Scott details Kacey has left out since our arrival. *How does she know all this anyway*? Dustin must be better friends with him than I'd previously thought. "You guys go ahead. I'll follow soon." I smile and hope it doesn't look forced.

Kacey nods. "Come in soon. You can't avoid us forever."

She means it lightly, but I still wince at the comment. I don't mean to make her and Rena feel that I'm avoiding them after they've gone to the effort to invite me here. Maybe I shouldn't have stayed out alone on the beach all day.

After Rena and Kacey close the sliding door, I stand up and clock the Tacoma. *So that's where Scott's truck came from*. It was Glen's truck. He must've inherited it.

I wander through the yard to the crest of the hill, peering over the bushes at the beach below. A light fog has rolled in over the bay, moon casting silver rays on the water. It's beautifully eerie, and while I try to tell myself that the view is the only reason I came over it's a lie. I stand there for a few minutes, waiting to see a shadow, a movement, anything. I hear nothing, not the scuff of flipflops on sand or the flick of a lighter or the slosh of beer inside a bottle. I'm about to turn away from the bay when a tall figure emerges on the bark dust trail beside me. I squeak, nearly jumping out of my skin.

Scott stumbles back. "Shit! What the—what the hell are you doing?"

"Standing, obviously, or trying to," I retort, hand on my own thumping heart.

He sneers. "Well, don't hurt yourself."

"Don't have to with you looking at me." It's a terrible

comeback. I cross my arms, huffing at the bay as embarrassment floods my cheeks.

He makes a passive sound, then continues across the yard.

"Scott?"

"What?" He throws his arms up as he spins around. "Jesus, am I ever going to escape you? First in Oregon City, then here at *my* friend's beach house, and now you're stalking me from behind the bushes!"

"Don't act like I planned any of this!" Except the spying from the bushes part. "You are the last person I wanted to get trapped with on my vacation, trust me!"

"Oh, puh-lease," Scott drawls. "I bet you've been seeing Noah for weeks! I see the way he treats you, how he can barely keep his tongue in his mouth when you walk into a room."

"Oh, shut up, that isn't true!"

"So is he everything you wanted? Is he the perfect beach-owning, money-making Prince Charming your family adores?"

Where is he coming up with this? "No, because we're not dating."

"Oh, so you're just sleeping with him?"

"Oh my God!"

"Wow, how your taste and standards have changed."

I hold both hands up as if to physically stop the conversation. How is it that after all this time he still knows exactly what buttons to push to send me off the deep end? "We're not going to have this fight. In fact, I'm done. Goodnight, Scott."

"Funny, I never pegged you as *easy*."

"For your information, I haven't slept with anyone since you." I let out a mumble of profanities, heading down the beach trail. I would go back to the house but he's in my way.

I'm ten steps down the path when the bark dust crunches behind me. "You haven't slept with anyone since we broke up?" Scott asks, shocked.

"Oh, piss off!" I desperately want to tell him that my mind and body have moved on to greater pastures just to prove he didn't leave such a deep impression on my life, but I can't.

He passes me and blocks the trail. "Why?"

I shove him out of the way. "Because some of us aren't sluts and we believe in being loyal to one person!"

He growls, dropping his head back. "God, here we go."

My building fury is scattering my brain. Another bout of nervous shakes takes hold of my legs so I sit on the edge of a lounge chair. My vision wobbles and it's not from the poor lighting. I drank my wine too fast.

Scott slowly crosses the beach. He's inches from the chair next to mine when I warn, "If you sit, I might really kill you." I don't know how or with what. There's a pointy rock parting the tide that I could probably lift.

"Fine, but at least hear me out," he demands. "What you think happened, *didn't*. You've made nothing into something and I'm telling you—"

"You want to tell me that what I saw was *nothing*?" I jump up like my chair is on fire. "She was sitting in your kitchen shirtless! Oh, yeah, that's a great indication of nothing, you lying bastard!"

"She had the wrong idea!"

"You're still going to feed me that crock of crap? What the f—"

"It was a mistake, Elle!" He's yelling so loudly I'm sure Jordan and Chris can hear him from the patio. "I didn't touch her, I didn't kiss her, I didn't want—"

"You and I both know what would've happened if I hadn't walked in!" My voice is shuddering and try as I might to keep the tears at bay, they start anyways. "You know the worst part about the whole thing? I still don't know why! Why, when it felt like we had everything, did you choose someone else?"

"I did *not* choose someone else."

"But you did! You alienated me for no reason at all and then you went to her! What did I do wrong?" I'm choking on my tears. It's shocking how much power his betrayal still has over me, how I can still feel the withered connection between us.

Scott sinks down on a chair, head in his tattooed hands. I wipe my face on the sleeves of my jacket, humiliated that I've lost control. Humiliated at the broken, hurting person I still am inside. How is it that I still carry this much grief over an event that happened five years ago? I've had professional counseling for this, for grief and betrayal in general. I have a roof over my head and a job and people who love and support me. I should be able to handle this with more grace, more patience, more understanding.

I'm angrier than ever.

"You don't understand," Scott whispers.

"I wasn't enough for you," I declare. "That's pretty easy to understand."

"You were more than enough, Elle. *I* just wasn't good enough for *you*."

I wave a dismissive hand. Oh, yes, not feeling good enough for someone who truly loved you is an excellent reason to cheat on them. "It doesn't matter now."

Scott pins me with a look. "It's been five years and this still has a hold on us. I'm pretty sure it matters."

"Look, I don't want to feel like this anymore. I see that we can't be in the same house and hope to have an enjoyable vacation, so in the morning I'm going to leave."

"Don't do that."

"I don't want Kacey or Rena to catch on. They deserve a good trip. If they ask you, tell them I got sick and went home."

Scott stands up from his chair. "I have a better idea: you stay, I'll go. Problem solved." He saunters across the sand, daring to come near me. I step back. "Can I make a request before I leave?"

"What could you possibly request of me?"

"Don't fall for Noah. He's a good guy and I like him, but he's not looking for the long term. He'll use you and then I'll have to kick his ass, which might compromise our friendship." Under his breath, he mutters, "Not that it isn't already compromised."

"You don't own me. I'll do whatever I want, just like you did," I coolly remind.

Scott lingers like he wants to fight my response, sighs, then turns away and begins the ascent up the sandy slope. "Scott?" I call before he's too far out of earshot. He looks over his shoulder. "What happened to Glen?"

His head tilts toward the bay, lips pressed into an unreadable line. For a moment, I think he's not going to answer, then he huffs a laugh. "A breakup," he says. "Followed by a heroin addiction."

June 9th, 2012

INTO THE GORGE

Mom is on a day trip to Seattle with her sisters and Dad is, conveniently, at a swap meet.

Scott's promise to take me hiking has me up at seven in the morning, which is highly unusual. I wake with my stomach fluttering, wondering if he will even show. After getting home from the Columbia River Gorge last Friday, he'd returned to his usual sealed-up self. He didn't say much to me at Dad's shop this week, though in his defense the shop has been busy.

Even as I become more and more certain that he's probably going to flake, I still prepare for him to pick me up. I dig out a pair of Nike tennis shoes, the closest thing to a pair of hiking boots I own, and a pair of leggings with black mesh up the sides. I opt for a push-up bra instead of a sports bra and a tank top with a hoodie. I wipe the dust off an old backpack that I used to use as a gym bag and fill it with snacks, a water bottle, and an extra pair of socks and pants.

Ten minutes after nine, I check my cell. No texts. No

calls. I start to fidget. I should've just asked him if we were still on for today. Isn't that what normal people do? But I didn't want to hear him reject me, especially not after I thought we had something in Cascade Locks.

Twenty minutes after nine, I am beginning to accept defeat. He's either forgotten or ditched me. His behavior this week would've been different if he had meant it.

I've just poured myself a cup of coffee to drown my sorrows when I hear an obnoxious rumble come up the road. Through the kitchen window I spot a hot blue Mazda pulling up to my house. Scott gets out of the driver's seat. *Oh my God.* He didn't flake. I throw my coffee cup into the sink and race to the bathroom to check my hair. My body jitters with nerves as the doorbell rings.

Scott stands there in black joggers and a Timberline hoodie, a Starbucks cup in his left hand. He extends the drink to me. "Sorry I'm late. The Cadillac in front of me thought it was okay to order ten drinks in the drive-through line."

I pick my jaw up off the ground. "You brought me coffee." It's almost a question. He nods. I slowly reach out and take it, reading the abbreviation scrolled across the side. It's an iced macchiato—with extra caramel drizzle. "You even brought me the *right kind* of coffee."

"I take notes. You ready?"

"Yeah." *No, I need ten minutes to convince myself this is really happening.* "Let me grab my backpack and I'll meet you in the car."

The trunk on the Mazda is roomy, though Scott's hiking pack takes up half of it. The bag is ten times the size of my little one, the kind you'd take on a five-day hike up the Pacific Crest Trail, not a daytrip. I pass him a suspicious glance, setting my midget bag beside it. "You kidnapping me for real this time?"

He can hardly contain the grin on his face. "Guess you'll find out."

We both buckle up and Scott burns rubber out of my driveway.

"Are you going to tell me where you're taking me in your new ride?" I'm trying to not sound giddy over the fact that we're actually doing this. I flick a button on the side of my seat and the leather begins to heat up. *Way nicer than the Honda.*

"How good of a hiker are you?"

"I'm great so long as the ground stays flat." I'm a panting dog going uphill, so secretly I hope he's picked something that isn't too challenging. His monstrous backpack says otherwise.

He nods, the gears almost audibly clicking in his head. "Perfect."

An hour later we are deep in the Gorge amongst a tight-knit community of pine trees and basalt formations. We snake down a rocky, one-way road that I mistake for someone's driveway and I nearly shield my eyes. At any minute, somebody could fly around a corner and wipe us out.

"Don't worry," Scott says, seeing me flatten against my

seat. "Few people know about this place. I doubt we'll see any vehicles."

The road climbs into a narrow, wooded lot. A red PT Cruiser is parked at the end, the only other sign of human life. The air is damp and cool as I step out of the Mazda. Shedding his sweatshirt already, Scott adjusts his tee. I watch his biceps flex as he shifts things around in his pack. I sling on the midget bag as he locks up then leads the way down a deer trail into the gully.

"What *are* you hauling in there?" I finally ask. "Or is that just a body bag for later?"

He chuckles darkly. "You think I'm going to kill you, huh?"

"Hard to say." Not that it matters now—we are well into the forest and even if I can navigate the deer trail back to the car, he still has the keys.

Scott faces forward but the smile is audible in his voice as he says, "I never start a daytrip unprepared. I've jinxed myself in the past and I figured today wasn't a good day to test fate." He puts his arm out in front of me, coming to a halt. The trail has washed out, leaving a ravine of dirt and clay three feet below us. He hops down, offering me both hands.

I brace my palms against his, his warm fingers wrapping around mine. A tingly sensation works its way up my arms from his touch. Jumping down, I wobble a moment and it's not from the uneven ground. "So why have you ignored me all week?"

"I didn't mean to." He shrugs. "I'm just trying to keep a low profile at work. I'm not sure how your dad feels about me yet and I don't want him to think I'm up to no good with his daughter."

"Oh."

At the bottom of the gully, the pathway ends at a wooden bridge crossing a creek. Crystal-clear water flows over a floor of colorful pebbles and I pause to admire, taking a deep clean breath. Scott leans on the railing. "What do you see?"

I smile. "Everything." Being away from the city always calms my inner chaos and awakens some slumbering part of myself. It's a deep and ancient place, almost mystical, like a piece of me has existed in these woods, in this water, forever and will continue to exist here long after I am gone.

Scott must feel it as well because instead of hustling me along, he stands quietly. We both watch as the trees wave in the breeze, as sunlight dances around the wildflowers. "Shall we?" He nods at the trail.

The Gorge is a wondrous union of wildlife and geology. The trees thin near the crest of the hill and the sun shines down over the rockier, more desert-like part of the hike. We pass four deer grazing in a meadow of clover and tall grasses that roll like waves when the breeze passes through them. The deer pay us no mind as we walk by, coming so close I can see the fuzzy nubs on a young male's head. I take a few pictures for my Instagram.

The temperature continues to rise so we stop for a water break around noon. Two fields of poppies and a steep canyon later, we break for lunch. I flop down on a fallen log in the shade, my tank damp with sweat and my Nikes covered in a fine film of dust. My jacket is wrapped around my waist. "How long is this trail anyway?"

"Are you dying already?" Scott chuckles.

"Already? We've been at this all day!" I laugh, though it hasn't felt like all day. Being out in the natural world erases time. The only giveaway for the hours that have passed is the sun's change of position in the sky.

Scott props his foot up on my log, taking a swig of water. "We're almost there."

"Any idea of what time it is?" I wave my phone around in the air but not a single bar is picked up.

Scott plucks the phone out of my fingers. "Does it matter?" He tucks it in his pants pocket.

My eyes follow it in there. "Don't think I won't go after that."

"Go ahead," he replies, somewhere between an invite and a dare.

I almost do, then chicken out. He laughs and sits down, unzipping his pack to hand me a sandwich. We eat while taking in our extraordinary view of the world below. The whole river is visible from up here, snaking between green patches of trees and the hills of The Dalles. The highway is no wider than my thumb.

"Scott?"

"Yeah?" He answers, mouth half full.

"Do you ever get tired of living in a fast-paced world?"

"I'm tired of it every day. Thank God school's over. I couldn't have handled another year." He shakes his head. "I've thought about just giving it all up and doing something crazy, like backpacking across America for a summer. Camp where I want, fish the lakes and rivers, live wild for a few months."

Strangely enough, I think he could do it. "I've thought about that, too." I would love to spend a summer in the woods, waking up to a campfire every morning, drinking coffee beside a river... but I can't go a day without having a shower, I can barely pitch a tent, and the idea of killing an animal—even for survival—deeply disturbs me.

Scott throws me a look that says *yeah, right,* then does a double take at my shoulders. "Elle?"

"What?"

"Did you not put sunscreen on before we left?"

I peer down my tank. A U-shape of scarlet skin stretches over my chest and up my collarbone. "Oh no—oh, my tattoo!" I struggle to see behind my shoulder but don't really need to. The black curve of my hummingbird's wing dances over a cherry-colored background.

"Don't panic. It'll be okay." Scott opens his bag and pulls out a tube of Banana Boat. "See? This is why I come prepared."

After slathering lotion across my chest, I reach to do my back and am met with a stinging sensation. The skin on my shoulders is already sore from the burn. I reach again but it hurts. I can't get the lotion past the balls of my shoulders and the U of my tank cuts low in both front and back. It can't be left this way. My eyes slowly drift up to meet Scott's. "Do you mind?" I hold out the tube.

He blinks at me, then shakes his head and takes the sunscreen. I turn around and pull my hair forward. His hands are tough, calloused against my back, though careful to not press too hard. His fingers rub circles of lotion into my burn, making every nerve I own zing beneath his touch. His thumb pauses on the birthmark between my shoulder blades.

"Okay. You should be good for a while." His cheeks are a little red, too, but it might not be from the sun. Clearing his throat, he stands up and says, "You want to keep going?"

"Yeah." I stuff my sandwich away and hop to my feet. My heart is beating so hard I feel lightheaded. We continue up the trail but my thoughts are no longer on the hike. Instead I'm imagining what those strong hands would feel like around me. *Pull yourself together, Elle.* I need to stay in control because while I'm ninety-six percent sure this is a date, I'm still not sure how he feels about me. I'm not sure *he* even knows how he feels.

Our pathway begins to curl up the mountain, growing

narrower and higher. The soil dissolves into layers of red and ivory rock and most of the plant life has died away. I'm even more grateful for Scott's sunscreen as the sun blazes down harder here than anywhere else on the trail. The backs of my legs begin to burn from the ground's steep angles, something I noticed earlier but now cannot ignore. Sweat gathers on my brow and I bat it away. The hike out has been fun but I'm secretly ready to head back. We're at least three hours from the car.

I lose momentum while Scott powers onward, unaware. He hasn't looked back for his routine check in a while and I wonder if asking him to put sunscreen on me bothered him in some way. I hate to appear as anything less than a champion hiker, but in this kind of heat the charade is impossible to keep up. I stop, hands on my knees, to catch my breath. I'm taking a long drink of water from my bottle, which is nearly empty, when he finally notices I'm behind.

He circles back. Sweat is glistening on his arms and face, too, which makes me feel a little better. "I know it's hot. This part of the trail is short, I swear."

I nod, swallowing a big swig of water. "I hope wherever you're taking me has water, because I'm going in."

"It does. And yeah you are." He's pokerfaced when he says it, but I hear the mischief in his tone.

I don't even have a swimsuit but at this point it doesn't matter—my clothes are soaked anyway. I cap my bottle and throw it in my pack. Later I would wonder what would've happened if I hadn't stopped right there, in that spot, and if I would've liked the stream or secret pool of water at the end of this long journey. In that moment, however, all I could think about was how much I liked the boy in front of me, how much it scared me, and how the rocky ground was suddenly shifting beneath my feet.

The trail below me gives out.

I dig my heels into the rocks, trying to slow my speed as I plummet down the hillside. I slide to a halt just inches from the ravine, lying face-up on the rocks. *Oh my God.* I lay still, panting at the sky. *Oh, God, did that just happen? Holy cow, holy cow.*

"Elle! *Elle*!" Scott is yelling somewhere overhead. "Don't move, do you hear me? Just stay still!"

My feet have stopped me on the last flat surface before the ninety-degree drop off. I close my eyes, willing myself to come up with something other than panic. My left thigh is pulsing like a heart. *Get out of here, Elle. Get up.* Despite Scott's orders, I can't ignore my intuition. I have to move. If the ledge gives way, it's over. My mother's face comes to mind, followed by my brother's and my dad's. *This is not how it's going to end.* Carefully, I sit up, judge my position. Hot red fluid stains the rocks around me. At first I think it's coming out of the ground, then realize it's me. My left pantleg is torn up the thigh. *It's blood.* I suppress my body's desire to hyperventilate. Digging both hands into the rubble, I pull up.

"Elle, don't move!" Scott swears to himself. "Just give me

a second!"

A gust of wind races through the canyon. *Move*, it seems to whisper while clattering through the rocks, pushing me upwards. *Move now*. Rolling onto my stomach, I proceed to do a polar bear crawl up the bloodied mountainside and away from the ledge.

Scott is frantically knotting something around his waist when I feel it again: the shifting and parting of earth. Over my shoulder, I watch as the ledge gives way, crumbling down into the valley a hundred feet below. My insides curl. *Not the time to throw up*. Nobody would survive a drop like that. My nausea and horrible thoughts are interrupted by a rope falling over my back. Scott kneels at the edge of the canyon.

"You won't be able to pull me up!" I'm no petite flower—I'm a full-grown woman and he would need a horse to drag me up this mountainside.

"Wanna bet?" Determination lights his features. He wraps his end of the rope around his hands. "Tie that around your waist and hold on! You hear me?"

Afraid of the earth moving again, I do as he says, sloppily knotting the rope below my chest and squeezing the nylon tight between my fingers. The rope jerks against me and I gasp as he pulls me from my spot. He starts dragging me up through the dust and rubble. Terrified that my weight is going to pull him over, I try to keep climbing but he pulls too fast. It's a rough ride up and I'm bumped and jabbed all the way.

Scott reels me right into him, all sense of personal space lost. He wraps his arms around my waist before I can slip out of reach and hauls me up. We scramble away from the ravine until our backs are against the rock wall. We sit there panting for several minutes, speechless over what just happened. I close my eyes, giving into a fit of shivers. *That was too close.*

Scott is sitting shoulder to shoulder with me. I feel his breath on my neck as he turns his head. "Elle, you're bleeding. Bad."

With the adrenaline wearing off, the pulsing pain in my thigh is more obvious. I open my eyes and look down. A pool of blood surrounds my legs, growing wider by the minute. "Shit."

Scott leans over my lap, placing a hand on my torn legging. Slowly, he tries to rotate my leg for a better look but fire rages through my veins. I let out a yelp. He jerks his hand away. "Damn it, I'm sorry."

"It's okay," I choke out, but it's most definitely not. Nothing about this is okay. Warring with the pain, I force my leg into a bent position to view the damage. A deep, jagged cut runs from the outside of my knee to just a few inches below my butt cheek. "Oh, wow, that's bad. That's really bad."

"Elle, I'm so sorry." Scott reaches for his backpack, which he had dropped several feet away. One of the front pockets is open and random crap including maps, compasses, and jerky sticks are spilling out of it. "I should've picked a different trail. I never thought this would happen."

The worst part about having an accident like this—besides the new, potentially long-term trauma on my psyche—is being so far from help. "We don't have cell service anywhere out here, do we?"

The dire look on his face tells me all I need to know. Pulling a half-filled water bottle out of his pack, he says, "You don't want to leave a wound that size dirty. Can you stand up?"

My leg becomes more immobile by the minute, each movement more excruciating. Using the rock wall, I force myself to my feet. The rope is still knotted around my waist and my hands are shaking too hard to untie it. Scott steps forward and takes over, removing the knot and putting the bloodied rope in his pack. Taking out a pocketknife, he stabs a few holes in the cap of a half-filled water bottle. He circles a finger in the air. *Turn around.*

I hesitate, eyeing his contraption. "You're going to blast me with that, aren't you?"

"You'll thank me later." He crunches the bottle and sprays the back of my leg.

The sensation of fire and ice nearly sends me to my knees. Bits of rubble wash out of the cut, flowing away with the reddened water. The trail looks like a murder scene by the time he's done, and I'm clinging to a half-dead tree sapling just to keep myself upright.

"It needs to be wrapped until we can get you to a hospital. Will you let me?" he asks, bringing out an emergency kit.

I open my mouth to tell him that I can wrap it, but the words never make it to my lips. My body is facing a new wave of shock and it's zapped my voice. His hands move carefully over my leg, smoothing gauze, winding tape. My nerves buzz with a mix of pain and pleasure as he works to cover the injury. *Thank God I shaved this morning.* This is not the person I thought Scott was. I can't imagine the boy on the dock or the one from the shop rescuing me from a collapsing trail and I certainly can't picture him as a caretaker of any kind. He rinses his hands off with the last of the water bottle, not even bothered that someone else's blood has stained his clothes.

I touch my mummified leg. "Thank you." He nods. I hop around for a minute, gauze chafing against my opposite thigh. If I felt stiff before, it's even harder to walk now. How am I going to get back down the trail? My eyes fall on the sun, hiding behind a cloud. "Scott?"

"Huh?"

"What time do you think it is?"

He follows my gaze to the sky. "Late." His tone is low, uneasy.

This doesn't comfort me. "How many hours to the parking lot do you think?"

"About three." He stands up, lifting his pack over his shoulders. "But that was before you got hurt."

Now I have a new reason to panic. Dad rarely ever goes looking for me if my car is in the driveway, but if Mom gets home before ten she'll want to say hi and tell me about her trip. She'll go to my room only to find that I'm missing with no way to contact me and no idea where I am. I didn't tell her I was going anywhere today—mostly because I thought Scott would stand me up—and I certainly didn't tell her that I'm hanging out with a guy.

My mind starts racing. "Did you bring flashlights? How far do you think we'll get before it gets dark out? Do you think there's any chance of cell service further down?"

"I think the first question you need to ask is can you walk."

"Oh." I take a few steps forward, trying not to flinch every time my knee bends. It's like someone is repeatedly jabbing me with a branding iron. "Yeah. No, sure, I'll be fine."

Scott shakes his head, seeing right through me. Knitting his hands behind his head he paces the trail a minute, muttering swear words beneath his breath. "Your dad's going to shoot me."

Actually, it will probably be my mother. "No, he'll be grateful that you pulled me out of the ravine and saved my life. I don't know if I could've climbed that whole hillside with this injury."

"I doubt you could've." He peers down the cliff at the fractured ledge that nearly swallowed me whole. "Try to keep up the best you can. At the very least, I want to get off this part of the trail."

"Excellent plan." I hobble past him and start back toward the meadows and the forest, wanting nothing more than to put distance between me and my new worst memory.

***

By the time we make it to the meadows, my breaks become more frequent. The longer I walk the more pins and needles fill my thigh and the branding iron seers deeper between my knee joints. Scott constantly looks back to make sure I'm there and every time I see the worry lines cut deeper into his forehead. I try to act like I'm only mildly uncomfortable and not like someone is sawing me apart with a dull bread knife.

We're coming up to the plateau before the denser part of the woods, where we'd stopped for our second water break, when Scott throws his pack off. "What are you doing?" I ask.

He sighs at the sunset that is trickling in through the trees. "Setting up camp for you."

"Whoa, *what*?"

"You are never going to make it back to the car like this. The trail gets steep and damp inside the woods. I'll set up camp for you and then keep going until I get cell service."

"You aren't serious! You can't just leave me up here in the middle of freaking nowhere!"

"What else do you want me to do, Elle?" He yells, throwing his arms in the air. "You need to get to a hospital and let's be honest: you aren't going to make it down into the gully in the dark with that leg. Let me go ahead and I will—"

"Oh, no, no! If you're going to make me stop then you're staying with me!" Like hell am I staying out in the wildlands of Oregon alone. These areas are home to all kinds of night-prowling predators, bears and cougars to name a few, and I'm no Cheryl Strayed. Being on the trails alone and in the dark frightens me almost as much as watching that cliff dissolve below my feet.

Scott rolls his eyes, waving at my leg. "You need stitches, remember?"

"And I'll still need them tomorrow!"

"What if you bleed to death?"

"I bleed for seven days straight every month and don't die—I'm not going to die now!" He wrinkles his nose up and turns away. "Look, I haven't soaked through the gauze yet so I have hope that I'll make it through the night. We are not separating out here! Either we keep going together, or we camp out *together*. End of story."

"Jesus, God." He rakes his hands through his hair like he's going to pull it all out. "I'm trying to help you! Why are you resisting? You're even more stubborn than your dad!"

"Never said I was easy," I spit back.

"Oh, don't I know it!"

His response rubs me the wrong way. "Hey, if you'd wanted easy maybe you should've gone after Kacey." It's a crappy thing to say and I don't really think Kacey is easy, but she might've been easier to coax into a relationship—or into bed.

"A little late for that now, isn't it?" He rips the knot out of his tent tie and throws the roll open with an unnecessary amount of force.

I want his words to roll off me but instead they sink in. I limp off to a fallen tree several paces away to sit down. Maybe I should think twice about making him stay. Perhaps being alone would be better than being stuck with a jerk all night long. My knee throbs as I carefully prop it on the log. I search out two Advil in the depths of my bag, trying to convince myself that I didn't waste my whole day and almost kill myself for an asshole.

We say nothing as he sets up a two-person tent and unrolls what I take to be a kind of nylon tarp. When the tarp begins to self-inflate, I realize it's some sort of high-tech sleeping pad. My stomach goes all wobbly when I realize the slim amount of personal space we're going to have inside that tent. We'll have to sleep arm to arm. *Maybe I'll just sleep outside*. I'm angry enough to do it, animals and all.

Scott throws a bunch of branches and broken tree limbs atop a pile of dirt and lights them, then lights a cigarette. It must not have rained here for a long time because the pile catches without the help of kindling. *Hopefully he won't burn the whole forest down*. From the corner of my eye, I see him glancing between me and the fire. I pretend to be watching the sun as it sinks behind the trees and tints the sky pink. At least it's a pretty sunset. *One I almost didn't get to witness.* The hair stands up on my back and it's not just from the sudden drop in temperature.

His footsteps walk slowly through the dirt. I wait for him to sit down next to me but instead he kneels on the ground in front. "Elle."

I know if I meet his gaze I'll melt and I don't want to. I'm not ready to forgive him. I pretend to be picking something off my shirt. "What?" His warm fingers creep over mine, pulling them from my lap and into the space between us. "You're a brave man to lay hands on a pissed off Irish woman."

"Wouldn't be my first poor judgement call today. Elle, I didn't mean what I said. I'm sorry. I'm sorry about all of it. I feel terrible because you're in this predicament thanks to me. If you had listened to me today and stayed put on that ledge..." He can't finish the sentence.

His soft, remorseful voice drifts through my ears and snakes its way through every inch of my being. I heave a sigh. "How were you supposed to know it was going to break? You were just trying to help me. Luckily for both of us, I *am* stubborn and I don't always listen to people when they're shouting orders."

"I promise the next hike will be your call."

"Who says I want to go hiking with you again?" He doesn't realize I'm teasing. Hurt passes over his face then hides behind that familiar ten-foot wall, which has been down between us all day and now threatens to rise again. Before he can take his hands away, I squeeze them closer. "I'm joking, Scott."

"I'd understand if you weren't."

"I *want* to hike with you. I want to do things with you." Despite the ending to our day, this trip had awoken what I can only describe as the call of the wild within; I want to go explore more, go on new adventures, and see new things. He has proven himself a worthy travel partner.

"Really?"

"Mm-hmm."

"Like what kinds of things do you want to do with me?" His hands slip up my forearms, testing to see if I'm going to push him back.

Maybe I should've worded that differently. "Like, um." My voice breaks. The energy between us is so intense it should've been audibly snapping in the air.

I don't know who leans in first, but either way his lips end up on mine. My arms wrap around his neck, something they've been longing to do all day—all *week*. He tastes like tobacco and sunscreen and something spicy. His hands slide to my back then down my waist, pressing his chest to mine. His kisses move to my chin, my jaw, then sear a luscious line down my throat that morphs me into the human embodiment of Jell-O. I've never kissed anyone like this before. Every nerve I own hums with desire and gathers low in my stomach, creating a warm, fluttery sensation. I want him as close as he can possibly get, which both excites and frightens me and I don't know which emotion is going to rule.

We don't get the chance to find out; my leg slips off its perch and slams against the log, sending pins, needles, razors down into my toes. I gasp and Scott pulls back. "Not that I want to leave you now," he says, one hand still resting on my hip, "but I wish you'd let me keep going. I bet that wound is worse than you think."

I grit my teeth against the aftermath of the hit, sweat gathering on my brow. "No. Stay with me." He runs a hand through his hair, which I've successfully tousled. My lip gloss shimmers on his cheek. A quirky expression shifts his face. "What now?"

"Does this mean you forgive me?"

"Heck no," I laugh, standing up. "Okay, maybe a little. Like fifty percent forgiven."

"What the hell, only fifty?"

"Yep." I whip my braids back and limp away.

He follows. "If I kiss you again, do I get a hundred-percent?"

If he kisses me again, my Jell-O legs won't make it to the tent. "No."

"So what do I have to do? The suspense is killing me." He cuts around in front, blocking my path to the tent.

I really want to pull him to me again, but instead I hold up a warning finger. "Don't rush me." Now that we've marred the Do Not Cross line between us, a few new rules may need to be set for both our sakes.

He tilts his head, catching the dual meaning in my response. "Alright."

"So." My hands go to my hips as I examine our makeshift camp. "Who's sleeping outside?"

He shakes his head once. "Not me."

I glance at the tent. "Okay. I'm sleeping outside."

"No. You're not." It's not up for debate. "Once the sun goes down our temperature is going to plummet. Don't tell me you don't already feel the change in the air."

The scorching heat lifted a while ago and in its place is an autumnal type of breeze that chills my nose when I inhale. I guess I don't want to add hypothermia to this venture. He drags a log over and sets it by the fire. Sitting down on one side, he gestures to the space beside him. "Come on," he says when I don't come. "It's going to be a long night. I suggest you get comfortable to the best of your ability."

Nothing about this is comfortable, from my injury to the close quarters in the tent to the realization that in a few hours my mother is going to be off the deep end and I can't do anything about it. Sighing in surrender, I limp over and sit with him. He hands me a beef jerky stick and a protein bar and we share his canteen of water. By the time the sun goes down, the stars are out in droves like I've never seen before. For all that the temperature falls and my leg aches, there is a wild magic in the night.

July 3rd, 2017

NEW BUDS AND OLD MEMORIES

A text from Noah wakes me up.

Good morning, Gorgeous! I have to run to Portland but I will be back this afternoon. Let me know when you want to go out on the boat.

I groan, returning my phone to the nightstand. I can barely read the message, my eyes still puffy and swollen from the faceoff with Scott. *You were just a pillar of good decisions last night, weren't you, Elle*? Not only do I have second thoughts about following my ex, I have second thoughts about my Betty Boop moves on the patio. Now I need to avoid Noah until he forgets about the boat ride. *Get real, he's not going to forget. Not after the flirty stunts you pulled.* I consider rolling over and sleeping half the day away when my phone rings. "Hello?"

"Well, gee, don't you sound like a bucket of sunshine," Mom's lively voice chimes.

I grunt. It's too early for me to have a comeback.

"I hope you aren't drinking your entire vacation away,

Daughter. It'd be nice if you actually had some memories to come back and tell me about."

"I'm not drinking my vacation away—you woke me up," I grumble in defense. "You know I'm not a morning person. Jeez."

"Oh." Her tone lightens. "Well, good! So are you having a fun time?"

If being stuck in a house with my ex and getting an unwanted date by flashing my boobs around is fun, then yeah I'm having a great time. "It's good. I went to the beach yesterday and the girls and I went to a cool restaurant the night before."

"That's great news, honey! Okay, well, I wanted to let you know the dogs are fine and everybody just had breakfast and now they're out romping around the backyard. Oh—Piglet, don't eat that!"

"Thanks for taking care of them." I hear Piglet's high-pitch bark in the background and the desire to go home and cuddle up with my pups is strong. "Is Dobby doing okay? Has he eaten anything since I left?"

"Not much. He finally ate part of a hot dog last night but it's had some, uh, unpleasant repercussions this morning. We've had to make a lot of trips outside. I'm going to try his dog food again tonight."

"Do I need to come home?"

"Don't be silly, Elle, he's fine. He's playing happily with his golf ball and chasing the squirrels around the yard. I know they're your babies but chill out."

"Okay, okay. Mom?"

"Yes, honey?"

I almost tell her about Scott. She would know what to do, what to say… She would also throw a fit, leap into her car, and drive out here. "Never mind. I'm glad you called to check in."

"You're welcome. Now tell me what's wrong. What were you going to say?"

Even when she can't see me she sees right through me. "I just—I don't know. I've forgotten how to be normal with people my own age. I'm used to middle-aged women who talk about hot flashes and Nordstrom sales and how they want their ugly, penis pendants redesigned because they're too old to wear something so phallic around their necks."

"Oh, hon, it's hard when you feel different," Mom says between giggles, "but if we were all the same what a boring world it would be, right?"

"I guess. Yeah."

"These people invited you because they like you. They want to spend time with you. Go take this chance to know them again! The older you get, the more you will need your friendships. Trust me. I love you."

Mom's pep talk is enough to get me out of bed. I twist my hair into a bun, then find some jeans and a long-sleeve top. I don't even bother with makeup. Maybe Noah will rescind his boat offer if he sees how plain and homely I can look.

Kacey and Rena are sitting at the bar upstairs when I appear. They both stop talking. "What?" I say, scanning the perimeter for any sign of extra company, but it's just us.

"Her eyes are puffy," Rena reports to Kacey. "She's pale, too."

Kacey sighs, looking like she didn't sleep well, either. "I'm sorry, Elle." There is a deep sadness in her tone that shouldn't be there. "This trip was never supposed to be like this."

"Everything is fine, really. It's been great here." I smile, but the action hurts my face.

Kacey sets a cup of fresh coffee down in front of me. "Scott left this morning. He told me I'm supposed to tell you that."

The relief rolls through me like a shot of moonshine. At the same time, however, there's a dull ache between my ribs. An ache that feels a lot like longing.

"Listen, Ms. Centerfold, Noah was also looking for you this morning." Rena grins widely. "After the moves you pulled last night, I think you've hooked your fish. Scott will be a distant bad dream once Noah is back from his run to Portland."

I nearly tell her that while I really like Noah I don't know if I can deal with him while I'm sober. Dating still frightens Sober Elle and despite Scott's weirdly possessive behavior with me last night, he's never given an unnecessary warning. *Don't fall for Noah. He's a good guy and I like him, but he's not looking for the long term.* "Yeah. Maybe."

"What is there to *maybe* about?" Rena asks in disbelief. "He's gorgeous, he's wealthy, and you don't even have to steal him or be his mistress—he's single! Just think: if you guys get married, this could be your beach house someday, too."

"Hold your horses, Re, the gate hasn't even opened on the track yet," Kacey reminds with a laugh. My face must've given away my discomfort. "Just test him out, Elle. He's not a Scott, I promise."

I take a long drink of coffee. "You're right." And really, I have mixed feelings about that.

After coffee, the girls and I decide to head into Lincoln City. The hub of the Oregon Coast, Lincoln City is the most commercialized of all Oregon's beaches and draws a variety of interests and businesses. We decide to hit a couple of places we've always talked about going, starting with a national landmark: Build-A-Bud.

Wedged between a shell shop and a thrift store, Build-A-Bud is the Rated R knockoff of the popular children's workshop, only instead of bears they have people decorate and clothe plush beer cans, wine bottles, or marijuana leaves. The conservatives that fill Lincoln City all hoped the store would fail quickly, but apparently adults like building stuffed toys just as much as kids, especially when provocative themes are involved. The place grew even more popular after they bought the shop next door and turned it into a bar.

Kacey, Rena, and I luck out and get a parking spot near the beach. Kacey attempts to parallel-park three times before turning off her engine. We all get out and look at the Subaru's tires. "Close enough," she declares, ignoring the two-foot gap between the curb and her vehicle.

Neon lights blink against Build-A-Bud's sign, which is done in swirly font the color of freshly printed money. Their logo and mascot, a cartoon marijuana leaf, winks at us as we enter the building. "Hello, ladies!" The hostess grins. "Welcome to Build-A-Bud! Can I see everyone's IDs please?" Blondie slaps bracelets on our wrists that read, *Welcome to the Play Bar.*

"Okay, what do we want to make?" Kacey's hands go to her hips as we stare at the wall of stuffed addictions, each sporting a different style.

"Mine needs boobs." Rena eyes a wine bottle plush with a Jessica Rabbit style dress and red lips.

I snort. "Of course it does."

"I like the Beach Beer." Kacey tilts her head fondly at the beer can plush with board shorts and sunglasses.

I settle on a purple bottle of cabernet, which has a cuter face than the other bottles of wine. We all move to the stuffing station where a woman with a lot of smiles and very little English floods cotton into our picks from a machine that looks like it's tumbling cotton candy. She sews them up and motions us into the dressing room, where we face a thousand accessories based off adult media influences like KISS, The Beatles, The Big Lebowski, Playboy, and more.

“I think my Bud needs this.” Rena holds up a pointy, metal bra that would've made Madonna proud.

“Not as much as mine needs this,” I joke, holding up a pair of underwear with a padded crotch. “Who comes up with this stuff?”

"People with dirty senses-of-humor like us. You guys, I'm in love with these flipflops." She holds up a pair of stuffed feet sporting pink sandals, which she's about to glue onto her Wine Bud.

I'm picking through a rack of wraps when Kacey pulls her phone out. "Oh my gosh, look at my stepmom!" She grins, holding her phone up.

A petite woman with long, blonde hair smiles up at us. She's wearing a knee-length white dress with lacey accents and rhinestones. Her text to Kacey reads, **What do you think of this one?** I knew Kacey's dad had found a new partner nine months after his divorce from her mother, but I had never seen the woman until now.

"Isn't she cute? She's picking out her elopement dress." Kacey chuckles while texting her back. "She and my Dad are eloping at this little country estate in Molalla so I can watch them get married. No big wedding ceremony or anything. Just a little event between us important people."

It intrigues me how much Kacey likes her stepmom. She babbles on about how they're going to get pedicures and drinks next week before the event, how her dad bought them matching fishing poles at Christmas and they're all going camping at Timothy Lake next month. A flicker of jealousy runs through me because it sounds like her dad finally found someone that made him not just a happier person, but a better person.

I can't picture myself getting pedicures or drinks with Bertie. Behind her pearly white smile and warm eyes, I sense a sharp, possessive quality. Instead of getting to know us, I think she would rather erase us and the past we're connected to. Three months after she and Dad got together, she quit her job and moved into the farmhouse where she promptly tore down my mother's artwork and turned my old bedroom into a storage area for her things. My brother's elementary school painting of Cannon Beach, which had overlooked our breakfast nook for a decade, was replaced with a large, gaudy cross and a bible verse about love being patient. The worst stab to the heart was seeing a blank wall in the living room where our family photos once hung.

"Gosh, all this fun is making me tired! I need to grab some coffee," Rena declares as we leave the play bar.

"Ocean Side Coffee is around the corner. I think I'll get one, too." Kacey shifts her Bud bag on her shoulder.

"How about you grab coffee and I'll take the bags to the car," I offer, since we're not far from the Subaru and I'm at that point where I need a few minutes to breathe without anyone watching.

"Thanks! We'll meet you." Kacey pulls out her car keys.

I jog across the road and up the boardwalk, packing bags neatly beneath the front seats. After locking back up, I stop to admire the sun on the ocean. The water glitters in blinding motion like a floor of diamonds, the tide rolling like molten glass against the sand. How someone can live an entire life without ever going to the beach, I will never understand.

A little girl in a mermaid suit plays in the dunes with a little boy who looks a lot like her. They're building a castle for her Barbies. I smile, suddenly seeing my brother and me. We would drip and carve sand for hours, never bothered by the mess or the wind or the gritty taste of it in our mouths. The small girl takes off her Jelly shoes and throws them into the sand.

I had jelly shoes like that once. I was eight.

They had been gifted to me on a beach vacation. I loved their teal color and the way they glittered in the sun, but the hard plastic cut up my feet. Saltwater had filled and burned my cuts, making it impossible to play in the ocean which deeply upset me.

Dad, the only man on the beach wearing socks with his sandals because he didn't like the gritty feeling between his toes, had scooped me off the beach towel where I had been crying. "Alright, Little Girl, how about some ice cream? Ice cream solves everything."

He plunked me down on a street bench then ordered a large mint cone from a street vendor. Most parents would've ordered a small, given that they were buying for a young child, but my father was an overachiever even in that category. Several mothers passed him judging glances as he handed me a chocolate-laden monstrosity. "I think we need a bigger one," he announced sarcastically then became serious. "I guess we'll be sharing. Bring on the heartburn."

We sat there for a while, eating and people-watching. I was entranced by the giant butterfly kites some kids were flying on the boardwalk. Dad noticed. "You want a kite? We can go buy one from Bobby's shop down the road. He's got lots to pick from."

"No," I mumbled. "I want to play in the sea."

Dad's brows furrowed together as he looked at my feet, at the bloody lines the jellies had carved into them. "I'm not liking those shoes." His eyes started roaming the street vendors. They came to rest on a booth selling rubber boots. "Get up, kid, I've got an idea."

We tossed the remains of the monstrosity then walked over to the Oregon Rainboot tent set up for a street faire. "Pick a pair, any pair," Dad said in an auctioneer voice, motioning to the row of youth boots on the floor.

The boots ran big so we had to try a couple different sizes. There was no sitting stool so Dad braced me against his knees and held my hands as I tugged boots on and off. I settled on a pair of blue ones with starfish print.

We walked back down to where the sea met land. The tide washed up around my boots and even though it was a little harder to walk in them versus the jellies, my cuts were untouched. I let out a whoop of joy, my day no longer ruined, and went splashing through the waves. Dad hovered just outside the water's reach, not wanting to get his socks wet. I plowed saltwater all over his legs as I raced up to hug him. He expelled a cry of disappointment at his sopping socks, but I only squeezed him tighter.

What happened to you, Dad?

"Beautiful, isn't it?"

I'm yanked out of the memory by a familiar voice. I spin around and see Noah walking toward me with two coffees in his hands. OCEAN SIDE is written across the cups in capital, scrolly font. "What are you doing out here?" I don't hide my surprise.

"Just dropped my sister off in town. She's going shopping with some friends at the outlet stores." He extends one of the cups to me. "I was grabbing a coffee before heading back when I ran into Kacey and Rena. They told me you like lattes."

"Oh, thank you." I smile and hope it looks genuine.

Noah's eyes glitter like the water as he joins me in observing the view. His eyes fall on the kids I've been watching. "Cute, aren't they?"

"I guess."

He chuckles. "Not a kid person?"

I shake my head. "No. I wish I could be one again though, just for a day. Isn't that funny?"

"Why's that?"

"So that maybe I can remember how to have fun without overthinking it or letting someone else ruin it."

Noah lifts his dark eyebrows, intrigued. "I get that. Kids always seem to know exactly who they are and what they like and don't like. Why do you think we doubt ourselves so much as we get older?"

"Peer pressure? Society's ever-crushing standards of what you're supposed to become when you grow up?"

He chuckles. "Ah, yes. Well, you don't seem to be a conformist."

I can't decide if he thinks that's a likeable trait or not. "I don't know. I feel like I've conformed a lot more than I meant to. I had big plans for my life, you know."

"Oh? Do tell."

"I was going to be a writer. A famous one, with novels that get mentioned in classrooms and turned into Hollywood box office hits. I was going to marry somebody famous and have a house that was really three houses, so my mom and brother would both have a place to live that could never be taken away from them. My property was going to have a view of the mountains on one side and the beach on the other, with a heated barn full of dog runs so I could foster all the tiny dogs that come off the streets of Mexico and Texas and California. I was going to write and live and be happy."

A long moment passes before he says, "So what's stopping you?"

I snort. "Reality."

"Alas, the true dream-killer."

"Always."

"Well, look on the bright side: you have all the makings for that kind of greatness. You have the nonconformity factor, which you'll need to rise above the norm. You have the dream, which is everything, and you have a strong voice, which you'll need to speak up for what you want." He slowly sips his coffee. "Speaking of strong voices, I noticed Scott left bright and early this morning. You alright?"

I grit my teeth. "You heard our tiff."

"That was more than a tiff, darling—that was a full-blown cat fight."

"I'm sorry." I should probably just buy a shirt with those words printed in bold font at this point, I say it so much around him. "I'm usually not this big of a drama queen. He just brings out the beast in me."

"Don't be sorry." Noah's eyes darken. "Nothing is worse than being cheated on. Trust me, I know."

"Someone cheated on *you?*"

"It was a complicated situation." He lifts a shoulder. "I stole her from another guy. I should've known that if she could cheat on him with me, she would later cheat on me with someone else."

I remember walking into Scott's kitchen, the stomach-curdling moment that I saw her stick figure wrapped around him. It still makes me nauseous. I shake my head as if I can shake the images away, but they will live within me forever.

"You don't really want to go out on my boat, do you?" Noah asks.

I scrunch my nose. "I really don't."

"That's okay. Would you be up for something else?"

"Like what?"

"I know this really great club on the water. Nothing wild; just a good place to go dancing and get dinner. Might take your mind off things."

There is a genuine quality to Noah's expressions, his

words, that reminds me of Nana. Not many people acknowledge the depth of my pain, of not being enough for someone and how devastating it is. Maybe it's time to finally try someone new. Maybe two broken birds can teach the other how to fly again.

"Okay," I say.

Noah grins ear to ear. "Perfect. I'll pick you up at seven."

July 3rd 2017

FOX AND THE OTHER FOX

The Elanza used to be a well-known art gallery that sat near the hub of Yaquina Bay. After the economic crisis of 2008, however, it went bankrupt and sold to an investor friend of Noah's who saw the hole in Newport's tourism for posher clients and wanted to give them an upper-scale dining experience by the water.

Noah parks his Audi in a narrow lot behind the club. "You must be very special, or a frequent flyer," I say, noticing the RESERVED sign posted in front of our spot.

Noah grins. "I helped him pay the contractor when he found out he had to rewire the entire building. In return, I told him I wanted all my money back plus a permanent parking spot up front." He offers me his arm as I step out of the car. He's wearing a cream button-down with designer jeans and I hope my hibiscus shampoo smells as good to him as his Armani cologne smells to me.

My heels click-clack across the pavement as he escorts me to the front of the building. I run a hand down the front of my dress, a salmon-colored bodycon with swirls of sequins—one of those pretty numbers you hoard for years in the hopes that one day you'll get the chance to wear it. There is a line waiting to get into The Elanza but Noah passes it. He knocks knuckles with the bouncer, who lets us in without asking for our IDs or passes. The smell of steak and hops fills my nose. The inside of the club is all Koa wood tables and white marble tile with panels of living plants growing across the ceiling. A drummer and two guitarists are playing on a platform by the tiki bar outside, where dancers and happy drunks cheer on the band. Noah steers us toward the stairs that lead up to a private bar in the loft.

"Noah, my man!" A bartender with a perfectly curled mustache and a fohawk points both hands. "I wondered where you've been hiding!"

"Hey, Nick. One scotch on the rocks, and whatever this lovely lady wants." Noah pulls out a chair for me.

Nick winks and pulls down a bottle of scotch with some unpronounceable name. "What do you drink, sweetheart?"

"Um, wine?" I glance at the drink list below my elbow but see only mixed drinks.

"You deserve better than wine." Noah nods at a cabinet below the counter. "Pour her a glass of Pour L'amour Du Vin, would you, Nick? The reserve bottle."

Nick slides a glass of golden liquid down the bar then opens the cabinet. "Only for you, Mr. Gonzales." He lifts out a faceted bottle with a French-looking title. The label features a Victorian era woman draped in gems and finery, a glass full of bubbles hanging between her fingers. Popping the cork, Nick pours a generous serving into a crystal glass. "For you, my lady."

The bubbly has a pink hue that almost matches my dress, an aroma like fresh peaches wafting out of the glass. I take a sip, it's flavor not dry or sweet but somewhere in the middle. It might just be the best glass of champagne I've ever had.

"Amazing, isn't it?" Noah's tone suggests he already knows my answer. "The owner's sister is married to a very prestigious Frenchman whose family has been producing wine for over a hundred years. When he opened The Elanza, he contracted out a select series of wines to be made specifically for this bar and this bar alone. You can't get Pour L'amour from anywhere else except the vineyard itself."

"That's amazing." I drink the whole glass before we've even ordered food. Not wanting to be the drunk date, I push aside my refill and read over the menu in search of non-alcoholic drinks. An iced tea sounds like a good idea. As I'm reading, my eyes land on the Reserved Wine list.

Every bottle of champagne is over a hundred dollars.

Oh my God. I look at my crystal glass. "Noah?"

"Yeah?"

"How much does a glass of Pour L'amour Du Vin cost?"

"Doesn't matter. You're not paying for it."

I try not to grit my teeth. "Come on, what do they typically charge for a champagne this fabulous?"

"Well, reserve imports can get kind of spendy so they only keep a few on hand."

I point at the most expensive champagne on the menu, which is priced at two-hundred and fifteen dollars. "Like this spendy?"

He mumbles under his breath, "More than that."

"Noah!"

"What? We're on a date!" He laughs it off like it's no big deal, like consuming a bubbly with that kind of price tag is normal. The most expensive wine I've ever tasted was from Mom's fiftieth birthday party, and the bottle cost a whopping forty dollars and ninety cents. "This is nothing!" He pushes the food menu in front of me. "Now, do you prefer halibut or razor clams?"

By the time we've ordered appetizers and dinner, I've guessed our bill at somewhere around three-hundred and fifty dollars. Noah talks to me about his Audi and how he's thinking about replacing it with a Tesla. I talk about my Suzuki and how it's gas efficient. We discuss his upcoming trip to London, Paris, and Ireland next year and my dream of seeing Antelope Canyon in Arizona someday. His furrowed brows tell me he doesn't understand my draw to a park in the desert when there are bigger, better destinations out there. He takes genuine interest in my job in diamonds but we still talk more about the cost of diamonds versus their unique gemology. Talk of money leads to talk of his job. His company in Portland helps new companies take off and his pay depends a lot on whether these new companies are successful. Several have been.

"Like a-million-dollars-a-year successful," he elaborates. Twice.

I'm handling things okay until the bartender tells us a joke and Noah laughs and puts his hand on my back. I pass it off as a friendly gesture but then there are several other attempts at physical contact. I thought I would be prepared for it—welcome it, even—but to my surprise I recoil. *It's just nerves. It'll pass.* Except, it doesn't. He holds my hand to admire my nails and my fingers twitch. He brushes my hair off my shoulder and a shiver runs down my spine.

At one point, I look down to fix my necklace and realize my chest is pasta-sauce red. My skin is blotching out. *Oh no.* I'm not good at letting people into my physical space. I'm not good at holding these kinds of conversations where I pretend to know what it's like to have money and want what people with money want. This is one of those rare moments where I wish I were more like my father, just so I knew the right things to say. Dad could make interesting conversation out of thin air. When he couldn't, he would just laugh and it was one of those contagious laughs that covered up any embarrassment. I've heard it so many times it echoes in my head now, mocking me, so real I start to sweat.

It's not until I see Noah's eyes light up at a familiar face across the room, rise from his seat to shake the hand of an older man who should've been dozens of miles away preparing for his own Fourth of July weekend, I realize the sound is not in my head.

I spit Pour L'amour Du Vin all over the floor.

"Jim, my friend! Fancy seeing you here," Noah chimes, delighted. "It's been too long!"

"It has, it has!" Dad's charismatic voice rings across the bar. "Business is good, I presume? The shop's website has taken off since you implemented that new car browsing option for us! We're selling three times as many cars now."

Oh my God. What is he doing here? What is happening right now? My stomach folds and I throw a hand over my mouth to prevent anything else from coming out. I had turned my head to the side before Dad could see me and am now hiding behind my free hand and curtain of hair. *What do I do now*? I would bolt but they're both blocking the stairs.

"Oh, we're being rude to your lovely lady here." There's that damned laugh again.

"Oh, of course!" Noah takes my hand and gently tugs it, encouraging me to get up and face our guest.

This trip is officially jinxed.

My legs shiver as I slowly rise. I haven't faced him since the Fox family Christmas party, and even then I barely said ten words to him. *God help me.* Taking a deep breath, I throw my hair over my shoulder and swivel to face him.

Dad chokes on his drink. My father has grayed a bit since Christmas, the color tainting his brown hair. He's wearing a cream button-down only a couple shades lighter than his skin and his Bluetooth is miraculously detached from his ear.

"Jim Fox, please meet—well, isn't this ironic?—*Elle Fox*, my lovely date this evening." Noah is gleaming, completely oblivious to our exchange. "She's a diamond specialist who designs wedding rings in Portland."

Dad stares. In his eyes I see the same I've-fallen-down-a-rabbit-hole into-another-dimension look that I've seen in my mother's time and time again. I glare—I can't help it— while inside my organs feel like they're being torn up by a raging storm. "Yes," he says, his tone less jolly than it had been a moment ago. "I know."

"Do you now?" Confusion passes over Noah's face, then his brows start to rise with understanding as he looks at me. It shouldn't be hard to figure out. I have Jim's nose, his dark hair, the same rosy cheeks, and green eyes. "Oh! Oh, wow, what a small world it is! So you must be Elle's, uh—"

"Her father," Dad declares.

Sperm donor, I nearly correct.

"Father." The word rolls around on Noah's tongue. He passes me this questioning glance that asks, *as in the father you don't get along with*? I give the slightest nod. After a moment of awkward silence, he says, "You know what how about a drink on me? What's in your glass, Jim? Let me get you another." He disappears downstairs to find our bartender before I can offer to do it, leaving Dad and I alone.

My heart is beating in my ears. I turn back to my chair and hastily dig out my wallet. I throw some cash on the bar —not even enough to cover one drink but oh well—then zip up my bag, throwing my shawl over my shoulders at the same time.

Dad launches forward. “Hey now, wait!” He reaches out to stop me from packing up.

I jump away, half tripping over a barstool. “Don’t you fucking touch me!”

“Why do you have to talk to me like that?” Dad hisses, peering around to make sure we haven’t gained unwanted attention. Luckily, only a handful of people are in the loft and most of them are on the opposite side of us. “I haven’t seen you in months, Little Girl. Can’t you sit down for five minutes and talk to me like I’m a human and not some beast out to get you?”

“I’m not little anymore and I have nothing to say to you.” Really I have too many things to say to him. So many that they’re jumbled up in my throat and I’m almost choking on them.

“Yeah, you do. You’re Jim Fox’s daughter—you have something to say about everything.” He pulls out a bar stool next to mine and sits down. “Five minutes.”

Once upon a time, I would’ve killed for five minutes of my father’s precious and rarely available time. Now the idea sounds like a cage... or perhaps an arena where the warrior has come to meet the lion.

“So where and how did you meet Noah Gonzales?” Dad lifts his brandy glass to his mouth and the lights flash off the face of his Rolex watch. The gold is shiny and unscratched, sure signs that it’s new. “He’s a smart young man. Got his own company and a good life going. A much better match for you then—what was that little hoodlum’s name that used to follow you around?—*Scott Darcy*.”

A sharp pain dashes through my chest. "Don't get attached—this is just a date." The last, as a matter of fact, because now that I've watched Noah and Dad's exchange all I can see is another Jim Fox in the making.

Dad's eyes wander over to my crystal glass of Pour L'amour. He lifts one furry eyebrow.

I change the subject. "Why are you here? Aren't you supposed to be home planning for some grand Fourth of July party?" I try to sound neutral but fail. My tone reeks of disgust.

"It's already planned, and we're heading home after this. We were only here for the day, picking up Bertie's daughter and son-in-law. Bertie wanted to see their new beach house. It's nice, about the size of Noah's over there on the water." Dad nods his chin in the direction of the bay. In a less enthusiastic tone, he says, "Matt says you don't want to come to the party."

"I don't celebrate the Fourth of July anymore."

"And why is that?"

He earns my sharp look. "Are you seriously asking?"

Dad starts to roll his eyes than catches himself. He becomes preoccupied with picking at the edge of the Koa wood bar, muttering something about precision and how the cut is off. "We can't move forward if you don't let go of the past, Elle."

A ripping sensation seems to go down the center of my body. "Wow. Is that how you say you're sorry?"

"You really want to get into this now? Right here?" He gestures to the bar, to the people surrounding us who might actually be enjoying their evening. "Why do you have to be like this? I'm trying, Elle! No father wants to feel this hated by his own daughter!"

It comes out of my mouth before I can stop it: "Most fathers don't shove their daughters down the stairs."

Dad sits back on his stool. Something shifts in his gaze and becomes dark and clouded, like an invisible tie has snapped between us and left in its wake a void a hundred feet wide. "You know that was an accident."

Angry tears burn behind my eyes. *So was it an accident that you threw Mom on the floor after she told you she wanted to move out for a while? Did your arm just swing out on its own accord when I tried to pull you away from her*? "Like hell it was."

"Oh, Jim, there you are!"

Bertie's voice interrupts us. My father's girlfriend appears at the end of the bar, wearing a black Audrey Hepburn type dress and a string of Tahitian pearls. A gold cross hangs below them, gleaming in the bar lights. She sees me and stops like she's run smack-dab into an invisible wall. "Oh, Elle." Faked enthusiasm. She passes Dad a skeptical glance. "I didn't know your daughter hung out here. What a small world!"

Dad is still gathering his composure, gaze focused on the floor. "Getting smaller by the minute."

I plaster on a smile, though it's tight and forced and probably makes me look like a mad woman. "He's all yours. I was just leaving."

"Noah's going to be back any minute, you know," Dad mumbles.

"Good. Tell him bye for me." I hoist my purse onto my shoulder and brush past Bertie. Dad doesn't stop me. He doesn't say another word. My heels click-clack across the floor, all the way down the stairs.

Noah is yakking with somebody else he must know at the first-floor bar, a tray of drinks in his hand. The main entrance is several feet behind him. A better person would've gathered her emotions and said goodbye, thanks, and could she pay for half the check, but I am not that person. Not right now. Veering out a side door to the patio, I weave through a crowd of dancers who are swaying drunkenly below the stage of a jazz band. I knock over two tiki torches while rounding the corner of the building and finally find a quiet spot in the alley near the outdoor smoking box.

I lean against the outside wall of the smoking box and pant. My stomach, throat, guts—they're all in knots and I can't seem to get enough air. My knees quiver, suddenly weak, and I have the urge to sit down. *Gross, not here*. I kick a few cigarette butts lining the edge of the pavement, which is stained with ash and scorch marks. For being a high-end club, I'm shocked they let this kind of filth slide. Up on the street I spot a bench that looks significantly cleaner.

You shouldn't have said it, Elle. My eyes water as I dig my nails into the backs of my arms and the scars there. I made myself look like a fool—an angry, rotten fool. Dad's probably telling Bertie how hurtful I had been. She's probably patting his head and handing him a drink from Noah's tray and they're all talking about how cruel and strange and terrible Jim Fox's offspring is. *Screw them all*. He had no right to corner me, to force me to talk to him, but can you tell the kid who stuck his hand in a beehive that it's his own damn fault he got stung? No. He's going to insist he had a right to the hive and the bee who stung him deserved its fate. There was never a thought for the harm or suffering he caused.

I've just emerged on the sidewalk of the main road and have stopped to look at the stars when I hear someone shout, "Hey! HEY! YOU in the pink dress!"

I turn around. A short, dark-haired guy with flash tattoos on his arms leaves a bar across the street. He's speed-walking across the asphalt, coming right for me, eyes ablaze. My already sick stomach drops. *Great, a hostile, crazy person.* Just what I need right now.

"*You*!" He stabs his finger through the air at me, voice a snarl. "You owe me a new paint job!"

Every inch of me freezes, except my heart which is racing a mile a minute. "I'm sorry," my wavering voice musters. "You must have the wrong person."

"Oh, no, I've been watchin' all over town for you, you crazy bitch!" He comes to a halt just feet away. I step back, my fist balling up at my side. "You're the drunk at Mother Shuckers who broke my antenna off and then scraped it across my truck's door panel two nights ago!"

This guy is either delusional or drunk—or both—although I *was* at Mother Shuckers two nights ago and pretty toasted myself. Could he really be telling… No, it can't be true. I've never damaged anyone's personal property, sober or not, and Kacey and Rena would've told me if I'd lost it, right? *Maybe they didn't see it happen*. I am known for skipping off on my own after too many drinks.

The guy is shouting insults, one slew of cuss words after the next. My body flinches, trying to decide whether it's going to remain a frozen lizard on the pavement or bloom into a dragon and summon my inner flame to defend myself. When I don't respond, he steps forward like he's going to grab me and I raise my fists. "You *back up*," I order.

"Oh, what are you going to do?" He spits. "You going to hit me? Really?"

I open my mouth but someone else speaks. "She probably won't."

I spin around.

Scott saunters up out of the smoking box beside the club, one hand in his pocket while the other taps ash off his cigarette. His stance is as calm and casual as someone going for an evening stroll, but his eyes spark like livewires under the lamplights. "I might though," he warns.

"This nutjob your girl?" The guy is back to stabbing fingers at me.

Of all the people to be witnessing this right now. Scott comes to a halt at my side. He has a full foot and a half over my attacker and at least thirty pounds. "What's it to you?" His voice is low, dangerous.

The guy puffs up like a blowfish but shifts back. "She scraped my Tacoma with my own antenna! She owes me a new paint job!" He goes off on another rant, calling me awful names and insisting that I am some breed of demon spawn whose insurance will pay out the butt for what I've done.

Scott calmly takes a drag off his cigarette, letting him rant. The guy seems to have a never-ending air supply. I peer sideways at Scott, trying to guess his next move. He's wearing a black plaid button-up with the sleeves rolled to his elbows. His forearms are wound so tight a few of his veins form raised lines beneath his tattoos. He steps forward, breathing smoke out of his nose. My hands clasp over my mouth as he drives the cigarette's burning butt into the guy's forehead, which stuns the jerk into silence.

All hell breaks loose.

The guy makes a swipe for Scott's face and I scream at the sound of clashing bones. For taking such a hard hit, Scott's fast to react. His own fist swings up and reams the guy in the gut, knocking the air out of him. He shoves him into the hood of someone's Honda Civic and twists his arm behind his back, the other pinned beneath him. "You need to learn some manners, Short Stack," Scott growls, smacking his face into the windshield for good measure. "Didn't your mother teach you how to act in public?"

"Hands off," Short Stack huffs, steaming up the glass. "Make you—pay for this!"

"No, dude, you're not making anyone pay for anything." Grabbing the back of the guy's jacket, Scott throws him to the ground. "Now get going before that broken antenna ends up in your ass."

Short Stack half stumbles, half runs away, choking and

wheezing.

I pace the sidewalk for a minute, lungs heaving. "*Holy crap*, did that really just happen?"

"What the hell are you doing out here?" He goes to rub his cheek and winces. "I'm starting to think you're my own personal demon sent to punish me for some terrible sin I've—"

"Just stop talking!" Black spots swim in my vision. I press a hand to my head, hoping this will steady me but it only makes things worse. "I think—I think I'm going to pass out." I reach out to hold the light pole and miss.

Scott grabs my arm, yanking me to him before I fall into the street. His hands are hot against the fabric of my dress as he steers me to a nearby bench. The smell of tobacco and sage drifts off him and makes me want to shove him away, but I'm seated before I get the chance. "If the seams on that dress aren't too tight you should put your head between your knees."

"Yeah, right." I'd probably smother myself with these thighs. I lean my head back, breathing in the sky. I focus on the smooth, well-worn lines in the driftwood bench, the wind as it passes through my sweaty hair. Scott lights up another cigarette. "Take your cancer stick over there if you're going to do that." I point at the smoking box. "Unless you want me to throw up on your shoes."

"Wouldn't be the worst thing you've done to me. You're here with Noah, aren't you?"

As if to answer his question, the front doors of The Elanza suddenly open and Noah comes racing over. "Elle! What happened? One second you're in the loft with your dad and the next—" He stops short when he sees Scott standing in the shadows nearby. "What are you doing here?"

Scott huffs at him. "Like you don't know." He nods to the alleyway, to an elegant bean pole of a woman in a fitted pencil skirt with a matching bandeau top who has just left The Elanza's patio. Her dark curls wave around her shoulders like something out of a Cover Girl commercial as she strides towards us.

"Scott, is everything okay?"

"Fine," Scott grumbles, looking at his reflection in somebody's car door mirror.

My heart slumps down to my feet as she grabs his arms. He straightens up to look at her and a gasp escapes her plump, glossy lips. "Who did this to you?" She shoots an accusatory glance my way then sees Noah. "Oh, Noah! I didn't know you would be here tonight."

"Didn't know you would either, Aliana." Noah's reply is rigid.

Aliana. Ah, so this is Noah's supermodel sister.

"Some freak was threatening Elle because she broke the antenna off his truck," Scott explains. "I stepped in and he didn't like that very much."

Noah cocks a brow at me. "You broke someone's antenna?"

I shrink down on the bench. "He had the wrong person." Drunk Elle is not in the building and thus cannot be held accountable for her actions. At least, not in front of these people.

"Didn't like it very much? Understatement of the century." Aliana tilts Scott's chin in her hand. His cheek is swelling fast, making his left eye want to close. "Count on you to try and be the hero. I'm taking you to urgent care. Where are the keys to your truck?"

Scott hesitates. "Inside, in your purse."

She rolls her eyes. "I'll go get it then."

I frown as Noah's sister disappears into the club, hair rippling down her spine in perfect, shiny waves, not an ounce of fat to jiggle as she walks. *More curves than a coke bottle my ass.* I stand up, the lightheadedness waning. Noah has just offered me his hands when I hear a clattering sound at my feet. A set of keys lays on the pavement like a dividing line between us.

They're the keys to Scott's Tacoma.

I look over at him, stumped. Didn't he just send Aliana into the club for these?

"I'm in this mess because of you," he reminds me. "*You* can drive me to urgent care, then you can come back and finish your ill-advised date."

"Are you serious?" Noah's nostrils are flaring, he's so mad. "Do you want me to hit you in the other eye?"

"Go ahead," Scott dares through gritted teeth.

Noah starts an aggressive stride toward him. I jump between them and put my hands up just in time. Noah's chest bumps against my left palm while Scott's presses into my other. “Alright, stop it, both of you! There’s been enough violence tonight! Noah, step back. Scott, have Aliana take you. Go make use of her like you say you always do.”

“Yeah, Scott, go take up my sister’s time instead of my date’s.” Noah leers over my head.

Scott presses harder into my hand, making it tougher to keep them apart. “I told you not her, damn it,” he spits as if I’m not standing here listening. “Besides, we both know Aliana can’t drive thanks to her D.U.I. She’s not touching my truck.”

“Everybody stop!” I’m getting squished between them.

Noah steps away first. He paces a moment, rubbing his hands over his forehead before facing us. A strange exchange of silent words passes between both men. Finally, he sighs at the ground. “Scott’s right. Aliana shouldn’t be driving. Someone else should go with him to the hospital.”

“You’re not seriously suggesting that I go.” What’s worse: going back inside The Elanza with Noah and my father, or getting struck in the same vehicle with my ex? I finally understand the term, ‘a rock and a hard place’.

Noah nods. “I am. It was you he was defending, after all. I’m sorry.” His apology isn’t aimed at me, but at Scott. “I’ll tell your father you had to leave and Aliana that her date found another ride.” His hand brushes across my lower back one last time as he walks away, following Aliana’s trail.

Scott picks his keys off the ground and dangles them in front of my face. “Did he just say your father?”

I rip them out of his hand. “Yeah, you want to go say hi?

I'm sure he'd love to see you," I drawl, being extra sarcastic. *What was that little hoodlum's name*?

Scott expels a disconcerting noise, spinning on his heel for the parking lot. "I'd nail my tongue to the alleyway before facing your father again."

***

The Tacoma smells like old leather and Lysol just as I remember it, though the dash has a fine film of dust that Glen would've never tolerated. The back ceiling still has a stain from where my Pepsi exploded half a decade ago, and the Ed Hardy steering wheel cover has been removed.

Scott is in the passenger seat, one arm draped over his eyes as I drive. I've heard horror stories about people who have fallen into a coma after a head trauma, and several minutes pass of him being utterly still. We're sitting at a stoplight when I finally reach over and jab his leg. He jumps. "Ouch! What was that for?"

"Making sure you're alive."

He exhales, pushing some hair out of his face. "Nice to know you care all of a sudden."

"Don't be a jerk. You're lucky Noah insisted or I wouldn't be here."

"I'm lucky, she says. I get hit in the face by an angry midget for her and she tells me I'm the lucky one. You think Noah would've put his fists up for you? He's never hit anybody in his life! What would you have done if I hadn't shown up?"

Honestly, I have no idea what would've happened if he hadn't been there. I still can't process the attack much less that it was Scott, of all people, who appeared to defend me… I also can't process the fact that I got so drunk at Mother Shucker's I tore off some guy's antenna and scraped his truck with it.

"I saved you from an evening of arrogant, boring conversations anyway," Scott continues. "The Elanza is filled with Noah's trust fund buddies who grew up with silver spoons in their mouths and big houses in Portland. All they know how to talk about is money. Your taste has sure changed a lot."

"Stop saying that," I snap back. "I don't have a *taste* anymore, thank you very much! And what about your taste? It's not like I was the only one of us there with the silver spooners. Since when did you go from curvy and pale to bony and rich? What does she weigh, a hundred pounds? Is there even anything to hang onto when you're screwing Noah's sister or is it like boinking a bag of bones?"

Scott laughs but it lacks humor. "I see five years hasn't made you any less blunt."

"Hasn't made you any less of a womanizer." My grip on the steering wheel is so tight I'm cutting off the circulation to my fingers.

He huffs under his breath, like he can't believe I'd call him such a thing. "Not that it's your business, but the only reason I got saddled with Aliana is because of Noah. He said he had important, prior engagements—I thought he meant work—and asked if I could drop her at the house because I'm his friend and everybody else was busy. Of course, by dropping her off he really meant taking the California princess who can't drive because she lost her license shopping and endure her numerous selfies and watch her spend ridiculous amounts of money on useless shit. You know how much I love that."

He's referring to the one time I took him Christmas shopping and it pretty much burned him out on shopping for the rest of our relationship. He was quick to sign me up for Amazon Prime after that and insisted I never needed to go near a mall again. "That sounds like a load of crap compared to the overt praise you were singing last night."

"No, the overt praise was a load of crap. I've never slept with Aliana in my life." He admits it without a shred of guilt or sheepishness. "You want to know what else I discovered was a load of crap?"

"Oh, please do tell I'm dying to hear."

He pins me with a serious look. "You're not that into Noah. In fact, you're about as into Noah as I am into his sister, and while we're being honest? The bathing suit move you pulled on the patio was slutty as hell."

I park in the emergency lot behind a well-lit white building that has SAMARITAN HOSPITAL displayed in red, glowing letters. I kill the engine and cold air instantly filters into the truck. Summers on the Oregon coast are generally mild and the evenings range from the mid to low fifties. I've been shaking since we left The Elanza but only now is it because I'm chilly. In the aftermath of my panic, I left my shawl on the bench.

"Are you cold?" Scott notices my trembling. Light shines

into the truck from the hospital and I see that his left eye has finally swollen shut on the ride over.

"I'm fine," I insist, not looking at him as I open the door. I'm still mad that he called me out on the bathing suit scheme. As I come around the truck bed, he's rummaging in the back seat. I tap my foot impatiently because the sooner I can get out of here and back to Rena and Kacey, the better. He stands up and holds out a Volcom hoodie.

My heart stutters. It's the same hoodie he handed me on Thunder Island in Cascade Locks so many years ago. "No, thanks."

"Why not?"

"Because I'm fine."

He sets his jaw then chucks it at me anyways. On reflex, I catch it. "Put it on before you freeze." He walks away before I can throw it back.

The hospital is busy, probably because it is the only twenty-four-hour emergency center between here and Lincoln City. I walk Scott up to the front counter, not sure if he needs help filling out paperwork. He can still see out of his right eye but the hand he punched my attacker with hasn't unfisted since the incident. A young receptionist whose nametag ironically reads PATIENCE sits up as we approach. "Good evening. What are we in for tonight?"

"Potentially broken eye socket," Scott mumbles.

"Ouch." She peers over the rims of her glasses, then starts typing on her computer. "That must've been painful. ID please."

"Meh." Scott pulls out his driver's license while nudging my arm. "She's hit me harder before."

Patience throws us a funny look.

"He—he's just kidding," I stutter.

She offers a strained smile then hands him a clipboard full of forms. "Fill these out for me, please. And I need a copy of your insurance card if you have one."

I follow Scott over to a pair of chairs between a guy with a bloody rag over his knee and a teary-eyed woman who is fidgeting with the keychain on her purse. "I can't believe you said that," I whisper. "What if she reports us as an abusive couple now? What is wrong with you?"

"We're a couple again, are we?"

"Shut up! You know what I mean!"

"She knew I was joking." He tries to write with his left hand and fails miserably. "Damn it."

I sigh. "Don't tell me I have to do that for you."

"No." He keeps going and makes a mess of the first page.

I reach over and snatch the pen from his hand. "They need to actually be able to *read* your paperwork."

He reluctantly surrenders the clipboard. "Fine."

I'm surprised at how much information I remember without having to ask, like his full name, Scott Alexander Darcy (named Scott after his mom's deceased brother and

Alexander after his grandfather), and his birthday—March first. He has the same phone number but his address is based up in Ridgefield, Washington, a farming town that is much like Oregon City in its quickly expanding population.

"So do you have a house up there in Ridgefield?" I make a mental note to Google it later and see how nice it is.

"I did. My lease is up in a couple of weeks so I'm at my mom's right now."

Please don't say you're moving back to Oregon City. We finish up the rest of the forms and I return the clipboard to the counter. Patience won't meet my gaze as she pulls it from my hands and lays it on her desk to process. Even if we aren't the abusive couple, I sense that we've been labeled as the annoying pair in the room. Scott smirks as he witnesses our awkward exchange. "You're an embarrassment."

"I'm not the one who ripped off someone's antenna," he retorts, stretching over the back of his chair. His tattooed arms flex and I see it's not an illusion like I thought it was in the kitchen: his arms really do have thicker, hillier muscles than before. "What prompted you to do it, anyways? You've always had a short fuse but you're not violent, at least not when I knew you."

"Stop talking." I don't want to think about the past—or his muscles—anymore, and I am most definitely not going to tell him alcohol and a broken heart were involved. I pull my phone out to signal the end of our conversation and start scrolling through Instagram.

An hour passes and we're still stuck in the waiting room.

The guy with the bloody hand and the teary-eyed lady were both called into the ER, leaving Scott and me alone near the back wall. "Do you think I can just ask for a bag of peas and go home now?" He asks, bored.

"A bag of peas isn't going to fix a broken eye socket." I pull Kacey's phone number up in a text message and begin to type.

Hey, any chance you or Re can come pick me up? I am at —

"Hey!" I squeak. Scott has swiftly plucked the phone out of my hands. "Seriously, what is wrong with you? You can't just take my stuff!"

"Watch me." He jams it deep into his jeans pocket. "Like I said, I'm in this mess because of you. You don't get to bail out yet. If they drug me up you might have to drive me back to my buddy's house near The Elanza."

I stare at his pocket. We've been in this situation before. Last time I was too shy to steal it back. These days, I'm not so shy. "You've got five seconds to return that."

"Or you'll do what?" He says, daring me to retrieve it. He lifts his brows, waiting.

I make a grab for the phone. He traps my hand inside his pocket. "And she's too slow," he declares in a mock sports announcer tone. "Zero points."

"Let go!" I yank my arm but he's stronger than me.

"Jeez, Scott, release! *Release*! Somebody's walking this way!" A woman at the end of our row has been called up to the counter and is walking down our aisle. As she passes by, she wrinkles her nose, disgusted by the girl whose hand is down her ex-boyfriend's pants.

"Not what it looks like," I say, but she ignores us.

Scott chuckles. "Not yet, at least."

"Ugh! You're horrible!" I pull back as hard as I can and he lets go. My knuckles smack into the wooden chair arm and instantly start throbbing. I get up and move three chairs over, praying they call us before I summon the audacity to walk back to Noah's house in stilettos.

They finally bring Scott in for diagnostics. A short nurse with beady eyes and a big nose leads us through a maze of lettered hallways and into a small, sterile room that smells like hand sanitizer. He takes Scott's blood pressure and examines his face. "My, my. That's a good bruise you got there." He chuckles. "Someone try and take this pretty lady from you?"

"He keeps trying but he's not the one who hit me," Scott answers, flinching as he shines a light into his only open eye.

"I'm not his girl," I make clear.

"Well, the doctor will be in shortly. It's been a busy night so I'll get him in here as soon as I can. Bear with us. I'll have Beatrice bring you in a cold pack and some painkillers while you wait." With that, the nurse scampers out of the room.

The ceiling light buzzes. I tap my feet, trying to ignore the radio as Chris Stapleton's *Tennessee Whiskey* starts to play.

I keep looking at the rectangular bulge in Scott's jean pocket where my phone is captured. "You really need to give that back."

"You really don't need it."

"Whether I need it or not is irrelevant—it's mine, you thief."

Scott rolls his eyes as he digs it out of his pocket. He launches it into my lap where it splats loudly against my bare thighs. "Fine, run off with Rena and Kacey and make the cyclops drive home by himself."

"I think I will." But I don't. I'm not sure if it's guilt that he got hit or something else that is stopping me from exiting this scene.

Ten minutes later, there's a knock on the door and a Nordic-looking woman with eyes as chilly blue as a White Walker's enters the room. "Hello, there," she greets warmly. "I heard somebody needed a cold pack."

"Can I get a beer, too, please?" Scott takes the pack from her along with a tiny cup cradling two pink pills.

The nurse chuckles, tugging free a paper cup from the dispenser on the wall. "Unfortunately, you cannot." She fills it in the sink. As she passes it to him, she notices me in the corner, slouching in my chair. Her pale gaze sweeps over my outfit. "Gorgeous dress."

"Thank you."

Her smile widens as she says to Scott, "I'm betting she's the girlfriend?"

I open my mouth to say absolutely not when he replies, "If circumstances hadn't turned on me, she would've been the wife."

My words jumble to a halt at the tip of my tongue. The nurse must notice my shock because her smile starts to show every sign of awkward discomfort, much like Patience's had at the front counter. She floats to the door while replying, "Okay, then. I'll check back with you guys soon. Take both those pills."

The second she's gone I shoot up out of my slouch. "Seriously?"

"What?" Scott dumps the painkillers into his water and throws it all back like a shot.

"You're just testing every boundary with me tonight, aren't you? *Wife*? What the hell, Scott, quit messing with the staff. And more importantly, quit messing with me! I am not yours! How can you joke about that after giving up on us?"

Scott scoffs, flopping the cold pack over his face. "You gave up on *me*. If you would've just listened and given me some time…" He doesn't finish.

He doesn't have to. I stand up, throwing my purse over my shoulder. "I'll see you in the truck." The door slams behind me and its sound ricochets throughout the entire first floor of the hospital.

March 10th, 2013

NOT ENOUGH WORDS

We stayed up most of the night talking while we were trapped in the Columbia River Gorge.

We talked about stars and forests and places we wanted to travel. We discussed family and parents, the pressures of society, and the all-consuming standard for what people are supposed to do when they grow up. Scott asked me about my hobbies, my interests, what kinds of books did I want to write and why did I want to write those books. I got him to talk about his fondness of street art, his dream of hiking Machu Picchu, and his strong objection to single-use plastics. When the first light of dawn brightened the horizon, I could no longer keep my eyes open and crawled into the tent for a nap. I woke some hours later to the buzzing sound of radios and muffled voices. When I opened the tent flap, he was coming out of the trees with two forest rangers and a pair of EMTs.

It took a long time for my family to warm up to Scott. My mother was a mess when we arrived at the hospital, sure someone had taken me from my house while she and Dad were gone. Watching me get carried in on a stretcher, leg covered in bloody gauze, with a boy she'd never met before earned me an immediate two-week grounding and Scott a detailed—and embarrassing—series of questions.

Dad was strangely cool about the accident, but I wonder if he felt as cool about it inside because he spent the next two months pretending Scott didn't exist, both at the shop and at Friday night dinners—which my mother insisted on hosting when she realized the tall, tattooed shadow I'd acquired wasn't going away. The first few Fridays were particularly brutal as she grilled him about his life goals and plans. Every Saturday, I expected to get a text or call saying sorry he couldn't keep doing this.

Every Saturday, he still showed up on my doorstep.

Fear of the Gorge trails still fresh in mind, we sought out a lot of state parks. We'd pick a new one every weekend, sometimes two, and spend the day exploring. He took me back to North Fork Reservoir, where our first uncomfortable meeting took place, and showed me how to string a fishing pole. We followed Jordan to the drag races outside the country flatlands of Woodburn and slow danced at the Blitz club in downtown Portland. We did return to the Gorge eventually—the safer, well-walked parts. I witnessed the cascading water of its signature landmark, Multnomah Falls, and the giant sturgeon who occupied the ponds of the local fish hatchery. We walked the windy, flower-covered flats of Rowena Plateau and swam in the icy sea that lapped against the hidden shores of Short Sand Beach. I learned that sushi from the right chef doesn't taste like slimy fish and family-owned, hole-in-the-wall eateries serve better food than the chain restaurants my family grew up on.

My senses were never more alive than when we were on an adventure.

He must've felt similarly, for a little more of his shell broke away with every outing. Over time his cold arrogance faded, giving rise to his subtle sense of humor and a surprisingly warm demeanor. He pressed a little closer every day, and I found it as thrilling as I did frightening. No one had ever been so physically and emotionally cozy with me, and before long I found *I* was the one putting up a wall—a blocked kiss here, a little jump to get out of his reach there. This seemed to confuse him at first but after Rena blurted the word "virgin" during a group outing (she and I didn't talk for a week after that) the bulb seemed to light up above his head.

"I won't push you," he assured, though longing still radiated off him like perfume. It would only be a matter of time before he asked for all of me, and I didn't know if I was brave enough to give it.

Then New Year's Eve came. We were tucked away in a cabin near Hood River, cuddled on the couch after being out in the crisp, snowy night, mapping constellations in the sky. The lights over the kitchen were bright and harsh, so we shut them off and filled the room with candles from the Dollar Store. Only a handful of minutes remained before midnight, the radio playing Chris Stapleton's *Tennessee Whiskey*. Scott leaned over and kissed my neck, which promptly turned into more kisses. His hands slipped under my shirt, winding around my ribcage.

I stiffened at the feeling of his thumb picking at my bra clasp.

"Elle, please just let me," he whispered, hugging me tighter to keep me from shying away. "Just trust me. I won't hurt you."

A dozen doubts and worries and insecurities raced through my head, loud as the fireworks crackling in the distance. For a moment, I didn't think I was going to let him, but the longer he held onto me the harder it was to tell him no.

I pressed my cheek against his shoulder, blood pumping in my ears. "Okay."

He slid an arm under my legs, carrying me to the bed. My muscles started to cramp from how tense I was, which I'd been told was the last thing you want to happen before your first time. He tugged my shirt off, my chest a mess of red anxiety hives but he didn't care. He kissed my blotchy skin, my blushing face, my nervous lips.

"Elle, you're not breathing." He was trying not to laugh. "Inhale. It's okay. Really."

I didn't feel okay. I just wanted it over with. Scott's shirt landed in a heap on the floor. His skin ran hot and I tried to focus on how good his chest felt against mine because the cabin air was cool and I was still chilled from outside. *Breathe.* He smelled like shaving cream and mint and something pleasantly spicy. *Breathe again.* My pants came off in one sweeping motion.

His eyebrows rose at the lacy thong I was wearing.

"That's cute," he remarked, then ripped that off, too.

I was naked. *So uncomfortably naked*. The last time I was so exposed around others was at my cousin's thirteenth birthday party and it was a dare that involved jumping in a pool. With nothing left to strip away except maybe my ego, Scott sat back. His eyes roamed my body, this odd expression befalling his features.

"What?" I snapped, because suddenly he wasn't touching me at all.

His eyes drifted up to meet mine. In an unusually meek and honest voice, he said, "You are so beautiful."

My fear of letting him in melted. Even as the first few moments together were burningly unpleasant I realized that close had never been close enough and some instinctual part of me had craved him too. Any remaining walls that had existed between us, physically and emotionally, were shattered to pieces and there was no going back. He was my one, my person, my other half. There would never be another him and no one would ever know the feelings that ran through me in those first new moments.

I fell asleep naked against him that night, his arms curled around me. I woke briefly from the pressure of his lips on my tattoo, his fingers tracing the jagged scar on my thigh. "I love you, Elle," he whispered.

I didn't say it then, but I loved him, too. Deeply, dangerously, deliriously so.

Which is why, when his grandmother flew into town from Arizona that March, I didn't understand why he didn't want me to go with him to the airport. "She's kind of a difficult old bitty," he explained. "It's better if you let me go by myself. We'll do dinner on Sunday together, okay?"

Sunday came and no dinner plans were made. I texted. I called. I left enough messages to make me look like one of those needy, worried girlfriends that I always insisted I wouldn't become, but we had never gone a day without talking before. Why wasn't he talking to me? His grandmother had come in Wednesday and was only staying through the weekend. Did he not want me to meet his grandmother at all?

Monday morning I walked into Dad's shop and found Scott's toolbox missing. "He up and quit," Dad said with a nonchalant shrug like it wasn't a big deal.

Except it was a very big deal.

***

All our months of adventures, memories, and feelings are pouring through my head as I stand outside the Safeway in Oregon City.

Scott walks directly in front of me, heading for the entrance, oblivious to my presence. My heart thunders in my chest, unable to believe it's him. He nearly gets away but I find my voice just in time. "Scott! Hey!"

He turns around just outside the store's entrance, the color visibly draining out of his face. I jog up, waiting for him to throw his arms around me, to kiss me and tell me he's sorry and there's a perfectly good explanation for why he disappeared. Instead, he just stands there and stares. "Hey." He gives a curt nod.

Hey, like I'm some long-lost acquaintance and not the woman he's shared clothing, adventures, food, and skin with these past months. I'm taken aback. More than taken aback. I have this terrible, heavy sensation in my chest like I'm coming down with the flu. For whatever reason, the walls have been fully rebuilt between us, only now they seem ten times thicker. "What the hell is going on with you?" My words take a lot of energy to force out.

He slowly tucks his hands in his pockets, looking out at the parking lot. "I've been… busy. I'm sorry."

"Busy?" I say, exasperated. My trembling heart is about to ruin my voice. "That's all you can say? You ignore all my calls, my texts, I walk in yesterday to find your toolbox missing from the shop and all you can say is you're *busy*?"

His gaze falls on his shoes while he rocks back and forth on his heels, anxious.

I'm two seconds from falling to pieces, so I turn to leave.

"Elle, wait!" He grabs my hand, squeezing it in his own. "Just—give me some time, okay? To figure things out. Please wait."

"For what?" If he's going to reject me he needs to do it now and get it over with. I can't take this kind of suffering, not again. Losing my first boyfriend was easy compared to the idea of losing Scott, like giving up an island versus half a planet.

Scott's expression changes and emotions swirl like typhoons in those blue eyes but they're unreadable. "Just wait." He lets go of my hand, backing away. "I'm sorry, Elle." It's a deep and remorseful sorry, the kind you don't want to hear out of anyone's mouth. It reeks of secrets and lies and, worst of all, some sort of betrayal.

Before I can get in another word, he turns and strides into Safeway.

I don't remember walking back to my car. I don't remember driving home, either, or what I said when Mom asked why I didn't bring dinner home. I only start to function after laying in my bed for a couple of hours, trying to recall in detail the last time he and I were together. Did I miss the signs that something was wrong? His mom was working late so we'd been at his house, wrapped up in his bed watching The Hangover. He'd seemed normal. His arm was around me and I was tucked into his side under the blankets.

A knock on my bedroom door ends my thoughts. "Elle?" Mom pokes her head in. "I brought you some Kentucky Fried Chicken. Are you hungry?"

I shake my head no. I still don't trust my voice to not crack.

Mom comes in and sets a plate down anyways. The smell sours my stomach. "What happened, honey? You look awful."

I close my eyes against the tears but they come anyway. Without a word, she pulls me into her arms and rocks me side to side like I'm a child again. "I think I lost him," I squeak.

"What?" Mom says, disbelieving.

I wipe my eyes on my sleeves then tell her what happened.

"Why on earth would his grandmother have anything against you? She's never even met you," Mom says, enraged. "If that woman has done anything to harm your relationship, she's got another thing coming! I will march over there—"

"I don't know that for sure," I interrupt before she launches into mama bear mode. "I just know everything was fine before she got here. She must've done or said something."

Mom lowers her hackles. "Well, then maybe this isn't about you. Maybe his grandmother is sick or something. That kind of news can be very devasting. I was your age when I found out my aunt Edith had cancer. They couldn't cure her. It was horrific for all of us to go through… You'd better be very sure it's about you before you cut Scott out. I know how you are. He might just need you to wait and be understanding."

Just wait. Scott's voice echoes in my mind. Why would he tell me to wait for him if he had no intention of coming back to me? Mom could very well be right: his distance might be caused by family matters and have absolutely nothing to do with me.

"I have to go apologize." I throw my comforter off and get up. "I was just as cold with him as he was with me." Once the shock of the bad news wears off, whatever this news is, he will need my support... and here I am, selfishly thinking this is all about me and that he wants to break it off. We have what neither of us has ever had in our lives before.

He wouldn't throw that away.

I eat a piece of chicken to appease Mom then leap in my car and head to historic Oregon City. I spend the entire drive practicing what I want to say and how to say it, starting with a dozen *I'm sorrys* and that he can have whatever space and time he needs with his family. I just need him to communicate versus block me out.

I steer down Monroe Street. An unusual car is parked in Scott's driveway. *Did his grandmother rent a car*? Scott's mom's car is gone, so he's either here alone or here with his grandmother. *Maybe this is a friend of the grandmother.* The problem is that the longer I stare at the Passat, the more familiar it looks. I walk up the driveway and spot a keychain hanging from the mirror inside. It's a metal picture with words printed around the outer rim.

The Big Locks Brewery.

Oh, no, no, no.

Flu like symptoms hit me again, worse than in the Safeway parking lot. My legs try to morph into pudding and it takes every ounce of my courage to walk up the porch steps. My first instinct is to knock down the door, but I need to be sure of what's happening this time. *Please God let me be wrong.* To my convenience, the front door is cracked open. The screen creaks a little as I creep inside. Voices drift out of the kitchen.

"I don't know what I'm going to tell her. I have to tell her soon," Scott's voice says.

"Parents are difficult, you know? They always think they know best," the voice of Nat the Tat drifts out of the kitchen. "Lucky for you, I don't have any to be involved."

It is *her.* I'd seen the Passat parked outside the brewery a dozen times in the last ten months. It had been a frequent pit stop on our way home from hiking. I want to tell myself it's no big deal because Nat isn't into guys but as I march around the corner, I find that I was right and women are not her primary interest as I'd been led to believe.

Nat's tattooed arms are wrapped around Scott's, which hang stiffly in her hands. She has one knee on a barstool and her front is pressed to his, their faces just inches apart. Her shirt lies in a skimpy blue heap on the floor.

My head spins like I'm going to throw up.

Scott's eyes shoot across the room. He shoves Nat the Tat back so hard she falls off her stool. "Elle!"

I race out the front door. He calls my name again, feet pounding across the porch behind me. I run faster, determined to make it to the car before he catches me but don't succeed. He grabs my elbow.

"Let go, you bastard!" I writhe against him, struggling to get free.

"Elle, you don't understand! Just stop and listen to—"

I loosen my arm from his grip and strike with full force. My hand makes contact with his face, palm burning from the impact. The sound echoes in my ears. He lets go. I should seize the opportunity to escape to my car, but the fury he's ignited is like none I've ever experienced. He stares at me, dumbfounded, hand on his already swelling cheek. There are so many things I want to say, scream, scold, but nothing would be enough. There are not enough words in the universe to describe the destruction happening inside me.

So I turn away, and somehow my pudding legs carry me to the car.

"Elle," he calls, words quivering. "I love you."

I open my door then give him one last look over my shoulder. I can hardly see him through the tears. "Burn in hell, you fucking liar." Mechanically, I start the engine and pull out of the driveway, trying to pull it together long enough to see my way home. Three miles down the street I no longer recognize the neighborhood. I'm so distraught that I've turned down the wrong road.

I pull over. My vision is swimming with black circles so I lay my head against the steering wheel. What I wouldn't give to just fade away into the upholstery of my vehicle, to turn to dust in the carpet and never feel again. I can't get the scene out of my head, can't stop seeing Nat's arms around him. This had nothing to do with his damned grandmother. My gut instinct had been right in the first place. How long has he been seeing her, I wonder? *Long enough to want to get naked in his kitchen.*

I open my door and throw up on someone's freshly-planted pansies. Images of him sharing his bed with someone else, of his fingers tracing Nat's numerous tattoos while she sleeps, has made me physically ill. I was so sure that he loved me, but I've been blinded by my own obsession. I now understand Marianne Dashwood's meltdown when she realizes that John Willoughby is a scumbag slut who isn't going to spend his life with her. It's a soul-shattering, all-consuming sorrow that cannot be fought. How laughable that Scott's last name is Darcy.

When my head stops spinning, I wipe the cold sweat off my forehead and turn the car around. *Come on now, Elle. You don't have time to be a paralyzed couch potato, remember*? I never loved anyone the way I loved Scott, but this place of hollowness isn't foreign to me. Somehow, someway, I have to find a way to get through this.

I'm coming back to the main thoroughfare when I see the flashing of police cars. Usually this isn't anything new, but I'm not used to seeing four of them at once. White Dodge Chargers are surrounding a hot blue Mazda that's sideways in the ditch with steam spilling out of the hood. *Wait a minute.* I pull up to the stop sign just in time to see a burly sheriff handcuffing the driver.

"Well, young man, maybe next time you won't drink and drive." The sheriff's voice drifts through my cracked window. He turns the boy around, marching him in front of me to his squad car.

I'm too overwhelmed to register any more emotion so all I do is stare at the boy who is bewilderedly staring at me. The sheriff tucks Scott into the back seat of his cruiser and closes the door. Another police officer walks out and motions for me to move along. I hit the gas and zip away from the scene, leaving the love of my life and the girl I had become with him behind.

July 4th, 2017

THE LONG-HIDDEN TRUTH

I wander the hospital until the smell of antiseptic and sick people drives me out. I venture into the night and salty beach air.

My eyelids droop as I climb into the driver seat of the Tacoma, stomach grumbling. Noah and I never did get to the main course at The Elanza. A drive-through with a sign mounted on the building that read 24 HOUR COFFEE had passed us on the way here. How pissed would Scott be if he came out and found his vehicle missing? What's he going to do? Jamming the key in the ignition, I start the truck and leave the lot.

"Good morning! Welcome to Beach Side Café, what can I get for you?" An annoyingly cheerful voice echoes from the drive-through box five minutes later.

I order a double-shot latte and a ham sandwich, which costs me a whopping eleven dollars and sixty cents. As I sit in line behind a white minivan, Noah and his pricey glasses of champagne cross my mind. The guilt over how things unfolded at The Elanza is settling in now. *Last time you'll ever be invited to his beach house, that's for sure.* I keep thinking of him shaking my father's hand then of his and Scott's showdown, how he backed off after Scott's comment. *I told you not her, damn it.*

The minivan is taking a stupidly long time to receive their order. I get bored and start snooping about the truck. It gives me a weird, childish pleasure to know I'm going through Scott's stuff without him knowing. The box between the seat is full of pocket change, napkins from various drive-throughs, a CD from Green Day and another from The Beatles. Crumpled up receipts are piled one on top of another. *He hasn't changed that much.* I open the glove box. A pair of clean socks falls out on the floor along with a folded map of Washington's state parks. Two empty cigarette boxes are lying on the car's user manual. I pick up the socks and stuff them back in their place only to dislodge a tiny black box.

I sigh, reaching down into the shadows of the passenger seat. The tiny box blends in with the floor mats. I feel around until a soft, velvet exterior rubs against my palm. The minivan is finally pulling away so I drop the box in my lap and steer forward.

The kid at the window—whose wide eyes and fast speech suggest that he, too, has probably had a lot of late-night caffeine—runs my card. As he gathers my coffee and sandwich, I examine the tiny box. It fits in the palm of my hand, the corners rounded and worn. *Looks like an old jewelry box.* Glen used to joke that if something happened to him, their grandfather's masonic ring would go to his brother. I pop the lid up.

My lungs hitch. It's not the masonic ring. It's not even a man's ring.

Five white diamonds of good size are set side by side, filigree cut outs running beneath them to form a unique undergallery. The diamonds don't flash with the harsh, consistent fire of modern brilliant cuts. Instead, they display a slow and uneven scintillation—sign of old cutting methods that didn't involve lasers.

This was a wedding ring straight out of mid 1900s.

"Ma'am?" The drive-through boy is trying to hand me my coffee.

His voice jerks me back into reality. I take my order and head back to the highway. *A ring*. Scott has a wedding ring in his truck. *Maybe it was Gwennie's*. I'm being stupid; Glen's wife would never give something like this to Scott. She loves vintage stuff and these stones would appraise for a pretty penny. No, this is an heirloom piece, the kind that little old ladies come into Portland Diamond with all the time. "I need to refurbish this so I can pass it down to my grandchild," they always say. Refurbish it because it is going to be worn, and pass it down because...

I try to stop the thought before it comes but don't succeed: *He's planning a proposal.*

It shouldn't hurt. It shouldn't make my innards roil and want to reject the bite of sandwich I just took, but it does. He had every right to move on; I couldn't have expected him to sit back all this time and yearn for me. I haven't been yearning for him—or have I? The time we've spent apart is five times longer than the time we spent together.

I've made myself unnecessarily ill by the time I return to the same parking spot in the hospital. I pull in just in time to see the devil himself walking out of the electronic double doors. He has a cast around one hand, a bag of ice in the other. His busted eye is open again but there's blood in the white. A jolt goes through me as I realize the ring box is still laying open in my lap.

I snap it shut and drop it in the side slot of my door just seconds before he opens his. He gets in then narrows his good eye. "What's that face for?"

"What face?" I use my irritated voice, hoping it helps to cover up the deer-in-the-headlights expression I know I just made.

He peers around the inside of his truck. The rumble of the engine rattles the ring box around in the plastic slot but if he notices he doesn't say so. I focus my gaze on anything but the door. "Did you drive off in my truck?"

I hold up the Beach Side Café bag. "I was hungry." Was, being the keyword.

"Gee, thanks for thinking of me."

"I didn't know how long you were going to take." I sip my coffee, which does not taste even remotely close to my beloved Starbucks, trying to play it cool like my hands aren't shaking. "What did they say to you?"

"Not broken." He picks up my coffee directly after I set it in the cup holder then takes a long drink without my permission. "But I'm going to look like a bar fight victim for the next few weeks. Bone's bruised but miraculously not fractured. Guess I have a hard head after all."

"You always did." He tries to pass back my cup, but I decline. It was a strange action for a soon-to-be-engaged man, drinking out of his ex's coffee like old times. My gaze drops to his casted hand, the one he'd kept in a fist the entire time we were in the waiting room. "Broke your fingers though, huh?"

He gives a menacing laugh. "Let's just say the other guy probably has a cracked rib or two. I'll take the busted fingers."

"What if that guy turns you in?"

"He doesn't know my name or that I drive a truck like his. I'll be gone tomorrow. I'll stay out of town and he'll never find me. I suggest you avoid town as well." His thumb traces the cup's lid, coming to rest on the lip gloss stain my mouth left behind. "Can I ask you something?"

"Do you have to?"

"Do you think you ripped that guy's antenna off his hood because, well, even though he was nowhere near as good-looking as me he had some similarities like the tattoos, the dark hair… the Tacoma truck. As I assume alcohol was involved, do you think you thought you were ripping the antenna off *my* truck?"

"I don't know." Except, I sort of do. That's probably *exactly* what drunk me thought she was doing: vandalizing the property of the man who'd vandalized her heart. "If I drive myself back to Noah's in this, can you drive to wherever you're staying? I think the girls have already gone to bed." Or maybe they haven't, but I'm not ready to face them yet. Noah will have told them what happened and they will have a lot more to say to me than just, *what the hell*. Maybe Noah will kick me out of his house.

Scott nods. We say nothing else the rest of the drive.

I park in the lot above the beach house fifteen minutes later. The exterior lights flick on, igniting the yard and the stairs to the patio, which is covered in empty furniture. A few embers still glow in the outdoor fireplace. Scott doesn't move to get out of the truck and take his driver's seat back. I want to gracefully depart this time, without tears or fury. I want to do it right now, but part of me is aching to speak. The sand in our fate-filled hourglass is done falling, I sense it, and it's unlikely the universe will mesh our paths a third time.

I clear my throat. "So, um, thanks. For saving me tonight. I really don't know what I would've done if you hadn't shown up."

He chuckles darkly. "Thanks for saving you from the nutjob whose truck you damaged or from your date with Noah?"

"Both," I admit, slightly sheepish.

This widens his smile. "Well, I owed you."

"You don't owe me a thing." I hate feeling like it's the opposite and I now owe him. I want to ask what prompted him to step in anyway, but he probably would've done it for any girl getting harassed in the dark, alone, wearing four-inch heels.

He mutters something that sounds like, *I owe you several.* I unzip his hoodie so he can have it back. "Don't. Just keep it."

"I don't want it." How can he think that I would want to keep a token from him when there is a wedding ring hidden in his vehicle? I lay the jacket over his lap. As I draw away, he grabs my hand. His fingers are hot around mine and slightly callused from years of working on cars. He strokes the soft, pale skin of my palm, sending familiar sensations up my arm.

"I'm sorry." It's a heavily loaded sorry, one that attempts to cover many offenses.

My throat is suddenly too tight to speak, so I nod—because I hear him, not because I accept his apology.

"I did love you," he goes on. "I want you to know that."

"Please just let it go." I pull my hand out of his.

"Why? You haven't. I can see it." His tone rises, angry. "Look, a lot more happened than met the eye. You never gave me the chance to—"

"Uh, topless chick in your kitchen—that was plenty to meet the eye." He throws his hands up in the air like my response is ridiculous. "Listen, you were important to me. Probably more important than any other man I might ever have, because you were there first. You changed how I looked at the world and how I looked at myself, but we're history. I was thoroughly reminded of that while watching Aliana fawn over you, lean into you like Nat did in your kitchen all those years ago. And let's not even get started on the wedding ring you jammed in your glovebox, which I assume is for some girl I probably don't compare to,"—my mouth tastes like tears and stomach acid at this point—"this is life. I've learned to roll with the punches." *Even when they hit you so hard you feel like you've fallen down five flights of stairs.*

"What are you talking about? I don't have a..." Scott's sentence trails off. He opens the glove box, hastily rummaging through its contents. Everything falls out, socks, map, cigarette boxes. A growl rumbles in his throat as it all piles at his feet. Everything except the tiny velvet box. "What did you do with it?"

Without turning my head from the windshield, I reach into the door slot and pull it out. He snatches it from my open palm. "I couldn't get it back in the glovebox before you opened the door at the hospital."

Relief sinks into his shoulders. He examines the diamonds for, I don't know what—damage probably, given my recent history—then tucks it back inside the padding. "Nosy much?" His tone is acidic, unnerved. "Why were you in there anyway?"

"Looking for a napkin," I lie. He returns the box to its spot then closes the flap a little too forcefully. His non-casted hand pulls through his hair. Either he's mad because I know about it or mad because I moved it and he thought he lost it. It turns my insides all the same. "I hope you're happy with her, whoever she is." I want to mean it, but really I just don't want to look like a jealous cow.

Scott leans his head back, expelling an almost manic laugh. The drugs must still be in his system. He mumbles something under his breath that sounds like, *God hates me*. "I haven't been happy with her in years. Things ended badly. The ring is in here because I'm preparing to sell it to cover business expenses."

"Oh. That's, um, unfortunate." I try to hide my sigh of relief. He sounds like he's as furious with this should've-been fiancée as he is with me for snooping around the truck. I should say something supportive, something that sounds like I'm sorry this happened to him. "Did your fear of commitment cause you to screw her over, too?"

He pins me with a look like I am the worst person on the planet. "Damn it, Elle, the ring was for you!"

Maybe it's the fact I'm stressed and exhausted, but a laugh escapes my lips. "Oh. Okay." I fling the truck door open and get out.

He kicks his own door open as I circle the bed of the truck. "I'm serious! It was handed to me in an airport five years ago," he calls from the passenger seat. "Don't you remember when my grandmother came to Portland? She was here gifting possessions she wanted to leave us."

"Oh, yeah, the one you didn't want me to meet." I remember little outside of that. That expanse of time is fuzzy in my mind. Shifting my purse onto my shoulder, I swiftly hold my arm out and dangle his truck keys in front of his face. I could've left them in the ignition but it's my way of saying, *you can get the hell out now*.

He doesn't take them. "That's not true. You just didn't get the chance." Pulling a lighter out of his pocket, he ignores my extended arm and tries to wedge a cigarette in between his casted fingers. A jumble of quiet cuss words rolls off his tongue.

I release his truck keys and they clang to the ground. "Oh, and why was that? Too busy letting her meet Nat the Tat first?" Oh please, God, don't let the ring be for her. I will vomit.

The cigarette falls out of his cast, joining his keys in the gravel. He throws me a look like I just shot him. "You know what? If you don't believe me, why don't you go back to The Elanza and ask your dad?"

"Ask my *dad*? What does he have to do with any of this?"

Scott hesitates, rubs his neck like he's suddenly in pain. His expression becomes guarded as he looks out at the bay. I start to walk away. "Ask him what he said when I told him I wanted to marry you."

It's like the ocean just came up and slammed me with a sneaky wave. "Y—you told him *what*?" He must be kidding. He couldn't have said that, not seriously. It's hard to believe for a multitude of reasons starting with A, the obvious (there was another female party involved) and, B, we were just kids, not even out of our teens. We didn't know how to apply for college much less plan a wedding.

"Ask him how he told me there was no way in hell," Scott continues bitterly. "How you were too smart to give up your future for some young, dumb shop kid with no college degree or savings account or way to support you. Ask him how he told me nothing at our age was permanent, that I'd be ruining your chance at a happy future. It'd probably just be best if I let go of those thoughts because, you know, he'd prefer you married a doctor or a businessman, some wealthy fuck. God, he must've loved Noah!"

His words hang in the air like the trickling remnants of fireworks, followed by an unearthly wave of silence. Even the crickets have stopped singing. I realize my jaw is hanging open. "M—my father said those things to you?" Dad hadn't been fond of Scott since the day we disappeared into the Gorge and I nearly killed myself, but I didn't think he'd ever verbally reject him. I didn't think he cared what I did or who I ended up with. I especially didn't think he was capable of something like this.

"Mm-hmm," Scott hums, finally managing to light a cigarette, though he's singed the bandage on his cast. He blows out a dragonesque puff of smoke. "He fired me, too."

"*Fired* you? He didn't fire you—you left!" I remember my shock when I entered the shop and found Scott's toolbox missing. Scott leaving was just more evidence that it was over between us and I had sunk to my knees on the filthy, oil-sheened floor. I did not know that grief could really do that, make a person so suddenly weak that they can't hold themselves up. It was Dad who'd peeled me off the cement. Dad who'd sat me on an old stool and wiped the oil off my knees and hands as I sobbed. Dad who'd cradled me and said, "It's alright, Elly. There are a lot of good men out there. Just because this one walked away from you doesn't mean the next one will. Everything is going to be fine."

"I never quit," Scott assures, then curses my father's name. "His best hope of ensuring I never proposed was to cut me off from you in any way he could."

"But then that means he…" *He lied to me*. Worse, he created an entire act around the lie, like he was this loving parent so genuinely hurt and concerned that his kid had been left in the dirt. I knew my father had multiple personalities, but liar to his own flesh and blood? *How could he do that*?

"Manipulated the situation for his own advantage? Yeah. Oh, wait, I'm sorry—for *your* advantage." Scott rolls his eyes. "Come on, Elle, don't look so surprised. Haven't you figured out your dad is a master manipulator yet?"

I lean against the side of the truck, suddenly very lightheaded. I've spent hours wondering what flipped the switch in Scott's head, what made him morph from an adoring boyfriend into a total stranger seemingly overnight. I thought it had been my fault. I had come up with all the classics like I wasn't pretty enough or didn't give him enough in bed, to wild imaginings like he secretly hated my laugh or couldn't get past the fact I dipped my pizza in tartar sauce.

I never imagined the switch was Jim Fox.

"You wanted to *marry* me?" Let's put aside that I can barely grasp that concept or the truth that Dad once again has succeeded in derailing an important aspect of my life, but this still doesn't address the big elephant in the driveway. "So you were hoping that, what, Nat and I would be happy as sister wives?"

"Oh, for Christ's sake!" Scott jumps out of the passenger seat so fast you'd think he dropped his cigarette in his lap. He thrusts it at the ground and it bursts into sparks. "Hear me this once: Nat and I were *never* together! The only reason she was there that night was because Glen was there!"

"Oh, of course, Glen was there! It all makes sense now! So, what, is Glen the cheater then?"

"Nobody was cheating, Elle! Good God, we've all been friends since junior high it wasn't unusual having her and Glen together in my house! They came over with pizza and beer because Glen was worried about me. It was only after he stepped out back to smoke and left us alone in the kitchen that things got weird." He rubs his forehead in his hand as if trying to fend off a headache. "I drank too much, said too much. I told her I was losing you, that I didn't know how to tell you what happened or if I should. She told me she could relate, as her girlfriend had just broken up with her over a family issue... She wanted us to be rebound buddies.

"I thought about it for a second—one stupid, split second because I allowed your dad to make me feel like trash, make me think he was right. Maybe there *was* someone out there who was better for you, someone who could offer you more than me. Maybe I'd be better off with a girl like Nat, someone without expectations or parents to judge me. The problem was that Nat wasn't you. She'd never be you, and I didn't want her to be. Before I could say this to her, however, you were standing in my living room.

"The look you gave me, like I had completely shattered you, I'll never forget it. It made me sick. I should've been faster to push her back, to realize it didn't matter what Jim Fox had said or tried to do to me—I should never have disappeared. I should've told you what happened, even though it would have changed how you looked at him and how you looked at me. It wasn't fair. How he and I handled the whole thing was not fair to you... I screwed up, Elle."

It's long been my biggest complaint that seeing past Scott's walls is a task comparable to rock climbing up a ninety-degree canyon. This is probably why I'm unprepared for the genuine devastation in his eyes. His regret, his suffering, is real.

This is the truth.

"So you're saying... you never hooked up with her?" I was so sure that's what happened, so sure I had been given up for another. The idea that he never did touch her feels impossible after the years of imaginings I conjured up. "Not even when we were getting lunch at the Big Locks Brewery all the time?"

"No. We tried to date in high school but I wasn't that into her and she wasn't sure what she was into. We were too different. She was ice and I, quite clearly, preferred a ring of fire." A smile tugs at the corner of his mouth.

I don't miss his reference. *The Ring of Fire* was not just a favorite Johnny Cash song that played in my house when I was growing up; it was a term coined by my grandmother referring to the hot-tempered gene pool from her side of the family. I came from a long line of emotional women who loved too hard and felt betrayal just as deeply. "It is a blessing and a curse," Grandma said to Scott at our dinner table once, "to be born with passion in your blood." If he had never been seeing Nat, if this entire thing had truly been a series of unfortunate misunderstandings, and Jim Fox jamming his thumb in it all...

Scott really had loved me.

"Ah, Elle," Scott sighs, because even though I'm hiding behind my hands, the tears are streaming through my fingers. He leans into the cab, rummages around in the center compartment, then walks over and extends a napkin to me. "Please don't cry. I didn't tell you this to make you upset."

"Well, you didn't tell me to make me feel better." I swipe the napkin out of his hand. I should feel better, like a burden has been lifted off me at long last. Instead I feel like someone kicked me in the stomach. The night I ended things, when I got into my car and fled his house, he had drunkenly gotten into his car to chase after me, which was why he'd crashed and gotten arrested. He tried to contact me when he was released from jail, but I swiped the red button on my cell every time he called. His texts were filled with anger because he'd just been slapped with an enormous fine and a DUI, something automotive employers avoid like the plague, and I wouldn't even talk to him. I didn't acknowledge that he existed anymore. He called a lot at first, then sometimes, then not at all. He showed up on the farmhouse doorstep once and I'd made Mom deny his visit. "Are you sure you don't want to hear what he has to say?" She asked me afterwards. No, I told her. I never wanted to talk to him or about him again.

I screwed up, too. Maybe even worse than he did.

"I had *hoped* it would make you feel better. You finally let me tell you the truth." Scott, at least, sounds relieved. "There are other crummy things I've done that I should tell you about but cheating on you was never one of them. Aren't you glad to know that never happened?"

"I am, but the truth hasn't lessened my grief." If anything, it's made it worse. Living with the fact you lost someone who was bad for you is one thing. Living with the fact you lost someone you should've kept has far more guilt involved. Why can't we have a rewind button? When am I going to be able to grab hold of my own temper before it grabs hold of me? If I had just talked to him, allowed him even a moment to explain himself...

Scott lolls his head, like he doesn't know what else to say. Shifting on his feet, he mumbles, "Well, then... I should probably get going. I'm staying with my friend Gabe who lives near The Elanza. He probably thinks I got shitfaced and can't find my way back." He laughs but it's strained.

I watch him bend down and pluck his keys off the ground. When he stands up, he's much closer than he had been before. For the first time in years, I want to reach out and pull him to me. "I should've listened to you sooner."

He lifts his good hand towards my face then his fingers coil into a fist. He drops his arm to his side. "We can't change the past." He tucks his hands in his pockets, slowly backing away to go around the truck. "Go get some sleep, Elle. It's late and I've given you too much to dwell on. Goodnight."

There is so much more I want to say, but I don't know how to phrase any of it and he doesn't give me the chance to try. He moves too eagerly into the cab. Exhaling a frustrated huff, I adjust my purse and start walking for the house, feeling like a bomb just fell on me and he's fleeing the aftermath. His truck rumbles to life, backing up to face the road that leads to the highway. I'm a few steps from the stairs when I hear his breaks squeal to a stop.

I turn around. The truck is immobile, headlights resting on the trees as the engine growls in place. The driver's side door is hanging open. Scott is striding across the gravel, his cool reserve suddenly replaced with an alarming ferocity. His good arm swoops around my waist at the same moment that his lips crash into mine.

His mouth moves against my own as if no time and a thousand problems haven't passed between us. Everything I've contained, all the suppressed suffering and wanting, bursts forth like prisoners from long-sealed cells. My hands lock around his neck as if they have minds of their own, drawing him in. He winces as I accidentally press into the bruise around his eye, but it doesn't slow us down. He tastes of the sea and the mountains and cozy cabins nestled in snow-covered hills —things I loved so much but forgot about. I purposely forgot because when he left, he took the person I was becoming with him—one who adventured and dreamed and believed the whole world was flowing with possibilities, a person I loved being. He breathes in the scent of my skin, my hair, his grip as tight as that of someone who's worried they'll crumble into the ground if they let go. I'm worried I'll crumble with him if he does.

His kisses suddenly slow down. His eyes have homed in on something over my shoulder.

I follow his gaze, seeing movement at the base of the steps.

Kacey and Rena unpeel their faces from the sliding glass door, which is cracked open for them to hear. Their shadows dart out of view but even from here I can hear stumbling and glass shattering across the floor. Kacey shouts, "Rena, damn it!"

Scott rolls his head back. "Seriously? Right now?"

As if to answer his question, Rena throws the sliding glass door open and shouts, "Hey, Elly! Doe ya stop on er counts!" She wobbles in the door frame and nearly falls over. Kacey is yelling at her to come back inside. "I knews yous likes them white tattoo meats! Er fill yar taco!"

"*Rena*!" Kacey's hands wrap around our friend's arm, hauling her back inside. The sliding door slams shut behind them.

I slap a hand over my face. Scott squints at the patio. "Did she just say *white tattoo meats*?"

"Don't ask." She is so dead when I get in there.

Moment spoiled, Scott loosens his grip, hands resting on my hips. "I, um." He pauses, trying to find words for what just happened. "I don't know what that was. I'm sorry."

My lips are zinging. My skin is, for once, on fire in a good way and the jolt I felt when he kissed me has rolled through my veins, attempting to rearrange every body part, thought, and belief I had thirty seconds ago. "You're sorry?"

He scrunches his nose. "Not really." He leans in to see if

I'll let him do it again. *Consider the repercussions, Elle,* my intuition warns but it's too late—he's already tugged on my waist. He draws me against him like he did in days of old, the bands of muscle beneath his tattoos folding over my shoulders like two straps of armor. Once upon a time, this was the safest place in the world.

A pair of lights flash through the woods, coming down the driveway. Scott looks up when we hear the low rumble of an engine approaching. "Ah, shit, here comes more unwanted company," he hisses.

"Noah?" The low, narrow headlights look like the ones on his Audi. Have he and his sister been at The Elanza this entire time?

"I should go. I've already busted one set of ribs tonight." He steps back, taking my safe haven with him. I stand up straighter and try to not look as vulnerable as I suddenly feel. His eyes dart around my face, searching. "Look, I know a lot has happened but... call me tomorrow?"

God, I want to. But I should really wait. "I don't have your number."

He smiles. "Yes, you do."

Ah, so that's what he was doing with my phone in the hospital. "Give me a few days."

"A few *days*?"

"I need to process all of this." My brain is malfunctioning at the idea that I might still be in love with somebody whose guts I've hated for years. I need to absorb what has happened, and he's doing way too good a job at overloading my senses right now.

He makes an annoyed sound. "Fine. Just don't take another five years." He pecks me on the lips one last time and turns away. He climbs back into the Tacoma seconds before Noah's headlights enter the parking lot. The Audi slows at the sight of the black truck and I can almost feel the heated tension as both vehicles pass each other.

I duck into the shadows of the house, making my way down the steps. I'm not ready to face Noah, either, though more out of embarrassment than anything else. The Audi doesn't branch off into the driveway but instead circles behind the house, into a private garage. I wait to hear voices but never do. They must've gone inside through another door.

Sinking down on the last step to the patio, I exhale loudly. I've been holding my breath a while, maybe years. I undo the straps of my stilettos and kick them off. The blisters on my toes and ankles are seeping and swollen but they don't hurt as much as my head. *What the hell just happened*?

July 4th 2017

THE GOLDEN BIRD

The girls had stayed up to wait for me last night, passing the time with snacks and wine. The snacks disappeared within the first hour, but the wine had kept flowing. Bets had been placed on when Noah and I would come home. Bets had not been placed on whether Noah and I would come home separately.

No one had expected the black Tacoma to pull into the driveway. There had been a lot of excitement and shock-filled confusion when it had been discovered that I was inside, and an explosion of it when Scott had flung his door open and strode over to swoop me up in what Rena describes as "The Notebook on steroids".

"I *knew* Noah wasn't your type." Rena tries to express enthusiasm but instead sounds tired. Her complexion is pale and dark circles loom beneath her eyes. She barely remembers last night and puked in the kitchen sink while we were brewing coffee this morning. She cleaned it up but we had to air out the first floor of the house. Now we're sitting at a cafe in Newport called Bea's.

"I tried to warn him," Kacey sighs, stirring her coffee. She isn't quite as pasty-faced as her partner in crime, but she keeps rubbing her head like she's trying to quell a headache.

"I didn't mean for our date to end the way it did, but after seeing my dad and then seeing that Noah *knows* my dad, I had to get out." I don't want them thinking Scott showed up and ruined the date on purpose.

"Completely understandable," Rena says. Her head is propped in her hand but it keeps drifting toward the starfish tablecloth. Kacey leans back in her wicker basket chair, frowning. Maybe her hangover is worse than I thought. They exchange glances. "So?"

I shrug. "So, what?"

"What was it like?"

"What was what like?"

"Come on, Elle," Rena drawls. "He looked like a starved wolf that just nabbed a caribou, for God's sake! What was it like being back in his embrace? Are you over the fact that he cheated on you?"

Kacey gives her the death glare. I'm turning my cup around in its saucer, searching for words. "I don't think he cheated on me."

Rena bursts out laughing. "Wow, that kiss must've been *really* good!"

"I'm serious. Our breakup was based on a big misunderstanding." I don't mean to sound snappy but I'm tired and I know how this all sounds—like the little kid who cried wolf is now confessing to her overreaction. If I were Rena, I'd think I was delusional, too. "Look, everything I went through last night was completely unplanned, including that kiss, and I don't know how I feel about any of it right now."

Hearing the testiness in my tone, Rena shuts up. Perfect timing, for a woman in an apron whose hair is coiled into a grey bun with a seashell clip comes to our table. "One bagel and cream cheese, one English muffin breakfast sandwich, and one Hangover Du Jour with lemon."

Rena wrinkles her nose at the pretty tomato-colored drink with an umbrella in it. It smells like Nana's legendary hangover cure. "I didn't order this," she grumbles.

Bea smiles and pats Kacey's shoulder. Kacey smiles knowingly. "On the house," Bea assures.

Rena makes a nauseated sound. "Oh. Gee, thank you." She sits up and gingerly sips the tomato drink. Her eyes twitch. "Oh my God, this tastes like death. Who can actually drink this shit?"

"People with more refined palettes." Kacey nibbles a piece of bacon.

"Refined palette my ass. I'd rather go lick the beach."

I purse my lips, thinking back to the night at Mother Shucker's. "Do you guys remember anything from our night at the seafood house? Did I—I don't know—disappear randomly for a long period of time?" I still don't want to believe that

I wrecked that guy's door panel. I want a shred of hope that maybe that crazy guy did have me mixed up with some other mentally unstable drunk woman.

Their silence is not reassuring. Rena stirs the umbrella in her drink, glares at Kacey like she should speak first, then says, "You did disappear at one point."

Kacey kicks her under the table.

My stomach sinks. So much for hope.

Rena's movements have become slow and controlled as she stirs the tomato concoction. "But who knows what you were doing? You might've been in the bathroom a long time or ran into somebody you knew. We were busy talking and didn't think much of it."

"I see." Judging by the sweat on her temple and her sudden interest in the hangover cure, I'd say that was a lie. Kacey is no longer eating. Instead, she stares at her plate like it just broke her heart. "Kacey, are you alright? You're not going to be sick, too, are you?"

Kacey inhales, then straightens. The look on her face says she's preparing to accept a death sentence rather than tell her friend she is an emotional basket case who should probably seek therapy. "I think it's great," she says slowly, "that you and Scott are back together—"

"We're not back together."

"Nonetheless." She squeezes her eyes shut as if trying to summon focus. "I need to tell you something."

No good conversation has ever started with *I need to tell*

you.

Kacey's thumbs turn white as they rub against the outside of her coffee cup. "I saw you pull off that guy's antenna in the parking lot. You scraped up his door panel good. You also tried to jam it through his tire but we dragged you into the car before that could happen. I don't know how we got away from there without that guy catching us. We're lucky there are a lot of white Subarus down here and mine isn't easy to decipher from others."

"You *saw me* pluck the guy's antenna off his Tacoma?" They didn't just hear me talk about it or notice the tail end of it—they *witnessed* the entire crime from start to finish and didn't say a word before now? "Why didn't you tell me the morning after I had behaved like an inebriated wild animal?"

"Because," Kacey stammers, "the next day you seemed to forget *why* you had such an outburst in the first place! You seemed to have forgotten everything. I wanted to leave it that way, for all of our sakes."

She's not making any sense. "Well, obviously I mistook the bar-goer for Scott. Weren't we talking about him and the breakup before I began the nonstop ordering of drinks? You guys, that dude would've *pummeled* me last night if Scott hadn't shown up! If I had known some psycho bar-goer was out there looking for me I wouldn't have gone out with Noah! How could you have kept this a secret?"

Rena is fanning herself with her napkin.

Kacey swallows hard. "Scott asked me to."

I'm faced with a strange, sinking feeling like the floor beneath me is made of putty. I suddenly want out of this conversation. "What do you mean?" Had Scott been at Mother Shuckers? Why would he ask anything of Kacey? They barely know each other. *Or do they*? It's been looking like Kacey knows Scott more than she has led on.

"I can't take it anymore!" Rena slaps her hands against the table, rattling our cups and plates. "Kacey got mad at Dustin nine months ago and slept with Scott after a company party. You two got toasted at Mother Shuckers and she told you this so you wrecked the Not Scott's vehicle thinking it was his! There, Jesus, now she knows!"

That newborn flame of hope that had started last night when Scott kissed me is smothered. In its wake, a darkness as hot and black as coal begins to rapidly spread. Kacey and Scott *together*? The idea roils up inside me, filling every pore and vein with a toxic, erratic sensation like when I'd caught him with Nat only this time it's real. There is no room for misinterpretation. *Control, Elle. You are an adult. Handle this with maturity and control. Reign your anger in before you—*

"Are you *shitting me*?" My voice rings across the entire restaurant, silencing the women's getaway group behind us and earning dirty looks from a family breakfast in the corner. "You got drunk and screwed *my* boyfriend?"

"You weren't dating at the time," Kacey cries.

"So?" I hate that she's defending what she did. I hate that she's also right. "Isn't there some silent clause about not fucking your friends' exes? You knew how much I loved him!

You knew how badly it ended between us!" My guts turn acidic with the images my head conjures up of Scott naked and pressed up against my best friend. Former best friend.

Kacey's eyes go glassy and she starts sobbing into her napkin.

Bea strides out of the kitchen and comes to our table. "This is a family restaurant! If you're going to talk like you're in a bar, go find one!"

"Gladly," I snarl then shove my chair back.

"You cannot leave like this," Rena says, more like demands as she folds one arm around Kacey's shoulders.

"Oh, I really think I can! How would she feel if I played hide the pickle with Dustin and didn't tell her?"

"It was a mistake, Elle," Kacey cries. "I've regretted it ever since! God, it's been weighing on me since the day I saw you at Starbucks! That's why I wanted you to hear it from me and not Scott!"

"So this entire trip was, what? To help make yourself feel like a better friend after what you did?" And to think that I believed she really wanted me here to reconnect, to help resolidify our once strong bond as friends. No, this wasn't because she missed me. This was about her guilt, her need to make herself feel okay again. She's getting married, after all. *I wonder if Dustin knows.*

"Ladies." Bea is on the verge of picking us all up by the backs of our shirts and hauling us out of her restaurant. "Your quarrel is going outside. *Now.*"

"Oh, don't worry. This quarrel is over. All of this is over." I swipe a hand through the air as if to sever my ties to the two women with whom I once shared some of the greatest moments of my life, then throw my purse over my shoulder.

Rena jumps up to grab my wrist. "She invited you on this trip because you are her friend and she cares about you! This has been on her mind for months! Are you really going to forsake us for that loser who cheated on you and is now trying to spin up your head again? Come on, Elle!"

I rip my hand out of her wrist. "Oh, go abort another baby." I turn around before I can fully witness the horror on her face.

By the time I get down to the beach, I regret my reaction. I walk and walk until my temper has fizzled out completely. Kacey might've earned my lifetime stamp of betrayal, but my anger shouldn't have come out at Rena. I should never have made the baby comment. *She will never forgive you for that, Elle.* I don't want her to. It was a hideous, ugly thing to say.

When the beach runs out, I call an Uber. I'm sitting on some bus stop bench near the mint arches of the Yachats Bridge when my phone buzzes. My innards twist at the idea that it's Rena or Kacey, sending out the initial blast for round two. The number comes up labeled, **Scott Darcy**.

I click open the message.

Elle?

I almost don't text back.

Not a good time, Scott

I know. I just got an unexpected text from Kacey. Will you talk to me if I call you?

I huff a laugh. Of course Kacey texted him, because someone who is engaged still talks to the guy she cheated on her boyfriend with. *Rena might be right.* Maybe I did just forsake them for a loser who is trying to spin up my head again after all this time. Maybe I just need to forsake everyone and go home to my mom and my dogs.

What is there to talk about? *Completely fucked up* about sums up the entire scenario. I feel like such an idiot, letting you kiss me when you were harboring this. How could you even show your face in Noah's house after what you and Kacey did to his brother? Shame on both of you.

I hit send. My phone starts ringing. I jump from the abruptness of the sound then send Scott to voicemail. A moment later, my phone dings again.

Dammit, this is why I told her to let me tell you. It *was* completely fucked up. That's why we swore to never talk about it. Dustin had just dumped her for the fifth time and I had just buried my brother. She wasn't stable and I wasn't

sober—bad combo. A lot of things have happened in five years, Elle. I've made poor choices. I can't change the past. I can only look forward, and now I'm looking forward at you. I'm up for another shot at this if you are.

A blue Prius pulls up to the curb and turns on its flashers. I get into the backseat of my Uber, fatigued, and it's not from my long bout of walking. What is Scott asking, that I just sweep this under the rug like he did? I'm not good at that. I've never been good at turning a blind eye to ugly truths. My mother never was, either. We both know the weight of unresolved disputes in a relationship. Worse, we know the weight of trying to cover them up for the sake of the other person and having it slowly eat at us until we're either numb or exploding.

Maybe we need to accept that too many things have happened in five years, Scott. We're not kids anymore. A lot has gone on in my life, too. Maybe we should just be thankful that we got to have a small period of perfectness in our lives and leave it at that. It's more than a lot of people get to have.

"Turn here, young lady?" The old man driving the Prius points to a turnoff that leads through a stream of old, weather-worn houses.

I nod at the rearview mirror. "Yes, please."

It's a long time before Scott responds. We're passing the ponds near Noah's road when my screen lights up.

And she shuts me out again. Okay then, if that's how you really feel. But I don't think it is. I think you're letting your insecurities get the best of you. I meant everything I said last night. If you can still believe that I would pick Nat or Kacey or anyone over what we had and could still have, then you're not different at all. Lose the number if that's how you feel.

I delete his number and all texts attached.

***

A shiny, newer Chevy truck is parked in Noah's lot when the Uber pulls in. Its owner is sitting on the tailgate talking to Allen and, besides the short hair and a few subtle facial differences, he looks like Noah. *That must be Dustin.* I instruct the Uber driver to drop me near the garage so I can take the bark dust trail around the back of the house. I'm relieved to find that Kacey's Subaru is not back yet.

The forest lingers against the back of the beach house, trees waving wildly in the wind. The sky has shifted from a silver cover to a menagerie of dark clouds. Those who were hoping for a sunny, warm Fourth of July are about to have their parades rained on, quite literally. The trail dips down and around a swampy area where I spot Nana, moving near a shed with cedar shingle siding. She's lifting what looks like bags of bird seed into a wheelbarrow. *She's too old to be doing that.* As anxious as I am to pack up and get out of here, I beeline down a stone-lined path. "Nana, can I help you with that?"

"Oh, hello, Elle." She grunts while picking up another bag. "Yes, that's great. Looks like a storm is coming." She casts a weary glance at the sky. "So much for filling feeders before she comes."

The breeze blows through my hair, sending a chill down the back of my shirt. Even for July in Oregon, this air is cold. I take the bag from her and set it atop the others then lift the wheelbarrow's handles. She directs me to a small porch where her sliding glass doors are. "Have you seen Noah? I really need to speak to him." He might hate me along with everyone else, but I at least want the chance to tell him I'm sorry for last night. I owe him that much.

"He's in my bathroom, replacing a light bulb," she says, leading the way to the house. "You can put it here. We don't need to unload it right now." She gestures to the flat gravel patch that rests between her porch and another garage. I park the wheelbarrow and brush some sand off my hands. Bird feeders of varying kinds decorate the walls here and line her porch rails. A euphony of avian song pours down from the old fir trees. "If you would kindly take this up to the porch, my little jewels would greatly appreciate it." She picks a container of red liquid off the ground and holds it out.

It looks like an upside-down laboratory flask set into a red plastic O with fake flowers as the feed holes. "Sure."

An old gate with a rusting lever guards the entrance to Nana's porch. I open the gate, stepping lightly on the mossy stairs. My nose twitches at Noah's shoes nearby, spotless with bright, white soles. *Can change a lightbulb but can't lift thirty-pound bags of birdseed or clear the slippery moss from his grandmother's stairs*?

I'm two steps across the porch when a high-pitch buzzing catches my ear. I lift my head toward the sliding door and come to a halt. Three large red feeders like the one in my hand hang over the deck, each swarming with tiny, emerald bodies. *They're hummingbirds*. Not just one or two like I'm used to seeing, either; they number in the dozens. They dip tiny beaks into plastic, faux flowers, stilling for only a few seconds at a time to suck the sugar water from inside. I stand only a few feet away yet none of them scatter.

"Beautiful, aren't they, my little jewels?" Nana chuckles, climbing the stairs with another sugar water feeder. "They return to me every spring and I see them almost every day of the summer. It's my favorite part of the morning. So peaceful to watch."

The hummers dive and flit and swirl around like torpedoes. My eyes don't quite know where to settle or if they even can settle on any one bird. It starts to make me dizzy. "Beautiful, but it looks more like total chaos than peace," I chuckle. "Sometimes I feel like that's what my brain looks like. What my *life* looks like."

"Life is chaos," Nana says brightly. "Just as it should be."

She picks a hook off the outdoor table and hangs the other feeder. "Should it be?" I try to hide my disagreement because she's old and has a right to her opinions, but I'm bothered at how positive her statement sounded, especially after the morning I've had.

A smile lifts her wrinkled cheeks. "Yup."

"Why do you think that?"

She shrugs like it's obvious. "We need it."

Personally, I could use less of it. A lot less.

"Without chaos, there's no growth. Everything would remain still, never changing, never moving forward. We need the discomfort of chaos to help us shift and evolve. It's as simple as realizing we are hungry, and our hunger drives us towards food." She lifts a glass jar off one of the plant tables, causing the hummers to widen their swarm. Again, I expect them to buzz off at her presence and return later, but they simply zip around her to get to the feeders. She removes the jar's lid and pours sugar water into her hand.

I watch in awe as three tiny jewels flit to her outstretched arm. With her other hand, she motions for me to come closer. "Won't they fly away?" I whisper.

"They'll come back if they do." She motions again. Three more birds have gathered around her hand, perching on her fingers like exotic, metallic jewelry. The hummingbirds' throats flash red at my approach. Up close, they aren't just metallic green but teal and gold when the light hits them just right. "Do you see their long beaks?" Nana points at their heads. "Perfectly formed to fit inside the flowers they love so. Lots of time and chaos pushed that to happen, to reshape them into what they needed to become."

"I suppose." A few are checking out the feeder still in my hand, hanging at my side. I lift it up, its bright color drawing some of the smaller hummers that couldn't fight their way into the crowds. "But how much suffering has to occur before something decent comes out of it?" Just because discomfort pushes us to become something other than what we are or do something different than we would've done, it's not always good. This morning was great proof of that. I cringe as Dad, the king of chaos, crosses my mind. I don't know if any good has come out of the chaos he's caused.

Nana lifts her gaze, an unreadable expression on her face. "There is a story that my mother used to tell me about a golden bird whose feathers rivaled those of the finest hummingbirds. She was the most beautiful bird in the forest, but one day her feathers began to change. Her golden glow was dimming, her colors fading to bronze and soon to black. She sought the wisdom of an owl who lived at the forest's edge. 'I'm dying,' she told him. 'I'm dying and I can't stand it.' The owl merely laughed. 'You are not dying,' he told the golden bird. 'You are simply changing. You have only fear to fear.'

"And fear she did. She was beautiful and loved and wanted to keep the security of those golden, gleaming feathers. She and her friends tried everything they could think of to help her; they stole gold paint from a nearby village and painted the black feathers. They plucked her remaining golden ones to prevent them from turning, gluing them back on with tree sap. Very soon, she no longer recognized herself. The gold paint began to flake. The sap wore off and the golden feathers fell away, leaving patches of wounded skin in their wake. 'This isn't me,' she said to Mother Earth. 'I give in. I accept the change'.

"In a burst of flame, the once golden bird plunged from her tree, turning to a pile of ashes. The sorrow of the forest could be felt in every grain of soil to the tip of every tree. As the woodland creatures came to mourn the loss of their friend, however, a glimmer of red moved in the ash. Standing from the golden bird's grave, a phoenix with feathers as bright as the rising sun stretched her new wings. The owl laughed from his perch overhead. 'I told you it was only change.'"

The sugar water in Nana's hand is gone by the time she finishes. The hummers have retreated. My arm, along with the rest of me, has gone weak from her story. My feeder now rests on the outdoor table. "That's beautiful, Nana."

"It is a good reminder." Nana wipes her hands on her jeans. "How we choose to embrace or reject the chaos that befalls us will decide our paths. The longer we fight, the longer it will take us to rise from it but, rise or fall, we are not meant to stay the same." With her free arm, Nana lifts a meaningful hand to my shoulder. "I see your chaos, Elle Fox. Elle Fox, whose very name means to lead during tricky and unpredictable change. Beneath that hard and worried gaze that I've rarely seen leave your face, I see a fox in you: her coat as bright as phoenix feathers with a burning heart to match. You have all the tools you need to overcome your struggles, whatever they may be." She grins while taking my feeder off the table. "Put a little more trust in chaos. It can push you in the right direction."

I want to tell her thank you but can't find my voice. To have her not only share such a powerful story, but to offer me —a girl she's only talked to a handful of times—such profound insight on who she believes I am has left me speechless. There are people who have known me all my life whose million words have not moved me as much as this old woman's just did. Nana disappears through the gate, heading back to her wheelbarrow. She hums her native chant as a ripple of lightning flashes above the house and thunder crackles loudly in the distance. "Oh, hear that? That was a good one," she laughs. "Even the sky needs a little chaos now and then!"

The cloud of hummingbirds begins to thin around the feeders, Nana's little jewels slowly dispersing into the woods at the probability of rain. A figure moves behind the sliding glass door and my muscles tighten as Noah steps outside. He stops in the doorway upon seeing me.

"Oh. Hey, Elle." He meets my eyes but is quick to focus them elsewhere. "Have you seen Nana? Dustin says a big storm is blowing in. I don't want her outside."

"She just went around the corner for birdseed." A raindrop splatters off my cheek. "Hey, Noah?"

"Yeah?"

"I'm really sorry about last night."

He huffs a laugh, smiling at his bare feet. "Don't be. I could tell there was a lot of tension between you and Jim—er —your dad. Plus, I knew better than to take one of my friend's exes on a date, especially when it was made clear there were still a lot of feelings for that ex."

"I'd like to write you a check for dinner."

"Absolutely not. I enjoyed your company and it was fun while it lasted." His eyes trace up my legs, like he's still imagining me in my high heels and sequined dress. A yearnful sigh leaves his throat. "Is Scott okay?"

"He will be." The bruise around his eye will heal and so will his fingers. I can't speak for the rest of him though, and I can't speak for any part—physically or mentally—of myself.

"So, you two going out for the Fourth?" He casts an eye to the sky, sounding like he doubts it.

I shake my head. "I'm going home."

"Well, then. It was nice to meet you, Elle." Noah offers me his hand and I shake it. He pats my shoulder as he walks by. I'm relieved, both for the fact that he isn't angry and that I don't have to give up next month's paycheck for our dinner.

A louder rumble of thunder rolls over the house as I pack my belongings in the spare room. Besides the lack of electricity and the scary portrait of the Indian chief, Speaks with Seas, I might miss the space a little. I left my good Wet Brush in Nana's bathroom earlier and go to collect it. By the time I come back, my phone is lit up with a missed call.

My brother's number flashes across my screensaver. *Why would Matt be calling*? My brother is a quiet soul who far prefers email and texting to using his voice. I'm even more unsettled by the voicemail symbol flashing at the top of the screen.

"Hey, sister. Where the heck are you?" My brother's message is frustrated. "Dad's been in an accident. Usually I wouldn't bother you, but… you need to come, Elly. It's bad."

***

Getting out of the coast on the Fourth of July is almost as difficult as getting into it. I don't remember packing the rest of my suitcase or leaving Nana's apartment. A new Uber in the form of an army green Jeep driven by a guy with mutton chops in a Harley Davidson shirt picks me up.

Most of the Fox family has gathered in one of the larger waiting rooms of Willamette Hospital's ICU on the second floor. My adrenaline starts rushing over the thought of a family reunion, for I have become almost as estranged to the Foxes as my mother these past two years. Since Bertie became a permanent fixture in Mom's chair, I haven't made many appearances at gatherings. Heads turn one by one, expressions of surprise lighting the features of my grandparents, aunts, and uncles. I'm offered warm greetings and hugs.

The only person who doesn't seem thrilled by my arrival is Bertie. Dad's girlfriend sits at the edge of the group, acrylic nails tapping on her phone. When she looks up, her gaze is steadily blank. There is no warm welcome in her eyes. I wonder if she's mad about how I treated my father at The Elanza, or perhaps just mad that I exist. Hard to say.

Grandma Johanna walks up and puts her arms around me. She's lost weight since I last saw her, her t-shirt bearing the logo for some 10K race in Seattle. "I'm so glad you are here," she whispers, relieved.

I squeeze her waist. "I'm sorry I didn't make it sooner. Is my mom here yet?"

She steps back, silver brows knit together. "Is your mother coming?"

Almost as if on cue, heads tilt to another approaching figure. Mom, walking like she has a board strapped to her spine, stops short of the group. *Matt must've told her what happened.* My aunts, Tera and Sheri, instantly cross the room to embrace her, new tears sliding down their cheeks. A few of my cousins follow suit.

Bertie's mouth flips over into a deep frown as they all hug Mom, pat her, tell her how much she's missed. My hackles raise. For a woman who reads the bible every morning and used to tell me "I'm all about love" Bertie looks like she could happily rip Mom's throat out. I step into her line of view and shoot her a glare. It took courage for my mother to come here, to stand beside her former family who she will never again have a true place amongst. We should all be rallying together in this dark hour, even those of us who do not like each other. I am not afraid to enforce that should anyone step out of line.

Bertie scowls, attention returning to her phone. Her hand clutches the golden cross around her neck and she mutters something under her breath that I can't hear.

I spot Matt sitting in the corner with his hood up, his Gameboy in hand. My brother is going through this late teenage stage where he wears a lot of black and hides behind electronics when stuck in busy social settings. I exit round one of Bertie Versus Elle and fold myself into the chair beside him.

"Hey, Bro. How are you? What's the latest scoop?"

He puts his Gameboy down, looks to a set of double doors on the left side of the room. "A blonde nurse with glasses came out ten minutes ago. She said he's stable but not enough, I guess. They still aren't letting anyone in to see him."

"Did you see him hit the U-Haul? You said the truck was backing out of the neighbor's driveway, right?" There hadn't been a lot of time to ask questions before the panic set in and I wanted off the phone so I could find a way home.

"No, but I heard it, so I got up and went outside. Dad had taken his motorbike out, showing off for Bertie's family. The bike was in pieces. There was blood on the road." Matt's expression remains neutral like it always does, but his hands quiver in his lap. "He had to have some sort of emergency surgery and a blood transfusion. Sounds like he broke several bones. I heard something about a wheelchair. If he makes it, they're not sure if he will walk again."

"Holy shit." Dad has always been a go-getter. To not be able to walk, to not work in his shop or drive his tractor would devastate him. He would've taken the U-Haul killing him over being put in a wheelchair.

An unusually tall man in scrubs and a white waistcoat pushes through the double doors. He walks toward my family, greeting my grandparents. Bertie jumps out of her seat and goes to join them, standing in front of my mother as if to block her from the situation.

"I think that's Dad's doctor," Matt mumbles. "I saw him earlier."

I rise from my chair. "Let's pray for some good news."

"We're going to keep him under anesthesia for a day or so, just to keep his stress levels down and protect his brain function," the doctor is saying as I approach. A lanyard around his neck is attached to a name card that reads *Dr. George Lawrence*. "We were able to get the bones to realign in his hip and pin those back in place. Looks like he knew he was going to hit the oncoming vehicle and tried to swerve, ultimately dropping the bike and skidding against the asphalt. He lost a lot of skin and a lot of blood. We did a skin graft from the top of his right hip to his knee, which was also dislocated."

The room starts to get fuzzy as Dr. Lawrence continues with his extensive list of injuries and corrections and long-term treatments and hints that suggest an entire lifestyle change for Jim Fox. The longer he talks the sicker I feel, and I can't decide if it's because of how upset I am over my father's injuries or the fact that I am upset. I always thought I would laugh when karma finally caught up with him, but now that karma has shot the fox who has been messing up the chicken coop it's no longer the chickens I feel sorry for.

"So when are we allowed to see him?" Grandma Johanna asks, pulling me back to reality.

"In a situation like this, once the patient has been stabilized we allow a handful of family members in. For now, it's best to limit it to a spouse and a couple of older children. For the sake of the patient, we can't allow more than that." Dr. Lawrence's big, brown eyes sweep all twenty heads. "Is everyone in this room part of the Fox family?"

Before anyone can speak, Bertie motions to my mother and loudly blurts, “She’s not.”

The Fox Family is not a confrontational bunch. In fact, they are the total opposite of confrontational and years can pass before someone brings up an unresolved issue. My mother and I have always tried to match this mentality, no matter how stirred over a subject we are.

I’m about to break twenty-three years of tradition as rage billows out of my pores. I take a step forward, toward this woman who in this moment has proven herself unworthy forever more of my mother’s stolen place, but someone grabs my arm. Mom firmly pulls me back as she prowls forward. She meets Bertie’s burning gaze with such icy coolness that the Devil himself would suppress a shiver. Bertie hardens her stance and clenches a fist at her side like she’s going to send somebody else to the ER.

Mom’s voice is quiet but dangerous as she says, “Then you *really* aren’t.” She points at her ring finger where a permanent indent circles her skin, left over from the three-stone ring she wore for more than twenty years. Her finger is bare now though not as bare as Bertie’s, which has never held a Fox ring.

Bertie is visibly vibrating. For a split second, I think she really might hit my mother but Johanna steps in, arms shooting up between them. “Enough,” she hisses. “We are all family here. End of story.”

It’s a glare off to see who will step down first. My mother holds steady, unblinking and unmoving. Bertie tries to match it, but her eyes start watering. Seeing her loss of composure and that none of the Foxes are going to back her up, she storms off in the direction of the women's restroom.

Dr. Lawrence clears his throat. "As I was saying, I know you all want to see him but in this state I can only allow a couple of people through. Perhaps his children would like to go in?"

My stomach jerks, and my brother sits up a little straighter in his chair. We exchange glances and in his eyes I spot the same insecurity I feel within. Neither of us is positive we can go into the ICU alone. Neither of is positive we want to go into the ICU at all.

My mother, still smoothing some frizzed hairs down, senses this. "Dr. Lawrence, these are my children and Jim's. I don't want them to face the ICU alone. They've never been in an ICU before. I want to go with them."

Dr. Lawrence observes the crowd. No one objects. "Alright. Follow me."

My brother and I slowly gather around Mom and she takes our hands as if we are still young. We follow Dr. Lawrence down a hallway lit by harsh white lights. The speckled tile has yellowed from age and more than one orange CAUTION sign marks where bodily fluids have been mopped up. Matt's nose wrinkles at the smell of bleach and rubbing alcohol clinging to the air. We pass a man and woman cradling each other, the woman sobbing into the man's shoulder. Mom's hand tightens around mine.

Dr. Lawrence stops at a recessed doorway with a golden plate above the handle: 2014. "Now just try to breathe and remember that he is unconscious but growing more stable," Dr. Lawrence says, but it doesn't comfort any of us. "We're keeping a close eye on him. Hopefully everything continues to go as smoothly as it can. I'll be at the desk at the end of the hall if you have any questions." The squeak of his shoes fades away.

None of us move to go in. We all stand there, aware that we're about to jump off the cliffs of our normal lives. Again. You'd think after a while we would get better at having to do this, as if handling trauma is an acquired skill much like learning to drive a car. It's not. I was scared to death last time and I'm just as scared this time. The fear shows on Mom's face even more so than on mine and Matt's.

We open the door.

Dad lays completely still, covered by white linen sheets. Various machines run lines to his body to transfer liquids and provide oxygen. Thick, gauzy bandages surround his head and a strip of bloody skin glares between the layers of wrap. He's missing some hair. Both of his eye sockets are deep purple, a sign of a broken nose, and his right cheek is sewn shut and swollen.

I barely recognize him.

Mom collapses at his bedside and sobs, hunching over his broken body. You would think a woman who endured so many lies, terrible deeds, and countless masks would hate the man who spoke them, committed them, wore them. As I stand back against the doorframe, however, I see a new unspoken truth: that inside the shambles of my mother's heart, despite her hatred for all his crimes committed both within and outside their marriage, she loves him still. My brother lumbers over and lays a hand on her back. His body is turned from me but I see his shoulders shake as they mourn together. Mourn this man who will never understand or appreciate or deserve the maddening, unconditional love they have for him. He doesn't deserve it. Not from them and not from me. *Especially not from me.* His lies, his deceptions, his violent tendencies when he loses control, his pushing the love of my life away from me...

Furious tears blur my vision. It isn't fair that we are all suffering for someone who deserves to suffer. Before they can notice, I slip back into the hallway. Dr. Lawrence does a double take as I speed by him and shove out the first exit I can find.

August 1st 2008

TAKE MY HAND

Salmon Shores Campground is alive with the rumble of RV engines, the dinging of bike bells, and the squeals of excited children.

Mom groans from the trailer, pulling the shade down over the window by the breakfast table as a large family of adults, kids, and dogs passes by. "Next time, I'm picking the campground and not your father," she growls into her coffee mug. "What is with everyone flocking to Oregon campgrounds anyway? It was never like this when I was a kid."

I'm not sure if she's looking for me to reply, so I stuff the rest of my English muffin in my mouth and take my plate to the sink. "I'm going to go find Dad."

"Don't get lost in the sea of animals and screaming children," Mom grumps.

An alpine breeze wafts through camp as I step out onto the bark chips. Pine and juniper surround our trailer in clusters thick as the summer tourists', their limbs waving at the world below. I inhale the scent of woodsmoke and adventures yet to be had.

Dad is sitting on our picnic table trying to show my brother how to string his fishing pole. Matt frowns at me as I approach, completely unenthused. "Here." He shoves it into my hands.

"Hey! You didn't even put the worm on it!" Dad calls as his son runs off to hide in the trailer with Mom. "He was doing fine. What's his problem?"

"He doesn't like slimy things." I eyeball the can of wiggling worms that Dad just bought from the store down the road. My brother also doesn't like people and he'd rather launch a fishing line via game controller versus in real life.

Dad sighs, shaking his head while pulling a hook from his tackle box. The box is rusting and the hooks inside are still wrapped in plastic and dust, purchased for a camping trip years prior that never happened. "I just don't get it, Elle. I put all this time and money aside for us to go have a good time and your mom and brother want to hide in the trailer. Kind of defeats the purpose of camping, doesn't it?"

"Well, you didn't really ask if they wanted to go camping." He sort of just told us that he'd booked the trip. There had not been any room for arguments, though Mom tried to pitch one anyway because Dad rarely ever puts time aside for family vacations and she would've liked to have had an input.

Dad scoffs. Gesturing to the fishing pole, he says, "I guess you'll be my star pupil then?"

I try not to look too eager as I nod. We never get to do

things like this.

"Alright, go put your boots on, Little Girl." Dad claps me on the back and stands up.

I follow him to the end of our loop, onto a narrow gravel path that takes us down through some berry groves and bike trails to the river. The sand is coarse and pebbly beneath my boots, not smooth and fine like my beloved coastal sand. People are already setting up umbrellas and chairs for their day by the water. We pass the family whose trailer is parked in the spot across from ours. Dad has already made friends with the man in the group and they both stop to shake hands. The man's son, a pretty, dark-haired boy named Zach, waves and comes over to offer me an Oreo. When we part ways, Dad hawk eyes the gangly youth. "A little old for you, isn't he?"

Blood rushes to my face. "No."

"What is he, sixteen?"

"Uh, yeah? And I'm fourteen so…"

A weird expression has taken over Dad's face. "You're not fourteen yet, are you?"

"Dad, seriously." I can't believe he's really asking and it's not just a sarcastic comment. He doesn't remember a lot of things outside of work, but he could at least remember how old his kids are.

Dad turns, navigating his way through the rocky tidepools near the end of the beach. He starts looking at me more than usual while demonstrating how to cast a fishing line into the water. It takes a couple of tries but I manage a decent throw, bobber landing in a calmer part of the river. We wedge our poles in between the rocks and I start checking the tidepools for agates and critters. Dad sits on a boulder nearby, sipping coffee from his canteen, still staring. "What's wrong?" I finally ask.

"Nothing." He shifts his gaze to the waterfall pouring down the slope across from us. "Time's just… going too fast. I swear it was just last year you guys were splashing around in the puddles at Uncle Tom's cabin, wearing nothing but diapers and duck boots." He pulls a hand over his mustache, which shines with its first strands of silver. "We should've done this more when you guys were kids. I should've been booking trips every year, taking you guys to Universal Studios and Disneyland. We could still do that next year. I can book it when we get back."

I chew my lip, not sure how to tell him that Disneyland was my dream two years ago. Now I'd rather be on a warm tropical beach with one of those colorful pineapple drinks in my hand.

"Just do me a favor and quit growing up so fast, will you? It's killing me. Pretty soon I'm going to blink and you'll be bringing home a husband and two kids of your own—then I'm *really* going to feel old."

"I don't know about that." I scrunch my nose, drawing in my fishing line. "Why does it bother you so much anyway?" He hasn't been this sentimentally strange since I was eleven and Mom went against all my wishes and told him I started my first period.

"How could it not bother me?"

"Because nothing seems to bother you?"

He huffs a laugh. "Lots of things bother me, like right now I really want a cheese sandwich and a root beer float but I don't think your mother packed the ice cream."

"It would've melted, and that's not what I'm talking about." I watch the hot red bobber on the end of my line float around in the river's current. "Dad, sometimes it's like, I don't know. Like you don't really care about anything or anybody." Except himself or things that affect his own wellbeing.

He picks at the algae growing on a limpet shell in the water. "Why is it that you and your mother constantly feel like I don't care about anyone?"

I shrug. He waits for me to explain and I don't want to. How is it that something so crystal clear to me is so cloudy to him? "You work like, every day of the week and we never get time with you."

"Who is going to pay for everything if I'm not working?" Dad retorts. "How do we afford food and your school and trips like this one?"

"I know that! I'm not saying you shouldn't work! I'm just saying that you don't even sit down for dinner with us when you come home."

"Well, I usually get home late. Do you guys want to eat at nine' o'clock at night?"

"No, but you're missing the point—"

"I suppose I could sell my shop and we could spend all that time together in poverty."

My hand tightens around the fishing pole. Now I understand why Mom says she never gets anywhere with him. "The least you could do," I mutter angrily, "is tell your family that you love them at the end of the day. You wouldn't even have to sell your shop or take us to Disneyland to do that."

When he doesn't say anything, I pop my rod out of the rocks and wander on down the bank. "Llewellyn," he calls but I ignore him, too busy trying to control the waterworks that are attempting to spill out of my eyes. He's hit a nerve by telling me he'd have to give up everything in order for him to spend time with us each day, yet he can stand and gab with people he's just met on the beach.

I climb up a huddle of large boulders, plopping down at the top to cast my line once more. *And now I'm ruining the one day I actually have with him*. That's my real heartbreak: I desperately wanted this to be a good day with my dad but he's so prone to pushing my buttons. Maybe this is the real reason he doesn't spend time with us. We finally get a weekend with him but we're so put off by all the other weekends and dinners and birthdays and holidays he's blown off that it's too easy for us to get emotional.

I'm still questioning if taking my brother's place on the beach was the right thing to do when Dad walks over. He stands at the base of my boulder, beneath my fishing line. "You're going to have a hard time catching anything from up there. Your line is too close to shore."

"You want it then?" I hold the pole down without taking my gaze off the river.

"No," he says calmly. "I want you to come down and go put your fishing pole back next to mine." He walks around to the narrow side of the rocks where I climbed up but I don't move. He heaves a sigh. "Elle."

"What?"

"I'm sorry."

"For what?"

"I'm sorry that I've made you think I don't care. I'm not good with sentimental shit—I mean, stuff. Sentimental *stuff*. Never have been. My siblings and I didn't grow up hearing our parents tell us they loved us every day."

"So you want us to have a relationship like your parents had with you?" I loved my grandparents, but Mom said Grandpa Lee had been in the military for the first part of his life. There were no hugs and kisses, no bedtime stories, no family movies nights. If Grandpa Lee's two young sons acted up, he'd take off his leather belt and beat them. If the boys ran crying to Grandma Johanna, she'd tell them to man up because they'd probably deserved it.

Dad gives one firm shake of the head. "No, which is why you need to crawl down from there so that we can go fishing, because my dad never took us fishing and I'm not going to have my daughter looking back ten years from now saying her dad didn't care enough to teach her things or take her places." He lifts his hands, motioning for me to come.

I relent and hand him my pole. He takes it in one hand but the other is still out. "I can get down by myself. I don't need help."

He doesn't withdraw. "I'm not going to watch you slip and crack your head open. Just take it." I scoff and roll my eyes, placing my palm on his while jumping down. He squeezes my fingers, which look like pale baby carrots in comparison to his scarred, oil-stained sausages. He holds my hand for a long moment. "Promise me something."

"What?"

"No matter how old you are, or how mad at me you feel, or how much you think I don't care—which you need to quit doing because I care a whole lot more than I say—promise me you'll always take your dad's hand when it's offered, okay?"

It seems like a weird thing to ask at first, but the more I think about it the more it makes sense. Dad has never been one for hugs and kisses, not even when I was little, but he always offers to hold our hands. "I promise."

"Good." We've just stepped away from the boulders when we see the line on his rod darting around in the water. "Oh, we've got one! Go, go!" He tugs on my hand. We run to get it before the fish retreats or takes the entire rod with it. He holds my arms as I grab it, instructing me when to reel and angle the pole. The trout weighs six pounds. He takes a horrible picture of me holding it, grinning too broadly with Oreo remnants in my teeth. I have no way of knowing that he is later going to frame and hang it over his company's front desk for the world to see.

I also have no way of knowing that it will be our first and last fishing trip as a family, and that we should've taken ten times more photos because, someday, memories will be all I have.

July 5th 2017

THE ONLY ONE

I wake with a gasp, laying in mush. The air reeks of sulfur and damp earth. My fingers twitch against the ground. The mush is grass and dirt. Water is falling from the ceiling. Wait—not a ceiling. Smoke and coils of clouds swirl above me and give it away: it's rain.

I am outside, on the ground.

Where am I? Where's the steak house? I'd escaped the hospital and wandered into a steak house some ways down the road. It had a comfortable, country-themed bar run by a cute bartender who kept giving me generous pours of wine. There might have been a few shots in there as well.

My head spins as I sit up. My limbs begin shivering with such ferocity I'm worried they're going to rattle themselves loose from their sockets. My jaw is doing the same. I'm so cold, yet so hot at the same time. Dark shapes on the hill below cause me to squeal, then I realize they aren't animals; they're gravestones.

I'm in a graveyard.

This is bad.

My shuddering hands pat around the grass for my purse or phone, but neither are here. *Shit*! My cell, my Visa, and my driver's license are all in that bag, sitting back in that bar or with God knows who. *What is wrong with you, Elle*?

The rain is growing from a drizzle to a heavy shower. My fingers latch onto the sharp marble ledge of a nearby grave marker and pull my body upright. My head whirls as I stand, stomach pitching. I throw up down the back of the gravestone and am reminded why I do not drink hard liquor: it burns even worse coming up than it did going down.

I need to get going but my forehead is pounding so hard it makes my vision swim. The shaking will not go away. *You got yourself into this—get yourself out*. I lift my leg, taking a step forward. It's like walking on two stiff boulders. My left foot keeps sinking into the cold, sloppy ground as I start down the hill. At some point during this evening's escapades, I tore my flipflop in half. *How does that even happen*?

A street runs perpendicular to the graveyard, one side running uphill to the woods, the other circling down into a trailer park. Nothing is familiar. *Did I walk here*? I nearly jump out of my tights as a loud bang rings through the night. The sky ignites with blue sparks. *It's still the Fourth of July*. That explains the lingering sulfur smell.

In the middle of the next street over, a familiar white blob glows in the dark, spilling its contents onto the asphalt. *My purse*! I try to run but thanks to my frozen muscles it's more like a fast-paced hobble. Tire tread marks the leather of my Dooney&Burke. The strap is busted and the inside is filled with chalky, gooey debris that were once expensive cosmetics and over-the-counter meds. My wallet is torn but somehow my driver's license and Visa have not been stolen. I swear under my breath, pulling out the sharp remains of my cell phone. Bits of plastic and shiny memory board fall apart in my hands. A slew of cusswords leaves my mouth. It was too much to hope that it'd been unharmed. Gathering the remnants, I peel my once prized possessions off the ground and toss them all into someone's garbage can on the curb.

A main roadway with streetlamps waits at the end of the trailer park. *Molalla Avenue*, I read on the green road plaque in the intersection. I know this road. I've driven it thousands of times and walked it a few dozen, though that doesn't bring me much comfort. I'm at least a forty-minute walk from the hospital. *I can't walk another forty minutes.* I'm not even sure I can walk ten, and finding a phone is going to be a challenge. Historic Oregon City is not one of those nocturnal adventure towns like Portland—its businesses are open from dawn until dusk and not the other way around. I start wandering down the lit street, watching for signs of life, and come to another familiar crossroad: Monroe.

My lease is up in a couple of weeks so I'm at my mom's.

It's a long shot to assume he's there, one I don't even want to take as I can barely stand to look at him much less ask for help. *Do you have a better idea, Elle*? I'm so cold I can hardly stand it and walking all the way home with a broken flipflop in the rain would be a fool's decision.

Fuck.

I guess we don't have to look at each other for him to call me a cab.

The old yellow house still has moss on its shingles. The blackberries, however, have been removed from the front of the yard and the wood-rotted fence beneath has been replaced with a classic white picket. Scott's mom's old Chevy Malibu is parked on the curb, a faded daisy sticker still clinging to the tailgate that reads, *Life is Good.*

And parked in the driveway in front of the garage is Scott's black Tacoma.

I'm flooded with an equal amount of relief and dread. Scott's bedroom used to be on the bottom floor on the south side, and I'm taking a huge risk by believing he would've moved back into the same one. I clamber over a pile of crap that looks like old wood—probably the old fence—wedged between the side of the house and the garage. I'm pulling my leg through the debris when a knife-like pain slices across my calf. A gasp escapes my lips. *Oh no.* Caught up in panic, I jerk myself through the rest of the junk pile and trip on my half flipflop. I go sprawling across the backyard.

The porch light flicks on.

I scramble backwards until my head hits the garage, just out of the light's reach. The *thunk* against the wall makes my vision spin again. *Uh oh.* Closing my eyes, I hope to prevent the second wave of nausea by not watching the world tip, but I don't succeed. I fertilize the pansy garden with a mix of stomach acid, wine, and tequila.

I have never felt more defeated, more humiliated, more *sick*. I try to pump myself up but really it'd be easier to just curl under the eaves of the garage and succumb to my fate. *What have I become*? *How did I let myself get to this point*? I can blame it on Dad. I can blame it on Scott or Kacey or just the general shittiness that sometimes comes with being alive, but at the end of the day none of those people made me walk into a bar and get blackout drunk. None of those people put me in a cemetery or forced me to sabotage a stranger's truck. I made those choices. It's all on me.

This is not who I am.

If I'm going to be defeated by life then so be it, but I'm dying in my own house. Worried that I'll set off nausea wave three, I crawl across the grass and onto the cement patio, passing the sliding glass doors that lead into the living room. Scott's mom still has all her old leather furniture, but a new, colorful rug covers the carpet. A flatscreen TV has been mounted to the wall and has bubbles floating across it, on screensaver mode. I'm about to crawl on toward what I hope is Scott's window when I notice a casted hand hanging over the arm of the recliner.

Scott is asleep in the front room.

Yes. I grip the door handle and drag myself upright, muscles rebelling all the way. I smooth my shirt down—why am I smoothing my shirt? Nothing is going to make this look better—then curl my hand into a fist.

I knock.

Scott looks over at the doors, lazily at first, then shoots

straight up in his chair.

I wave. Well, more like vibrate.

He doesn't come to the door. His shadow disappears into the hallway, fumbling around near the coat closet. When he comes back he is no longer shuffling but striding, and a baseball bat is clenched in his hands. He flicks open the lock and cracks the back door.

I step back. "Y—you're really g-gonna hit me w—with that?" My voice is broken, ruined by this uncontrollable shuddering, but I manage to sound unimpressed.

The bat falls to the carpet. "*Elle*?" His eyes go wide as saucers. He shoves the sliding door open, looking me up and down. "What the—what happened to you?"

The horror on his face and in his voice are wounding. I must look even worse than I feel. My lips part to offer another sarcastic comment, something to break the complete awkwardness and embarrassment of this situation, but my brain is glazed and my jaw is chattering too hard.

Scott pulls a hand through his hair. "Come on." He folds his arm around my shoulders and pulls me inside before I can tell him I just need a ride. His eyes roam the yard suspiciously before closing the door.

The house smells like mothballs and tobacco, just as it always has. He whips the Seattle Seahawks blanket out of his chair and bundles me in it. "W-will you c-call me an Uber or a c-cab? I don—have my—phone." I hate how small and pathetic I sound. I hate that I'm asking and that I'm here at all. This is suddenly looking like the wrong decision. Perhaps crawling all the way home down the street wouldn't have been as humiliating as this.

Scott huffs incredulously. "Not a chance." His eyes dart to the tiled part of the floor, to the pool of blood and water forming at my feet. "You're bleeding. Why are you soaking wet and bleeding? What is going on?"

"Doesn't m-matter." Hot. This blanket is too hot. Beneath the rainwater that saturates my clothes, I swear I'm sweating. "Look, I-I just need to g-go home. I w-will pay you to c-call me an U-Uber." Except all the cash was missing from my wallet when I found it and it's hard to say whether that's because someone stole it or I was feeling rich and threw it like confetti across the bar. Both are possible.

"*Doesn't matter*? Seriously?" Scott reaches out to touch my arm then jerks his hand back. "You're cold as ice. How long have you been outside like this?"

I don't know.

"You can't stay cold like this. Come on." He starts to cross the living room. I follow but not very gracefully or fast. There must be something in my movements that is alarming to him because suddenly he comes back, pulls me against him and sweeps his arm under my legs. I'm carried into the bathroom and set on the side of the tub. He turns on the shower.

"We're g-going to w-wake your mom." Water pounds loudly into the tub, the sound beating against my ear drums. I catch a glimpse of myself in the mirror by the sink and jump. The girl staring back at me is gaunt and hollow-eyed, all her makeup washed away. A red egg has emerged on her forehead. Between that and the torn flipflop I am beginning to wonder if I sat down and passed out against that gravestone or if I tripped and knocked myself out. Bits of twig and other tree debris are tangled in my locks, dark grass stains mar my sweater and jeans. A trail of blood snakes across the floor to where I'm sitting.

"My mom is in Arizona." Scott's mouth presses into a thin line as he looks at my reflection in the mirror. A collection of hard lines has settled on his face. Wet, red stains dampen the sleeves of his AC/DC sweatshirt from where he carried me but he doesn't seem to care.

"Scott, I d-don't need you to—"

"Take off your flipflops." He does a double take at my feet, sees that one of them isn't whole. I don't have the strength to rebel so I kick them off. He picks them up and launches them into a trash bin without asking. "Give me the blanket. Lift your arms. You can't stay in those wet clothes." I sit there like a stump. "Elle."

I release a frustrated noise, forcing my frozen fingers to grip the hem of my sweater. He is *not* going to help me take these clothes off—I refuse to be that helpless. The sweater is heavy with moisture and takes more effort than it should to pull over my head. I thrust it down and it splats loudly against the floor. Peeling my pants off is an equal challenge.

Scott squats down to examine the cut on my leg. It's long but not deep. "Where did this come from?"

"Your j-junk pile against the house. I'll p-probably need a

tetanus shot."

"By the garage? Nah, it's all wood and plastic piping. My mom tore out the do-it-yourself sprinkler system my dad rigged up years ago. You probably caught yourself on one of the broken pipes." He pulls a bottle of Bactine from the cabinet behind the mirror. Sitting on the floor, he soaks down a washcloth and presses it to the wound. My leg stings and I gasp, trying to jerk it away, but he holds it in place.

The shower water also stings. I crawl into the bottom of the tub and lay there, getting pelted by razor droplets. Dirt and debris swirl into the drain, forming tiny whirlpools beneath my feet. Scott has disappeared with my clothes, which have left muddy stains on his mother's new flooring. The floor in here used to be tile, robin's egg blue to match the trim around the mirror, but now it's faux wood that reminds me too much of the cabins Scott and I used to rent together. The only nice thing about being this sick and numb is the memories don't hurt so much.

He comes back with another band sweatshirt and lays it on the counter. It would be great if he would just leave and let my suffering continue in private but instead he sits down beside the tub and locks his hands around his knees. "Did someone do this to you?"

"No."

"So you just, what, fell down the stairs in the rain?"

It's probably because I am so tired, but his question summons a small laugh out of me. "Not exactly."

Several minutes pass where we say nothing and the only sound in the room is the shower running. Water begins to gather in the bottom of the tub and lap against my thighs. Circulation buzzes back into my limbs. I rinse the acidic residue off my teeth then scrub at the patches of dirt on my feet. The shivers have finally slowed to a manageable state.

Scott's nose twitches, eyes suddenly lighting up. "You smell like a winery." I don't respond. "You blacked out, didn't you? Is that why you were out in the rain?"

I hate how he still, after all this time, can read me like an open book.

"Did you just party too hard or did something happen? Knowing you, I have to assume that something really bad occurred to make you want—"

"Just *stop*." I throw my hand up. "Can I have a towel please?"

He pulls a clean one from the linen cupboard. I turn off the shower then squeeze the excess water from my bra. He at least offers me the privacy to dry off alone. I pick up the spare sweatshirt from the counter and reluctantly throw it over my head. The material is nubbly, rough from years of wear, and carries the aroma of cigarettes and Tide detergent. The sleeves engulf my hands, hem sliding over my thighs. He's also left a pair of sweatpants but they're too long for me and pose another tripping threat. I leave them on the counter.

He's sitting on the couch in the living room when I step out, rubbing a tattooed finger across his chin. "Will you please call a cab for me *now*?" I emphasis the last word like this has been a real inconvenience.

He drags a hand over his face, then heads for the front door. "Get in the truck."

His flipflops are three sizes too big for me and they slap like duck feet across the flooded lawn as I head to the Tacoma. We rumble into my driveway fifteen minutes later and the porch light flicks on to greet us. He parks beside my car and cuts the engine, admiring my property. My four-hundred square-foot house on a quarter acre is probably a shocker compared to my family's former three-thousand square foot farmhouse on ten acres. A cacophony of wild barking resonates inside the walls. Piglet pops her head through the living room curtains, sitting on the back of the couch.

The sight of Piglet sparks a smile on Scott's face, but it disappears quickly. "Elle?"

"Hmm?" The truck's heat is blasting and I've gotten comfortable in my seat, wrapped up in the Seahawks blanket. I could fall asleep right here, right now.

He gives me a look that is annoyingly like the one my father used to give me as a teenager. It's an I-need-to-know-and-you-need-tell-me type of expression. "What happened tonight?"

His words even summon an emotional response in me like my father's used to, like he's wide open and I could tell him anything in the world. I choke down the lump in my throat. "He's dying."

"Who's dying?"

"Dad." Maybe I'm being overly dramatic but even if he does escape the clutches of the grim reaper after this one, some part of him is gone. I saw it in that hospital room.

"Oh," Scott says, shocked. "What happened?"

I roll my eyes. "He was showing off, drove his motorbike into a U-Haul."

"Damn." He reaches across the console to take my hand. "I'm sorry, Elle. I know how hard it is to—"

I pull my hand away. "Don't be." No one should be sorry for Jim Fox, Scott least of all. The thing to be sorry for is his family, who never lived up to his expectations yet were all there for him tonight, heartbroken at his bedside. He wouldn't have appreciated it if he had been conscious. He wouldn't have come if the situation had been reversed and it were my mother in that hospital bed. I unbuckle my seatbelt and get out of the truck. "Thanks for taking care of me. Sorry I intruded on your night. Again,"—*and in one of the worst ways possible*—"I promise this will be the last time you have to endure me."

He glances at my empty seat, the space I've put between us. "It shouldn't be this way."

"And yet, it is."

"This is over the Kacey thing, isn't it? Would it help if I told you I was too drunk to remember? Because that's the truth."

In comparison to the horrifying events that occurred this evening, the situation with Kacey should seem less significant. Unfortunately, it doesn't, for I am an excellent grudge-holder. "How would you feel if I screwed your best friend?"

He winces like I physically hit him, then drops his head to the steering wheel. "Like shit," he drawls.

The rain is soaking through his borrowed sweatshirt and I'm starting to shiver again. "Goodnight, Scott." I shut the door then plod barefoot to the porch, leaving his oversized flipflops in the truck. They would've slowed me down and I'm too anxious to get away. Besides the growing patches of ivy, my deck is also home to a pair of matching planter pots, each packed with a variety of succulents that are usually floral-shop gorgeous when not half-drowned by a summer storm. I'm unearthing my spare house key from beneath some drooping hens-and-chicks when I hear his truck door shut. Scott jogs through the rain and up the steps. He stops abruptly in front of me, holding his arm out. Something small and black is clutched between his fingers. "What is that?"

"I don't think you took a close enough look at this when you were snooping through my stuff." He shakes it at me.

My heart jolts as I realize what it is. "I don't have the energy for this right now."

He opens the velvet box and pulls out the five-stone ring. "There. I just did half the work for you. Now will you please read the engraving?"

The ring glares at me, diamonds scintillating like clusters of stars beneath my porch light. I heave a frustrated sigh and pluck it from his fingers. *This thing is what started all the trouble.* I've been trying to not think about the ring, not think about what it would've looked like on my finger or what my life would be like today if I had known about it sooner. Words I had noticed previously but hadn't bothered to read are etched into the metal, taking up the inside of the shank.

To my marvel-worthy motion — S.D & E.F

"I'm not perfect, Elle. I'm human," Scott says. "I've made poor choices, drunk choices, choices I wish I could take back same as you, same as everyone. You were *not* one of those regrettable choices.

"I've shared my bed with plenty of women. What I haven't shared is trips to the mountains with them, or hikes in the Gorge. I haven't shared my clothes with them, or my dreams, or my deepest thoughts." He takes another step across the porch, leaving inches between us, raising a finger. "*You* were the only one who had those things, the only one who had *me*. Trust me when I say that is a far more intimate thing to give. So stop looking at me like I'm a traitor. Everything I said to you yesterday was true, and that kiss in Noah's driveway..." He doesn't finish. He doesn't have to—despite his frustration, the longing is still clear in his gaze.

It's still in mine, too.

Most people hit a certain point where their hearts have bled so much in a short period of time there isn't any more blood to spare but mine always seems to find a way. I bite down on my lip. *Marvel-worthy motion.* It's what I said to him on Thunder Island when he asked for my thoughts on the world, the very sentence that broke down the wall he kept between us.

Now he's breaking down my wall, and I'm terrified.

He steps away to look at the pond forming in my yard. The downspouts on the house are spewing rainwater so hard they look ready to fly off. He rubs the back of his neck. "Is that your house key?" He gestures to my hand. I nod. "You have a roommate or someone who can keep an eye on you tonight?"

"No." Just because my mother is next door doesn't mean I'm ready to call her. *Oh, boy, Mom.* She's probably awake right now, worried and wondering where I am. The moment I plunked myself down on that barstool in the steakhouse I had turned my phone off.

"You live by yourself?" He sounds surprised, then again not many people can afford to live alone in Portland.

"No. Don't you hear the ruckus?" I wave at the cacophony of barking beyond the front door. It's mostly Dobby now. Piglet has gone silent, frozen to the back of the couch like a gargoyle staring through the drapes. Her hackles are like patches of spring grass, pointed straight at the sky.

Scott shifts on his feet, glances at his truck. "Well, I doubt they can dial nine-one-one. I don't think you should be alone after having signs of hypothermia."

Hypothermia. Count on me to be the one person who ends up hypothermic in the middle of summer. "So are you staying then?" It's not really an apology but it's something. It's also late and the dark grooves beneath both our eyes are getting deeper.

His brows perk, surprised. "Um."

I unlock the front door and leave it open. He stands outside for a moment, then slowly follows.

Dobby and Piglet blaze around the front room like two knights defending their castle, noses coming to attack Scott's feet. "She's gotten big," he says, bending down to look at Piglet. "She looks just like her mom. Ouch!" He jerks his leg back, getting bit in the toe.

"No, Cheerio was nine pounds. She's barely six." A ceramic bowl that I bought from an art show last fall sits on a table near the door. I lay my key—and the ring—together inside it. "She was the runt, remember?"

"You'd never know it." Scott glances at his ring, shimmering in the bowl, but doesn't take it. He sits on the floor of the living room where Pig is growling. Most dogs tuck their tails to their butts when they're panicked but mine is weird and curls hers over her back like a scorpion. He clicks at her like he used to when she was a pup and offers her his hands, which are reluctantly sniffed.

I walk around my bar, the only structure separating the kitchen from the living room and pull a glass from the cupboard. Dobby is perched on my shoulder, staring unblinkingly at our intruder while I fill the glass with water. "Do you want a cup of coffee or something?"

He shakes his head. His eyes roam my house, taking in the yellow popcorn ceiling, the faded vinyl floors. His gaze stops on a bookcase in the nook, which had originally been designed for a breakfast table. He gets up and wanders over to it. "Did you ever publish your work?"

"No." My reply is gloomy, implying that he'd better not start another emotional discussion this late at night. Dobby fusses in my arms so I set him down. He trots over to Scott and Piglet growls at him. Pig's memory must've jogged because she's pressed up against his leg, flashing fangs at her brother. The new human is hers and hers only.

"You should." Scott bends down to scratch Piglet's head and notices one of my old journals. Pulling it free, he starts flipping pages. "You were a good writer."

I'm flattered that he thinks so. "Someday." *If I can pull my shit together long enough to focus.* I chug down the last of my water then stick the glass in the sink. Leaving Scott to rummage through my old work, I wander into the bathroom and brush my teeth. Dobby follows, guarding the door. My face has a little more color when I look in the mirror this time but the bump on my head is now a hill instead of a hump and has turned a dirty shade of lavender. By the time I come out, Scott has disappeared from the living room. A wave of disappointment washes over me at the idea that he just got up and left. Dobby emits a single, shrill bark and darts into the bedroom. My desk lamp has been turned on.

Scott is staring at my bedroom wall. Tiny canvas prints are mounted from floor to ceiling by my bed, each containing a different picture of a place I've gone or want to go to. "So how many of these places have you made it to?" There's a roughness to his tone, like he's bothered I've traveled without him.

"Very few." I turn down the sheets and crawl into bed. My fleece-lined comforter gets pulled up to my neck and I sigh in relief. I've never been so glad to be in my house, on my own mattress. "When we broke up, the brave girl I was went with you. I haven't wanted to travel much since." I kept hoping that by putting up a wall of dreams and memories I would get the urge back, but it's been slow. I shouldn't need another person to make me want to travel, but part of the joy of adventuring is having someone there who loves it as much as you do.

He gives me a meaningful glance then pulls one of the canvases off the wall. It's a picture of sunset over the rocky hills of Salmon Shores Campground. "Isn't this the big campground on the way to the Gorge?"

"The one that burned? Yeah." Salmon Shores, as well as most of my memories of the place, disintegrated years ago. A forest fire swept through the woodlands and took out half the camping area. "That picture is really old." Equally old is the picture next to it of me standing on the riverbank, holding a fishing pole.

Scott puts the picture back then picks up another one with a big, silver bridge. A smile tugs at his mouth, thumb running across the structure that watches over Cascade Locks. "I haven't been here since you and I were together."

"I haven't been to any part of the Gorge." It wasn't for lack of trying, either, but every time I started to make the drive I worked myself up and turned around. Between losing him and losing my family, my life is full of places and destinations I can no longer return to. It's no wonder I want to hide out at home all the time.

He purses his lips, sitting down on the bed. He waits for

me to object to this closeness, but I offer him a pillow. It feels more like I'm offering a truce. Pulling it under his head, he gets comfortable beside me. "If we got up tomorrow and left everything behind, which of these places would we go to?"

I hum, looking at my collection of deserts, oceans, and snow-covered mountain trails. "Antelope Canyon." I point to the beautiful, wind-worn tunnels of red rock near the center of my wall. "And Vermillion Cliffs afterward." A portrait of blue sky overlooking incredible wave formations of scarlet and vanilla hangs next to the canyon.

He grins from ear to ear. "And after that?"

"What do you mean?"

"We're going to Antelope Canyon and Vermillion Cliffs, and then where?" His eyes shimmer with mischief and anticipation, like this is a real plan we're setting.

This is what I missed the most: how he could make me believe that tomorrow held something amazing amidst the fear, chaos, and boring normality of everyday life. *Wherever the hell we want,* I used to say. He was supposed to take me to Australia for my twenty-first birthday. We had planned to swim in the Great Barrier Reef and walk the arid grounds of the outback. We were going to rent one of those glass cabins in the Netherlands and watch the Northern Lights dance across our ceiling. We were supposed to taste true Italian pizza in Italy and touch the rocks of Stonehenge and laugh and love and spend our painfully short lives experiencing the world and each other.

I hate being apart.

I'm still mad about him and Kacey—I might always be mad about it—but I slide closer anyway, resting my knees against his thigh, my head on his arm. He brushes a tangle of hair off my forehead. "You're confusing as hell, do you know that?" He mutters.

"Yeah." Heat radiates from where he lays on the bed, soothing my chilled, clammy skin.

He lifts his arm and pulls my pillow toward his chest. He folds me into his side, as close as I can get without being on top of him. My limbs soften at his closeness, his warmth. "Why are you so intent on pushing me away?" He asks. "Do you really believe I meant to hurt you?"

"No. But do you have any idea what it is like to love someone so much and have them stop loving you?" I whisper. "Like you are suddenly a stranger, no more important to their life than a passerby on the streets. It doesn't matter if you were their lover or their best friend or their child. Do you know what a mindfuck that is, how hard it is to want to love somebody knowing that could happen again?"

Rain is pattering lightly against my window, the downpour finally slowing. Piglet and Dobby have curled up together in their dog bed against the wall, half buried in blankets. Scott is quiet for a long time. His thumb is brushing softly over my arm and the sweatshirt I borrowed. I don't realize I've dozed off until he lifts the blankets, sliding in beside me. He rolls me onto my side, spooning his legs behind mine. His breath ruffles the hairs on the back of my neck. "For the record," he whispers, "I don't think I ever stopped loving you."

July 5th 2017

ONLY HUMAN

I wake up because of the pressure on my chest. Piglet is draped over my neck like a scarf and is pushing her head into my cheek, her morning greeting since puppyhood. Dobby expels a pitiful cry, like his whole world is crashing down because she's lying across my windpipe and he's not. I push them both away, hand slapping down on the rumpled blankets beside me. The sheets are cold and empty.

He left? Discomfort rains over me like a shower of needles. I throw the sheets back and get up, stumbling out of the room. He isn't in the kitchen or the living area and his grandmother's diamond ring is missing from the bowl by the door. Piglet leaps onto the back of the couch, gargoyling out the window at the empty patch of pavement where his truck should be. *How could he leave without saying goodbye*? I should've seen this coming. It's not like last night was some beautiful reconnection worth staying for. *You wouldn't have stayed for you either, Elle, you damn train wreck.*

I float numbly onto a bar stool. A notebook that I haven't

used in weeks is lying open on the kitchen counter.

Duty calls. Sorry I couldn't stay.

For your new cell phone, in case you forgot:

730-6695

No blackouts today. You've got this.

Piglet lets out a piercing bark and wags her tail, focused on something across the yard. I figure it's a squirrel until the sound of flipflops slapping against stone grows louder outside.

The front door swings open. Mom exhales a breath that sounds like she hasn't breathed since yesterday. Her face is tissue-paper white and the dark circles below her eyes could eclipse the sun. "Sweet Jesus, *there* you are!" She's relieved. And livid. "What the fuck, Llewelyn? Do you not know how to answer your phone? I've been looking for you all night!"

My lips part to make up an excuse but I can't. My head hurts and I hate lying to my mother, but how do you sugarcoat a night like mine?

She watches me flounder. Her eyes scroll up and down my figure, as if scanning for anything that would clue her in to what I had done, where I had gone, whose car carried me home. "You look like hell. Is this just going to be a new thing with you?"

"What are you talking about?"

"You know exactly what I'm talking about," she roars. "I am your *mother*! There ain't shit that happens between this house and mine that I don't know about, like how your porch collection of wine bottles grows with every emotional meltdown you have! And don't think I didn't see that boy leave your house this morning!"

Crap. "You did?"

"You bet your drunken ass I did! What bar stool did this one come off?"

"Jeez, Mom!" I can't believe she thinks my standards have sunk to barstool level, though I suppose I myself am not much above that these days. She hadn't seen 'that boy' very closely then.

"The Elle I knew never did this—this whole running off with a boy during family emergencies garbage! A boy she doesn't even have the decency to introduce to her own mother —"

"Mom, it was Scott Darcy!"

Her rant comes to a screeching halt. "W—what did you just say?"

"I said it was Scott Darcy. You remember, tall, dark-haired, tattooed love of my life? The one Dad *fired* and sent away because apparently he wasn't good enough for me?"

I might as well have slapped my mother upside the head with a frying pan. She just stands there, stunned. My mouth trembles because we never fight like this and I hate it, but I'm not going to back down. Not when I see in her eyes something I didn't think about before.

"You knew," I realize, the shock running through me like

a bolt of electricity. "You *knew*, didn't you? That he wanted to marry me so Dad got rid of him?"

Mom lays her face in her hands. "This is *not* the time for this conversation." Her voice is a low snarl. "You were eighteen. What kind of parents would we have been to allow such a thing?"

"So you both agreed to get him out of my life?" Her betrayal cuts so much deeper than Dad's. At least I knew to expect crummy behavior on his end but for my own mother, who I trusted more than any person on the planet… I can barely contain the swirl of swear words on my tongue.

"I did not agree to *that*." She points a warning finger, like I don't dare accuse her. "What I agreed on was that you two needed some space from each other long enough to consider your future—"

"Yet you never told me. Never, not even after he was gone." That's the part I'm angriest about. "I don't care how much you both hated him—you are my *mother*. You above all people in this screwed up family should've told me!" I understand, of course, why she didn't: it was a toss-up between allowing me to hate Scott or making me hate my father, and blood runs thicker than water in her book.

"He was a cheating shmuck! You deserved better than that inked up hood rat—you *still* deserve better, Llewellyn! How is he even back in your life? Of course he's going to show up *now* when the last thing we need is another problem!"

"He might be exactly what I need right now, thank you very much, and he didn't cheat on me," I billow back. "And you want to talk about taste in men? Look at you, woman who wept at Jim's bedside after everything he's pulled, after he replaced you with horrid Bertie, after he shoved your kid down the basement steps!" I pinch the back of one of my arms, jiggling the scarred, white flesh at her.

My mother has only ever looked at me in true disgust one time before this—when I was twelve and stole money out of her wallet because some shady friends of mine at the time told me to. She didn't trust me to hold or watch her purse for a year after that.

I would've taken that all over again if it meant not having to endure the look I'm getting now; her expression is almost animalistic, the kind that reminds me how some wild creatures eat their young. I wait for her to scream, behead me, do something.

She does the worst thing of all: she turns away, silent, and walks out the front door.

I collapse on a kitchen stool. I don't know how many minutes or hours pass, but it must be a long while because the sun is fully overhead by the time I find the strength to rise. I end up back in the shower, like I can rinse this fight off the way I washed the dirt and grass away from the graveyard, but both experiences have left permanent stains. I put on a pair of clean leggings but keep Scott's oversized sweatshirt on. Carrying a piece of him with me today feels important. While dabbing makeup over the ugly bump on my head, I practice what I'm going to say to Mom. I can't leave it like this, despite how upsetting it is to know she kept a big truth from me.

Her car isn't in the driveway when I finally gather the courage to go to her house. I'm wondering if she'll pick up her phone if I call, then remember I no longer have a phone. Or a purse. I'm not even sure I have all of myself.

What would an emotionally stable person do right now? I return to my house and pull a cardboard box out of the pantry, then start opening my cupboards. At first glance, my shelves are filled with soups and spices and other dry goods but at closer inspection it is clear I am more Betty Ford than Betty Crocker—an assortment of unopened wine bottles are scattered throughout the kitchen. I take every bottle out and put it in the box, then drop it next door with my neighbor, Mrs. Marigold, who is elated to have a month's worth of afternoon wine ventures paid for. It won't stop me from buying another round should something terrible happen but getting rid of it all feels like a start.

I feed the dogs a generous breakfast then dig out an old Coach handbag to replace my deceased Dooney. Peeking over at Mom's driveway—she's still not home—I jump in my Suzuki and head to the phone store where I spend an hour with an annoying salesgirl who keeps trying to upsell me with gadgets and tablets and doesn't seem to comprehend that I. Just. Want. A. *Phone.*

Mom is still not back when I come home but there is a white Subaru in my driveway and a blonde head standing behind it. Kacey stiffens as I pull in, a hand on her car's open hatch. My makeup bag and one of my hoodies is clutched in her other.

I squeeze my steering wheel, debating whether I'm going to get out of my car. When I continue to sit there, she slowly walks up to my driver side door. I roll down the window. "You left these." She extends them. "I thought you might want them back."

"Thanks." I set them in the passenger seat. I'm having a hard time looking at her. "Why aren't you at the beach?"

"It was time to come home." She shrugs, then starts picking at her nails. It dawns on me that her blingy ring isn't on her finger and her eyes are puffier now than when I left Bea's. "I, um, I told Dustin about what happened with Scott. I want you to know I came clean with him, too."

Now I'm looking at her. "What did he say?"

Her lip twitches, eyes turning instantly glassy. "He said he needed some space."

Of course he did. I wonder who took the news worse: me or the engaged man—formerly engaged. I release a heavy sigh, then reluctantly push my door open and get out of the car. I wrap my arms around her fragile shoulders and let her quietly sob against me. "I'm sorry." Despite the fury still simmering in my veins, I mean it.

"Not as sorry as I am," she whimpers. "I would take it back if I could, Elly, I swear. I never meant to hurt you or Dustin and Scott didn't, either. We were being stupid and mad at the world."

You think you *were mad at the world.* At least she didn't wake up in a graveyard at one in the morning. I think about

Scott standing on my porch, how that diamond ring glittered in my porch lights last night. "We're human, Kacey. We make poor choices, angry choices, drunk choices. What we have to decide is if we're going to learn from them and move on."

She lets go of me. "I understand if you can't move on with me but know that I didn't invite you to the beach for the purpose of making myself feel better. I invited you because you and Rena are two of my longest running friends and I wanted that time with you."

"I believe you." My gaze drifts to the Subaru. I spot Rena's figure shifting in the passenger seat. "How mad at me is she?" Kacey grits her teeth. "That bad, huh?"

"Well, I've never seen her just stop talking about someone like they never existed."

"Great."

"Give her time. She'll come around."

I start walking to the passenger side. "I don't have time."

Rena sees me coming in the side mirror and locks her door. She pretends to be engrossed in her Pinterest app and is scrolling through boards of gourmet food while I stand at her window. "I'm sorry, Re," I say to the glass. "Truly, deeply sorry. It was a fowl, horrible thing to say. I regretted it the second it came out."

"Go tell it to your slut of an ex," she says, keeping focused on her screen. "I'm sure he'll make you feel better about it."

"I don't need him to make me feel better about anything." Honestly, between him, them, and my mother, I've never felt lousier about myself. "What do I need to do to make it up to you?"

"Nothing. We're over, remember?" She slices her arm through the air just like I did in the restaurant.

Ouch. This might be harder than I thought. My eyes must be "flickering", as my mother would say, because Kacey comes over and tugs on my arm. I let her, not wanting that flicker to burst into a flame and snowball the very situation I'm trying to undo. "You're right. She's mad as fuck," I mumble after we step away from the Subaru.

"I'm sorry, Elle." Kacey glances over her shoulder at the car, at Rena shaking her head. "Sometimes we just have to wait until the other person is ready to talk."

"I hate the waiting game." Waiting only allows people time to stew in their own emotions. The longer it remains unspoken of, the harder it's going to be to sort out. My stomach rolls as I suddenly envision my dad, the emblazed yet desperate look on his face at The Elanza. *Can't you sit down for five minutes and talk to me*?

"I should probably get going." Kacey glances at her Fitbit. "Rena's car got a flat tire on the drive home and we have to go pick it up from the shop. What are you doing later? Hey—oh, God, how's your dad? Nana told me why you left so fast!"

"He's… it's not good." I quickly change the subject. "Anyway, I need to get going, too. I'm trying to find my mom."

"Your mom?" Kacey's brows knit together. "Well, isn't she out hiking?"

"Hiking?"

"Yeah." She whips out her phone and pulls up Instagram. "I mean, I assumed she was hiking." She shows me her screen.

Mom's Instagram profile flashes a new post, a large white trillium flower next to a smaller bud that hasn't opened yet. The shot has been taken at an angle, the terrain behind it green and mossy. A waterfall pours down a hilly embankment with a maple tree growing beside it, some sort of large nest in its branches.

I know exactly where she is.

"How long ago did she post that?" I ask.

Kacey shrugs. "About an hour ago?"

It's a long shot to think I'm going to make it there before she leaves as it's a forty-minute drive, but I can't bear to just stand here and wait. "I have to go. I'm sorry." I pat Kacey's shoulder then race back to my car.

"Hey," Kacey calls as I fling my driver side door open. "Are we okay?"

I wish it were that easy. "We're better."

The 205 freeway is busy this time of day, but luckily traffic thins out when I hit the east-bound roads. Nearly an hour later, I turn off on a dusty drive surrounded by old pine and juniper. A large parking lot near the front is roped off, surrounding trees logged and burnt. An old, carved sign, scorched black on one side, still reads: **Salmon Shores**.

At the end of the drive, a square patch of asphalt appears

seemingly in the middle of nowhere. I park and get out of the car, alpine air and the aroma of bark dust instantly transporting me back to the summer I was fourteen. I do a quick sweep of the parking lot, looking for Mom's Mustang. My heart jumps at a bright blue dot nestled amongst a series of white and silver sedans. *She's still here.* But where?

The main pathway has been paved since I was here and is swarming with families, joggers, and bicyclists. I veer off on a lesser-known side trail. Mom wouldn't take the road most traveled. Bark chips crunch below my feet as I admire the wildflowers, the moss, the mushrooms peeking out from carpets of fallen pine needles. The trees are bigger now but still creak and moan the same way, waving their limbs in unison like people at a concert.

My hangover headache begins to wane the longer I walk. The stiffness in my shoulders disappears as I breathe in all the rich, wild smells. Returning to places like this one had felt daunting before last night, but now that I'm here I am more soothed than distressed. This isn't just the place where my family had a surprisingly good camping trip; it is where I first felt excited about what my life could be and the adventures that could be had. It is the first place where I picked up on the energy of the land, felt its ancient magic that made me believe I am an eternal piece of everything that was and will be.

I stop walking. Closing my eyes, I do something that I am not very familiar with: I pray. *Please take me to my mother. It's important.* I open my eyes and start walking again, following the trickling sound of river water.

Shores Campground Store—the one where Dad bought the worms for fishing—is charred, covered in yellow tape and KEEP OUT signs. Much of its surrounding foliage has been cut down and removed. I cross the cobblestone path that leads up to the bathrooms, the same ones whose showers ran either icy cold or piping hot. A gentle slope runs behind the restrooms, grass fading away to a mix of mud and sand.

I step onto the pebbly beach. Unlike the rest of the park, the river has remained the same, weaving lazily between beaches and cliffsides, glittering in the sun. The sky is clear after last night's storm though still unexpectedly cool for July. The temperature has cut the number of picnic blankets and camp chairs in half, though I'm still forced to weave through a dozen groups of them to get to the water. I peer through a throng of teenagers playing ball and a group of gossiping women sharing margaritas and life stories, but there is no sign of my mother.

I'm wandering down the rockier side of the beach, checking the pools for agates and shells, when I come across the base of an old rock quarry, remnants of a landslide from before I was born. The boulders nearest the water where a common sit place for me during our vacation. A woman is sitting there now, at the base of a rather square one that I once fished from, her elbows on her knees as she gazes sadly at the river.

Mom does a double take as I tip-toe across the flatter river stones, trying not to get my Nikes wet. Her expression is neutral but the skin around her eyes is raised and watery. She slaps a few tears off as I sit down on the boulder next to her. A waft of smoke is drifting up from her left hand, a cloud of it flowing out her nostrils as she looks downstream.

"You're smoking again?" It's been six months since her last pack, which had been a big milestone for her.

She taps some ash into the river. "You want to talk to me about addictions right now?"

I shake my head. "Nope."

She takes another drag off her Camel then douses it in the rocks. We listen to the trickle of water as it runs through the pebbles, forming curly, bubbly patterns. Her gaze lifts to follow an osprey circling its nest in the old maple tree. The nest has been rebuilt from its original, probably many times over, and contains a pair of new hatchlings who are calling to their parents. "How did you know?" She finally asks. "How did you know I was here?"

"Your picture on Instagram. The same waterfall is in Dad's picture of me from when we were here camping." I try not to think too hard about that trip or about what he said to me in this very spot. Of all the places in this park that I could've found her, I wish it hadn't been this one.

"Oh." Mom tries to not sound too impressed with my detective skills. "You could've just called, saved yourself the gas. It's a long drive out here."

"I didn't want to talk over the phone." I'll tell her the someone-ran-over-my-phone part later. Or never.

Mom snorts, suppressing a flicker of a smile. "You're like me in that way, always wanting to confront things face to face." Her breath shivers out, eyes glassy with a new round of waterworks. "I'm sorry, Elle."

My throat is tight so I pat her knee. "Me, too, Momma. It's okay."

"No, it's not okay. I've fought like hell to make a good life for my kids and my husband and everything still turned out like shit." She folds a hand over her face so I can't see it crumble, but it doesn't hurt me any less. She collapses into a fit of sobs almost as heartbreaking as the ones I heard in the hospital last night.

I cradle her as if she is now the child and I am the adult, just as I did when she filed for a divorce and as I will always do when she suffers. We sit like that until her sobs tone down to intermittent gasps then sniffles. "This wasn't how things were supposed to go," she finally says. "I never imagined that I would be fifty years old, starting over from scratch."

"Mom, you're not starting over from scratch," I calmly reply. "You have a home, a car, a job, and two kids who love you. You're doing fine."

"Yeah, I'm *fine*. I'm behind on my property taxes, my health is questionable, I'm about to be sent to collections for two stupid, unpaid credit cards, and my daughter hates her father because he's a sociopathic fuck who replaced us all with some holier-than-art-thou gold-digger—one who had the audacity to remind me in front of my family that I'm not really family to anyone in that room except Jim's poor bastard children." Mom takes a breath then jerks her cigarette box out of her pocket, whole body vibrating as she lights up another. "But other than that, I'm doing perfectly fine!"

I want to say something brilliant, something truly inspiring that only a daughter could say, but all I have is, "It's going to be okay."

She snorts smoke like a dragon, wagging her head. "I shouldn't have gone to the hospital. It was a mistake."

"It was not. And I think the Foxes were happy you did."

"They didn't know what to think. Your grandpa kept looking at me like he'd seen me a hundred times but couldn't remember my name. Twenty-five years in that family and not one of them stood up for me against Bertha or Bird Shit or whatever her name is. I was more their child than Jim. I sent birthday cards, brought food when they were sick, showed up to holiday events with you kids even when Jim didn't."

"Grandma Johanna stood up for you," I remind her, remembering the fierceness of the old woman as she marched over and threw her hands up.

"Johanna didn't want a fight in the middle of a hospital. If Bird Shit had punched me first though, I promise you I would've jammed that cross down her throat until she choked to death. For someone so Christian, where was the care or the attempt at understanding where I was coming from?"

"She isn't worth going to prison for. Or Hell." I smirk, trying to lighten the mood.

"You're probably right about prison," she reluctantly admits. "But I'm pretty sure there's already a seat in hell with my name on it."

"Mom, you've already faced hell. Cut your losses and

start a new life. It's not too late, and you deserve it." I think again of Nana's story, of the sickly golden bird who finally allowed herself to turn to ash and be born again. "Nothing is meant to stay the same. This is a new chapter. There is something good for each of us on the other side of hell." I stand and brush off my pants then offer her my hand so she can stand, too.

She doesn't take it. "I'm sorry for what I said about Scott Darcy. I don't think he's an inked-up hood rat. Well, I mean he's inked up, but I didn't think badly of him when you two were together. I thought he was a unique young man that loved my daughter. I didn't tell you what your dad did because he needed to tell you himself. I told him to come clean because you deserved to know the things he said to that boy, things that I'm sure are responsible for his choosing someone else. The thing is, I had convinced myself that if Scott could pick another girl over my daughter, then maybe your dad did the right thing by getting rid of him. It's hard being married, Elle. It's even harder when you're young and you start out with nothing. Trust me —I did it. Everything we had we struggled for, starved for, sacrificed for."

Mom doesn't say the last part that I can practically hear resonating from her thoughts: *and it was all for nothing*. "I understand," I assure. "I'm not angry with you, but there was more to Scott's side of the story. That's why you both should've allowed me to hear his proposal. I don't think I would've said yes, but it was wrong of both of you to let me think he didn't love me. I hate Dad for that." The word *hate* comes off my lips louder than I meant for it to.

Mom takes my hand, squeezes my fingers. Her eyes turn into those big, glossy Mom eyes that she gets right before telling me something I don't want to hear. "Lew, your dad has done a lot of screwed up stuff but it's time to face the fact that despite all of that, he cares." I try to pull my fingers from her grip but she holds them tighter. "No—listen to me. Your father has made terrible mistakes, but that doesn't mean he doesn't love you."

"My father loves his company and his cars. Next topic," I say impatiently.

"You know one of the reasons it was so hard being in that room last night? Before their giant remodel, that area of the hospital used to be the delivery wing... You were born in that room."

"Please don't," I beg, because the past twenty-four hours have been hard enough and I don't need this on top of it.

She rubs her thumb over my hand, looking at it in hers. "You were so tiny, so full of fire even though you were just hours old. Your dad would sit in the delivery room's bay window and just stare at you. I'd never seen him look at anything like that before, like he held the entire universe in his hands and nothing else mattered."

"I said stop," I whisper, but the words are cracked and broken.

"That's what kept me going all those years, even when our marriage was hanging by a thread. I would remember the warmth in your dad's eyes when he saw you, the love that radiated from him when you smiled or took his big bear paw in your tiny hand." Mom, despite her streaming, puffy face, grins. "You want to know what's hiding behind all of those masks he loves to wear? Do you know why he drove the love of your life away, or why he so viciously attacked me on the Fourth of July when I told him I wanted to move out for a while?"

I wag my head. I don't want to hear another word or think about the past, because now I'm the one crumbling and I won't be able to stop the outpour once it happens. The need for a glass of wine, an escape, hits me like a house.

"Fear," Mom declares. "Fear of losing that which he truly, deeply loves."

A few tears have escaped from my ducts. I can't look at her.

Mom stands up and hugs me, returning me to the position of child and her the parent. "You can do whatever you want to do," she says, kissing my forehead. "But I think you will regret not telling him how you really feel."

"I'm not going to tell a potentially dying man that I hate him," I say, appalled that she could suggest such a thing.

She tilts my chin up, looking me dead in the eyes. "You and I both know that hate is just a cover up word for a whole lot of unsettled emotions. Do as you will but think about what I said and, God help me, don't you drink to forget my words."

"But what if there aren't other emotions? What if I really do just hate him and that's all there is to it?" It's a dark statement, but a genuine worry of mine.

Mom stops walking down the beach, frowning over her

shoulder. "Well, then I guess you'd better go find out. It'd be a shame if he died and you realized too late that you were wrong."

***

The hospital smells extra sanitized today.

My eyes sting from it as I walk down a hallway with gray tile and wide glass windows. I pass a nurse and a woman in a wheelchair who looks like a living skeleton, then share the elevator with a teenage boy on crutches who won't stop staring at me. "Wow, you look just like Emma Stone."

His eyes are bloodshot and he's swaying where he stands. *Pain meds.* "Thanks," I say, even though I don't look remotely close to the Hollywood star.

The Fox family has dispersed from the waiting room.

"Ms. Fox." Dr. Lawrence's voice rumbles behind me. He's standing at a check-in desk with two nurses. "If you're looking for your family, they've moved into our new waiting room down the hall. It's closer to your father. Would you like me to show you?"

It'll be easier to do this without them knowing I am here. Plus, I don't want any chance of seeing Bertie right now. "No, thank you. Actually, I was hoping I could just go straight to my dad."

He studies my face. I know he's thinking about watching me rocket out of the hospital as fast as I could last time. "Of course. Do you know how to get back there from here?" I shake my head. "Come. I will show you." His shadow passes over my whole figure as he takes abnormally long strides to the double doors.

I summon a deep breath and follow.

"He has been in and out of consciousness today," Dr. Lawrence says brightly. "We have him on a mild sedative to help reduce stress, but his body is responding well to the surgery and treatment."

"So he's awake?" The challenge before me now looks even more intimidating.

"On and off." Dr. Lawrence pauses. "He'll probably be asleep now."

He'd better be. My fingers curl into my hand, desperately wishing I had Mom's or Matt's to hold. I follow Dr. Lawrence around a corner when the walls start to wobble. Even as I'm walking over tiles of a hallway that reeks of bleach and Purell, all I can envision is the pale tiles of my family's farmhouse basement.

Dr. Lawrence passes a desk full of alarmed nurses and office staff, a few of which are running over to an adjacent hallway where an irate woman is screaming, "Get off! Get away from me!"

My body locks up as I watch a male nurse try to restrain a very frightened blonde woman in a plastic gown. I see him towering over her, his hands squeezing her arms as she tries to shove him back. She's half laying, half sitting on the floor, tear lines fresh on her cheeks. "Get back! Take your hands off me!"

Suddenly the woman isn't a stranger but my mother, and the brawny nurse is Dad.

And I'm back in the farmhouse, back in that moment two summers ago.

Dr. Lawrence stops at Room 2014. "Here you are, Ms. Fox."

I stare at the door. A cold sweat has broken out beneath my hair. I'm not ready. I can wait to do this. I don't have to confront him. The problem is, just like that day in the Gorge when I fell down the cliffside and my entire life hung in the balance, a voice deep in the recesses of my mind is shouting.

Move now.

My hand rises to the smooth, brushed brass of the handle. I pull down.

The room is a big, blue square with blaring white trim and ugly, floral wallpaper. The big bay window overlooking the trees of the south parking lot is its only redeeming quality. The door closes silently behind me, sealing me in.

The heart monitor beeps quietly, evenly. Dad lays quietly, eyes closed, beneath scratchy linen sheets that he probably would've complained about if he were awake. After a while I'm brave enough to take a few steps forward, feeling nothing at first. By the time I've reached his bedside, however, the hatred is seeping in dark, ugly puddles around me just as I feared it would. I hate him so much that I can't swallow, can't breathe. This is the man who broke my mother's heart, the man who lied to us and replaced us, the one we had put faith in. This is the man who I believed, deep down, had loved us and wanted to do right by us despite his questionable traits and multiple personalities... the one who struck me, both physically and mentally, and left me with ugly, gnarled scars.

I mean nothing to this man.

I'm about to turn and leave the room when his eyelids lift. His gaze lands on me, freezing me where I stand. It takes him a moment to focus, to realize who is standing beside him. The heart monitor starts clicking faster. He croaks a word that sounds like my name but is unclear. His soulless, hollow eyes become deep and glassy, filling with things I do not recognize. He tries to speak again but it's garbled. It sounds like, *Hi, Little Girl.*

His shaking hand reaches up to take mine.

I want to brush his hand off, return to that safe, numb place behind the fortress I have kept for so long but it no longer exists. My walls have somehow disintegrated, leaving the truths I couldn't bear to look at out in the open. I now understand what Mom meant: hatred *is* a cover up word. Beneath it lies the real feelings, the disappointment, sorrow, desperation, fear, envy, longing.

Love.

Love that I have been trying so hard to detach from. Love that I don't even know what to do with because he doesn't deserve it and I don't want him to have it, but to deny it would be to deny that the grass is green and the sea is made of salt water. If he dies, part of me dies with him, a bigger part than I wanted to believe existed. Our memories of the beach, of him buying me boots to protect my cut-up feet, of catching my first fish at Salmon Shores, I would become the sole bearer of those moments. There would be no one else to remember how precious they were, no future to even consider making new memories. I thought I had been okay with this.

I am not.

So I squeeze his hand back. He doesn't speak, which might have something to do with the drugs. I realize then and there, as I hold his weary, calloused fingers, that I have two choices: I can spend the rest of my life battling and being broken by the truth, that I love Jim Fox even though I am strongly, deeply disappointed in him as a father and a husband and a person, or I can accept it. I can accept that it's okay to love him knowing our relationship will never be the same and I may never forgive him for his sins. I can give in.

Nana's laugh echoes in my head like an old, wise owl. *I told you it was only change*. The drugs must be kicking back in because Dad closes his eyes, though his hand stays around mine. I don't know how long we sit like that. Maybe it's minutes, maybe it's hours. What I do know is when I finally rise from his bedside, the weight on my shoulders no longer presses down like a brick building. I catch a glimpse of myself in the mirror over the sink, my natural hair glimmering red in the sunlight. When I walk out the door, a trail of ash and golden feathers is left in my wake.

July 5th 2017

WHAT WILL NEVER CHANGE

I've just pulled into my driveway when my new phone lights up. Two texts from Scott flash on the screen.

Got your message. Glad you got a new phone. Don't suppose you're up for a party around five-thirty? I've got a bottle of dealcoholized wine with your name on it.

I glance at my car clock and see that it's nearly seven-thirty. *Drat.* I punch the phone emblem on my screen.

Scott picks up on the first ring. "Ah, so you're not avoiding me. We were starting to place bets." Male voices mumble and chuckle in the background.

"Sorry. Just came back from the hospital."

"The hospi—oh... Did you go see your dad?"

I swallow the lump in my throat. "Yeah."

He makes a sound of approval. "Good girl. What are you doing now?"

"Besides getting out of my car and unlocking my front

door? Not a clue. Sorry I missed your party."

"It's okay. The afterparty is still going… if you're interested." He hushes Jordan, who is yelling in the background, telling me to hurry up and come down.

My reflection frowns at me from the front windows of my house. My hair is slopped into a greasy bun and I've cried off most of my makeup. "I'm not really in a partying mood."

"Fine. If you won't do it for me, do it for Glen. He would've wanted you here."

My heart stutters. "For Glen?"

"I'll text you the address. See you in fifteen minutes?"

I sigh, getting mobbed by the dogs as I walk into my living room. "Make it thirty."

***

The address takes me to the parking lot of a small strip mall. The light up L in the Plaid Place sign has finally been fixed over the super mart and the Teriyaki joint is now an upscale Sushi bar. I get out of the car near the end of the building, sure the GPS has taken me to the wrong place, but the address matches the one Scott gave me. The brickwork along the end of the building is just as black as I remember, the trim newly painted white. The floor-to-ceiling windows are open, drapes tied aside. A few shadows linger within the low-lit interior.

A brand-new sign hangs above the door that reads, RAVEN EYE TATTOO.

No way. I stand there and stare at it for several minutes. The giant decal of the golden eagle with the crown on its head still covers the left side window but a new one, this one a raven with a broken crown hanging from its talons, adorns the other. The raven carries so many of Glen's detailed shading techniques but the angles are sharper, the linework thicker. There might be a smile on my face as I walk up to the door.

A neon green print out is taped to the glass: VIP PARTY – RSVPS ONLY. The door is locked. I peer in through the window and spot a group of people sitting around a table in the waiting area. A patch of red hair sits up at the sound of me knocking. Jordan grins and waves, then taps the shoulder of a dark-haired guy in a button-down shirt with the sleeves rolled up to his elbows.

Scott, looking much more put together than I'm used to seeing him, turns around and does a double take.

I hold my arms out to the sides of my red chiffon dress as if to say, *here I am*.

A slow smile creeps across his face. He makes a slow saunter to the door, scanning me up and down through the window. His shirt is tucked into a pair of black Levi's. There's jell in his hair and the stud in his ear has been replaced with a tiny hoop of silver. He turns the lock and it releases with a loud click. The smell of Old Spice and curiosity rolls out as he leans against the doorframe, blocking the entrance. "I'm sorry, Gorgeous, this is a VIP party only. You'll have to convince me to let you in."

"How about I know the owner?" I flick my eyes at the

door, at his name tattooed in gold foil beneath his shop title.

For a man who is known for rarely ever showing emotion, he can hardly contain it. Those blue eyes dazzle like the sea at sunset. "Oh, really? Do you know him well?"

Heat is blooming across my cheeks. He's lucky he has an audience or I'd pull him forward and remind him how well I know him. "Well, we got naked in the woods once and made love under a waterfall, so I'd say pretty well."

He snorts, closing his eyes and shaking his. *Still subtle as a gun*, he mouths. I have a feeling he's wishing we didn't have an audience, either. "Well, in that case I guess I should let you in." He holds the door open for me.

The tattoo studio smells like hand soap and fresh paint. The fireplace is lined with lit black candles but the velvet chairs have been traded out for two beautifully carved, wooden benches, currently occupied by a handful of tattooed men ranging from teen to middle age and classy to mountain-manish—the type of group I am more used to seeing him with versus Noah's crowd of silver-spooners. Jordan is sitting among them and whistles as I walk in. "Hot damn, there she is," he calls. "'Bout time! We were starting to think you snuffed us."

I give a nervous wave, aware that I am now the focus of the room. The skin between my boobs automatically starts sweating. "Hi."

The palm of Scott's hand presses against my lower back, propelling me forward. Wood planking lines most of the walls except for the one above the fireplace, where a painting of the Columbia River Gorge stretches to the ceiling. "Males and

Gents, this is Elle Fox." He introduces me to everyone, to his teenage cousins, Max and Morgan; to Ben, a heavily tattooed thirty-year-old who was Glen's best friend; Uncle Lars, who is wearing plaid and has a beard that sits in his lap when he bends forward; a gentleman who has tattoos instead of hair and a name I already forgot; and Jordan's dad, Dale Cane, who is the mirror image of Jordan only with crows feet and a head of graying curls. They greet me with pleasant heys and hellos and the raising of half-empty beer glasses.

"You're not too late," Ben says, clapping Jordan's shoulder. "He drank the last of the beer but there's still champagne and whiskey up for grabs."

"I'm good. Thanks." It's the first time I've turned down alcohol in an uncomfortable situation since moving out of the farmhouse. A weird rush of triumph runs through me. "I'd take a water though, if you have one." I turn to Scott.

"Come on back." He walks around Glen's old desk, into the hallway. Glen's tattooed muse with the eagle on her shoulder still occupies most of the desk wall. I notice a few new birds have been painted beside her, a hawk of some dark-feathered variety and a hummingbird with stars in her wings. As I start to follow him, my eye is caught by another piece of art—a huge black frame on the opposite side of the room that is not yet hung but propped up on a folding table. My breath hitches as I look at it.

Glen Darcy smiles at me, his arm wrapped around Scott's shoulders. They each have a hand up in front of them, tattooed fingers split to form two Vs. Scott's expression appears bored but a hint of a smile lifts his cheeks. He's wearing a black tee with sweatpants tucked into Carhart boots, his ridiculously huge hiking pack sitting against his leg. The landscape they're standing on is dry and rocky, perhaps some place high up in the Gorge, the smooth limbs of a madrona tree waving behind them. This picture must've been taken a while ago because Scott's left arm isn't all tattooed yet. The frame matting around the photo is exposed, not yet tucked behind the safety of glass, and is covered in black and silver scribbles. *Words*, I realize. Wishes and memories for Glen, from the people who knew and loved him.

This party is not just a celebration for Scott's new business. It is a celebration of life.

"What do you think?" Scott asks as we step through the last door of the hallway.

I lean against the edge of a padded tattoo table, its pleather as red as the boots of a strip club dancer. It's probably seen just as much skin. I'm still trying to swallow my realization about the party. "I should've known."

"Known what?" He chuckles, tossing me a water bottle from the fridge.

I clumsily catch it. "That you would share Glen's incredible art skills."

He shrugs, hands in his pockets. "Had to do something different after getting a DUI. I couldn't drive cars for a living anymore." I cringe. "I have no regrets." He lifts a hand to touch my hair, its curls already starting to unwind. I wait for that hand to slide to my face and bring me in for a kiss but it doesn't happen. He steps back, a strange force pressing between us like the repel of two magnets. "So. What now?"

"What do you mean?"

"I mean, you show up at my house bleeding and near-hypothermic after telling me off, you try to shame me for taking you home, then we end up in the same bed spooning for most of the night." He shrugs, folding his arms as he leans against the wall. "So what now?"

"I... don't know."

"You don't know?"

"Well, wait—"

"If last night was a one-time thing, you can say so. I won't hold it against you." His tone and body language say otherwise. "But we should probably be smart about this and end it now if you're really not sure. For both our sakes."

"Okay, hold for a second. I didn't mean *I don't know* I'm saying this is the first chance all day that I've had to think about you instead of my parents, so can you give me a second to gather my thoughts?" His expression softens, gaze dropping to the floor. "I, um..." *God, so many things to say but where to start?* "I liked having you there last night, even though the circumstances weren't pretty. I liked that, for a moment, despite all the terrible things surrounding me you made me feel normal again. I haven't felt right like that in a long time.

"I know a lot has happened in five years. I'm sorry for telling you off—more than once, and neither time for the right reasons. I'm sorry I've been too busy being closed off and angry and... scared."

"Scared?" Scott tilts his head. "Of me?"

"Yeah."

"Why?"

"Because. Love is complicated and I'm taking a huge risk by putting my heart back in your hands. I feel like I'm handing you a loaded gun and praying you don't shoot me with it."

He slowly nods. "I feel the same way about you."

"So what do we do about it?"

He hums. Peeling himself away from the wall, he walks over and puts one hand on either side of me, on the table. My skin comes alive at his closeness, buzzing from one end to the other. A smirk curls his mouth. "Do you ever go hiking?"

I laugh, and almost cry at the same time. "I used to."

"Would you go with me?"

"Right now?"

He glances over his shoulder at the hallway, towards the laughter and chatter coming out of the studio. "Right now, tomorrow, next week, you name it. I've learned the best way to conquer fear is to take one step at a time."

"Seems like a fair plan." I smooth the ends of his hair behind his ears, watching the shiver go down his neck. "But what if you don't like me? Let's be honest—I've changed a lot in the past few years and it's not all good. I have a lot to work on."

He chuckles, then brushes a kiss across my lips. "Don't

we all? Change is part of life. Nothing stays the same and I don't expect it to—we've been through a lot. I'll work with you through everything if you can promise you'll talk to me when things get harry instead of shutting me out."

"I promise." I seal it with another kiss. He pulls me in for a few more but we're interrupted by Jordan's voice, calling for us to hurry up and come say goodbye to the cousins. Scott pulls away to open the door to the hall, then offers his hand. I take it, curling my fingers through his tattooed ones. "Just for the record, there is one thing you should expect to stay the same. Something that I don't believe ever really changes."

He hums, curious. "And what is that?"

I squeeze his fingers. "Love."

Author's Note

This book… it made me cry. It made me laugh. It made me remember why I love writing, and that I *can* still write even after years of writer's block.

While this book is a work of fiction, I cannot deny the bits of nonfiction woven in between. Loss in any form is single-handedly the worst thing we're forced to go through in this life. It rips us to the core, crumbles everything we think we know about ourselves and our existence. It can also, however, bring about strange and incredible revelations and opportunities, if we are brave enough to look up from our grief.

I want to thank my editor, Marla Daniels, for the hours she put into editing this novel and her words of advice. This book would not be what it is today without your help, guidance, and enthusiasm. Thank you from the bottom of my heart!

I also want to thank my mom, Gudrun, for her words of wisdom and for being a pillar of knowledge and love throughout my life. I would not be the person I am today without you. I have watched you go through hell and come out on the other side, still smiling, still ready to take on life. I am so proud of how far you've come.

About The Author

Sarah Kraft

Sarah Kraft is a native Portlander currently living in Oregon. By day, she designs jewelry for Portland's up and coming brides. By night, she writes novels and designs prints for her athletics line, Kouture De Le Kraft . Follow her on Twitter or Facebook @SB_Roozenboom for cute dog stories and Oregon travel recommendations.

CPSIA information can be obtained
at www.ICGtesting.com
Printed in the USA
LVHW092302220921
698528LV00005B/271

9 798519 749626